Books by Rebecca York

KILLING MOON
EDGE OF THE MOON
WITCHING MOON
CRIMSON MOON
SHADOW OF THE MOON
NEW MOON
GHOST MOON
ETERNAL MOON
DRAGON MOON
DAY OF THE DRAGON

BEYOND CONTROL
BEYOND FEARLESS

Anthologies

CRAVINGS
(with Laurell K. Hamilton, MaryJanice Davidson, and Eileen Wilks)

ELEMENTAL MAGIC
(with Sharon Shinn, Carol Berg, and Jean Johnson)

DAY OF THE
DRAGON

REBECCA YORK

BERKLEY SENSATION, NEW YORK

THE BERKLEY PUBLISHING GROUP
Published by the Penguin Group
Penguin Group (USA) Inc.
375 Hudson Street, New York, New York 10014, USA
Penguin Group (Canada), 90 Eglinton Avenue East, Suite 700, Toronto, Ontario M4P 2Y3, Canada
(a division of Pearson Penguin Canada Inc.)
Penguin Books Ltd., 80 Strand, London WC2R 0RL, England
Penguin Group Ireland, 25 St. Stephen's Green, Dublin 2, Ireland (a division of Penguin Books Ltd.)
Penguin Group (Australia), 250 Camberwell Road, Camberwell, Victoria 3124, Australia
(a division of Pearson Australia Group Pty. Ltd.)
Penguin Books India Pvt. Ltd., 11 Community Centre, Panchsheel Park, New Delhi—110 017, India
Penguin Group (NZ), 67 Apollo Drive, Rosedale, North Shore 0632, New Zealand
(a division of Pearson New Zealand Ltd.)
Penguin Books (South Africa) (Pty.) Ltd., 24 Sturdee Avenue, Rosebank, Johannesburg 2196,
South Africa

Penguin Books Ltd., Registered Offices: 80 Strand, London WC2R 0RL, England

This is a work of fiction. Names, characters, places, and incidents either are the product of the author's imagination or are used fictitiously, and any resemblance to actual persons, living or dead, business establishments, events, or locales is entirely coincidental. The publisher does not have any control over and does not assume any responsibility for author or third-party websites or their content.

DAY OF THE DRAGON

A Berkley Sensation Book / published by arrangement with the author

PRINTING HISTORY
Berkley Sensation mass-market edition / December 2010

Copyright © 2010 by Ruth Glick.
Excerpt from *Shattered Destiny* by Rebecca York copyright © by Ruth Glick.
Cover art by Shutterstock.
Cover design by Bruce Springer.

ISBN: 978-0-425-23818-9

BERKLEY® SENSATION
Berkley Sensation Books are published by The Berkley Publishing Group,
a division of Penguin Group (USA) Inc.,
375 Hudson Street, New York, New York 10014.
BERKLEY® SENSATION and the "B" design are trademarks of Penguin Group (USA) Inc.

PRINTED IN THE UNITED STATES OF AMERICA

10 9 8 7 6 5 4 3 2 1

To Norman,
who keeps me thinking straight.

CHAPTER
ONE

WAS HE DEAD or alive?

Ramsay Gallagher supposed it depended on how you defined life and death. He was breathing. His heart pumped blood through his body, and his brain could process information.

But though a crowd of people swirled around him, he didn't feel alive. Not when the mental abilities that he had taken for granted all his life were lost to him.

When coins clattering into a metal tray broke through his dark thoughts, he turned to his right to see a fifty-something woman in a bright orange dress scooping quarters from the spout of a machine with flashing lights.

"I told you the slots near the door were the good ones," she crowed to the balding man beside her. "They want people to see the winners."

Outside it was well past midnight, but time had no meaning inside the casino. Ramsay looked around the vast room, struck by the contrasts of crystal chandeliers, marble floors, and bright neon. In ages past, this might have been the palace of a monarch who had drained the royal treasury to create a universe of opulence and pleasure for himself. In fact it was in a hotel called Versailles. But instead of the Sun King's courtiers dressed in their best silk and satin, it was filled with people wearing everything from T-shirts and jeans to strapless gowns and even a few business suits.

He stood for a moment watching the crowd, wondering if he had made a mistake in coming to Las Vegas. But his e-mail had brought an announcement of a conference here, New Frontiers in Archaeology, and one of the seminars had intrigued him. A Dr. Madison Dartmoor was giving a paper on the excavation of an ancient tomb discovered in a remote mountain site in southern Italy, the area where Ramsay had been born.

Or rather found there as a small boy, wandering alone. He had always wondered why, and perhaps Dr. Dartmoor could give him some clues.

Had his parents tossed him away? Had they been forced to give him up? Had they gotten separated by accident?

He'd have to wait until tomorrow morning for the seminar. Tonight he strode toward the craps tables.

The dice game, he knew, dated back to the Crusades and was a simplification of the English game of hazard. The modern American version had been born in New Orleans around the turn of the nineteenth century, and he had first played it there. Black Americans had spread it throughout the U.S.

He reached one of the tables just as a man in a cowboy hat crapped out, punctuating his failure with a loud curse.

The faux cowboy passed the dice to a guy with a belly that made him look nine months pregnant. Ramsay felt the man's tension, which was hardly less than his own. He focused on the dice as the shooter flung the small cubes across the table, where they bounced against the side bumper.

Pair of fours, he silently chanted, willing the combination to come up. Instead the man rolled two threes.

Ramsay clenched his fists in frustration. A few months ago, it would have been easy to manipulate dice with his mind and get them to come up any way he wanted. Now such a simple task eluded him.

But he had never been one to give up without a fight. He stayed at the table for several more minutes, trying to influence the outcome of the action. Finally, when a new shooter stepped up, Ramsay felt a small stirring somewhere inside his mind. Gathering every ounce of power he could muster, he focused on the white cubes, willing a winning combination.

When they rolled to a stop with a three and four showing, he felt a spurt of victory. He was almost sure he had been the cause of the successful throw.

But even that amount of effort had sapped his energy. He needed to recharge before he tried any more experiments.

He stepped from the casino into the marble and gold lobby where a three-story-high replica of the authentic Versailles facade adorned the back of the registration desk, with parterre hedges and flower beds defining the check-in lines.

A slender blond woman turned away from the desk, catching his attention. She was attractive, perhaps in her late twenties, with straight hair cut just below her chin, light eyes, and an intelligent face that made him want to get to know her better. She appeared to be alone—and not the usual patron of this establishment, at least from the people he'd seen. She was wearing a beige pantsuit, with a green-and-white striped knit top under the jacket and an expression that was a combination of determination and wariness.

When she started talking to a bellman, Ramsay could see she was worried about a small trunk the porter had just placed on the cart.

Edging closer, he heard her say, "Be very careful with that one."

"Certainly, ma'am. You can go up to your room, and I'll meet you there."

"No, I'll stay with the luggage."

The ring of command in her voice sparked his interest. Obviously, she was used to giving orders. Was she here with expensive merchandise to sell? Or was she carting a boatload of money to the gambling capital of the world? Still intrigued, he strode toward her, watching her reaction as he approached the cart.

When she stepped between him and the trunk, he kept walking toward the concierge desk, where a middle-aged couple was trying to buy tickets for the night's upscale circus show performance.

Turning, he saw that the blond and the bellman were headed toward the elevator.

On the other side of the lobby, partly hidden by a decorative pillar, two men were watching her. They were dressed in casual sports shirts and slacks, but their hard-looking faces and tense posture made him think they weren't here on a gambling holiday. They seemed more like Mafia tough guys staking out a mark. One was short and chunky, with curly brown hair that gave his head the appearance of a mop. The other was over six feet tall and bald as Yul Brynner.

Moments after the woman disappeared into the elevator with the bellman and the cart, Mophead pulled out a cell phone and made a call. It was a brief exchange.

So what's going on? Ramsay wondered as he watched the men head for the bar. It looked like someone was keeping tabs on her. Was she in danger?

He should warn her. He started across the lobby, then stopped in his tracks, since he wasn't going to find her room by picking up her scent in the elevator. Besides, her problems were none of his business.

Still, he stayed where he was for heartbeats before exiting the hotel onto the famous street called "the Strip," lined with massive hotels, each with a theme decor. It was early April and the night air was chilled, but he welcomed the bite of the desert wind. To his right he could see an

Egyptian pyramid, and to his left was a replica of the New York City skyline. As he started down the street, a volcano suddenly shot flames into the air.

This was fantasy land. Any fantasy that would draw gamblers to the casinos.

Turning right, he headed for the low rent part of town and came quickly to an area of downscale motels and low-rise apartments.

He walked between two of the buildings, fading into the shadows, waiting. A man in a white shirt, bow tie, and black pants came from the direction of the Strip, shoulders slumped after a long shift, Ramsay supposed.

He let the guy pass, then focused on the sound of a woman's heels clicking along the sidewalk, coming rapidly toward him.

A few months ago, he would have been able to probe her mind. Now he had to rely on his senses as he watched her approach. Her bright red hair hung in thick waves around her shoulders. She was wearing a knit dress that rode up her thighs and clung to her ample curves. A glittery purse was slung over one shoulder.

He was almost sure she was a prostitute back from plying her trade along the Strip. She looked to be in her late twenties or early thirties. Too old for the type of life she was leading. Still, her stride was brisk and her posture was erect, signs that her profession hadn't undermined her health.

Stepping out of the shadows, he waited for her to see him.

When she did, she stopped short, and he knew she was evaluating him. She saw a man who appeared to be in his thirties, with dark hair caught at the back of his neck in a short ponytail and dark eyes, dressed in expensive jeans, a black polo shirt, and Italian loafers. All signs of his prosperity. Still, he could be an ax murderer for all she knew.

"Hello," he said, sending her a silent message. *You like my looks. I'm okay. I won't hurt you.*

She answered, "You're out of your element."

"I just got into town. Can you take one more customer tonight?" He continued to send her reassuring messages, knowing that any working girl would love to make a little more money before the evening was over.

When she stepped closer, he led her into the shadows. Turning toward him, she pressed her hand against the fly of his jeans, making him instantly hard.

"Fifty dollars for a blow job," she murmured.

"That's fine."

He let her rock her hand against him while his own hands went to her breasts, lifting and shaping them.

"What's your name?"

"Yvonne."

Probably her working name, but he didn't challenge her as he stroked his thumbs over her nipples, back and forth, urging a response from her, knowing that she usually kept herself detached from the men she serviced. But he wanted to drag her into a web of sensuality. His mind reached out to hers, and he was gratified to feel her falling under his spell.

"Where would you like to be, if you could go anywhere you wanted?" he asked.

"Back home," she answered in a dreamy voice.

"Where is home?"

"Santa Monica. I love the beach."

He sent her an image of sand and ocean, complete with waves breaking against the shore, rushing up to lap at their feet and then receding.

She shivered. "I feel the water tickling my toes. It's so cool and nice. And the sun is hot."

"And you and I are naked," he added.

"Um. You've got a great body."

"Thanks."

He backed her against the wall, then pulled down her low top, lapping at her nipples, then teasing himself by nipping at the tender place where her neck met her shoulder.

He stoked her response, his own arousal rising to meet

hers as he sank his teeth into her neck and began to draw blood.

"Oh! You're so sexy."

He let himself go into his own fantasy, imagining he was with the blond from the hotel lobby instead of the woman in his arms.

One hand slid downward to the juncture of her legs, pressing against her clit, urging her to climax.

Her blood tasted wonderful, mingling with her sexual excitement. He wanted to go on and on, drawing the sensuality and the life fluid from her. He knew his evil twin—Vandar—had lived for that pleasure. And long ago the old Ramsay might have indulged the need to drain the last drop from this woman. But he'd conquered that impulse.

When she climaxed, he felt a spurt of pleasure.

She raised her head and blinked, looking around the darkened grounds of the apartment complex. "The beach . . ."

"A wonderful fantasy."

Her voice was high and shaky. "What did you do to me?"

"I wanted to make it good for both of us," he answered.

"You did—for me." When she reached for his cock again, he dragged in a shuddering breath, ready to let her perform the service she'd suggested—until he heard footsteps approaching.

She stiffened, and he stepped away from her so that they were standing three feet apart when a man sauntered down the sidewalk and gave them a smirking look.

The sensuality of the moment had been broken for Ramsay. He no longer wanted this woman, but he wasn't finished with her.

"You will forget me. Forget what I look like. Forget that I was here. Will you forget?"

"Yes."

"Say it."

"I will forget you."

"And you want to go home, to Santa Monica. You're

tired of this life. You want to get a real job. What would you do if you could pick your profession?"

"I'd like to work in fashion."

"Good. That's good. You want to go home and work in the fashion industry."

He reached for his wallet and counted out two thousand dollars, which he tucked into her purse.

"You've saved enough to go home," he said. As she swayed on her feet, he led her to the steps of the apartment building and helped her sit down. Leaving her staring into space, he turned and walked back toward the Hotel Versailles, elated that he had connected with her on a mental level—not simply the purely physical.

CHAPTER
TWO

RAMSAY WOKE FEELING better than he had in months.

Since Dr. Dartmoor was scheduled to speak at ten, he had time for an hour's workout in the hotel gym. After a shower, he grabbed a casual shirt and a pair of khakis.

In the lobby restaurant, he bought a steaming cup of Jamaica Blue Mountain coffee and inhaled the aroma. In his experience, coffee always smelled better than it tasted. He took several sips of the strong brew as he walked through the casino—which was between the guest rooms and the conference area. Although blood was his main food source, he could survive on a human diet. He'd done it as a boy, until the day he'd killed the man who was working him to death.

He carefully deposited the two-thirds-full coffee cup into a trash can before finding the room where Dr. Dartmoor was to speak. It looked like it would hold about two hundred people, and most of the seats were filled ten minutes before the talk.

After claiming an aisle spot about halfway back, he listened to the buzz of anticipation around him.

In the front row, a trim, gray-haired man dressed in a blue sports coat set down a briefcase and glanced at his watch. After craning his neck toward the back of the room, he stepped to the lectern and introduced himself as Matthew Westfield, professor of archaeology at the University of California at Santa Barbara.

"I see Dr. Dartmoor is running a little late," he said. "But I'm going to start. It's an honor to be here this morning, and a pleasure to see so many of you in the audience. It's not often that I get to introduce one of my most promising students. Dr. Madison Dartmoor earned a PhD in my department in Santa Barbara, then went directly into fieldwork."

Ramsay felt a buzz of anticipation around the room as some of the audience twisted around in their seats and the professor continued.

"Dr. Dartmoor was an undergraduate archaeology major at the University of Chicago, then came to our department on a full scholarship. Among my colleague's publications are papers on ancient Italian civilizations and the coastal regions of Albania. You can see a more complete list in the conference bio."

The blond from last night came striding up the aisle toward the front of the room, the same mixture of determination and wariness on her face that he'd seen in the lobby.

Westfield smiled at her. He and the woman exchanged a few low words before she stepped up to the lectern.

She was dressed much as she had been the evening before, only now her beige suit had a skirt instead of pants. Was she here to make excuses for the doctor?

She cleared her throat and said, "Thank you for that generous introduction."

It wasn't until that moment that he realized that *she* was Dr. Dartmoor.

She looked uncomfortable, and he wondered how much experience she had at public speaking.

He would have expected her to have a PowerPoint presentation with slides taken at her excavation site, but he saw nothing on the large screen behind her.

"As Dr. Westfield may have told you, I was fortunate to go right from the doctoral program at Santa Barbara into fieldwork, with a generous grant to research an area in southern Italy where an ancient civilization may have flourished well before the Roman era."

He could see that her knuckles were white as she held on to the top edges of the lectern. "I have been working in that area, and I was eager to share my findings with the archaeology community, but I had no idea I was going to create such a stir with the mere mention of my lecture topic." She stopped and took a breath. "Unfortunately, I am no longer able to proceed with the discussion."

A current of sharp-toned conversation sprang up around the room. Up until now they'd been a group of polite academics giving a colleague the space she needed, but they suddenly turned hostile. Ramsay wondered why she hadn't simply canceled her talk.

Or had she thought she was going to go ahead with her plans?

Someone in the audience shouted, "You were rumored to have found startling artifacts at the excavation. Can you comment on that?"

"No. I'm sorry."

"What did you have with you last night?"

Ramsay flashed back to the scene in the lobby. Apparently he wasn't the only one in the room who had seen her protecting the luggage cart.

A heavyset man stood and demanded, "Did Dominic Coleman put the kibosh on your presentation?"

As Ramsay listened to the turmoil in the room, he

thought there hadn't been so much excitement in the archaeology community since the discovery of the bodies in the cave at Herculaneum.

She raised her voice to speak above the din. "No. There was an attack on the excavation site last night. Some of our security force were wounded. I'm not going to put anyone else at risk."

The buzz in the room changed to astonished exclamations.

"I'm sorry. I can't say any more."

A couple of rows in front of Ramsay, a tall, lanky man stood and glared at the speaker. He had thinning hair swept to the side across the top of his shiny pate. When he turned to look back at the audience, Ramsay saw his conference badge identified him as Kent Spader.

Facing the speaker again, he said, "Some of us came to this meeting specifically to hear your presentation."

"There are many other fascinating topics on the program," she answered.

Ignoring her, he went on, "This is exasperating. We'd like to know what you found in that tomb."

"Dr. Dartmoor," someone else shouted, but she turned away and spoke in a low voice to her professor.

Spader stared at her with angry eyes, then pushed his way along the row where he'd been sitting. From the reactions of the people he shoved past, it appeared that he'd stepped on several toes. When he reached the aisle, he hesitated, and Ramsay tensed, wondering if the man was preparing for a physical attack. But he seemed to realize that everyone was now focused on him. After several charged seconds, he turned and strode out of the room, reaching for his cell phone as he walked.

KENT Spader held the phone in his hand, anxious to dial and yet aware that there were too many people in the hallway.

Dartmoor had advertised that she was going to talk

about what she'd found in that tomb in the hills of Calabria. He'd taken time out of his busy schedule to come to Las Vegas to hear what she had to say, but she'd had the nerve to blow off a whole room full of people who'd paid good money to come to this conference. Although what did you expect when someone was totally immoral?

An attack! Well, that made a convenient excuse.

He knew for sure that she'd discovered something significant within the past six months. Now she was closed up tighter than a clam in polluted water.

He had to discover what she'd found—no matter what it took.

Muttering under his breath, he hurried down the hall and into the casino. You couldn't get out of the damn conference center without walking past the clattering slot machines and the gaming tables. And breathing the air heavy with cigarette smoke and the odor of stale alcohol. If God sent down a lightning bolt to destroy this city, it would serve the sinners right.

He stopped to look in a mirror. His hair was mussed, and he swept it back into place. Satisfied, he stepped into the desert sunshine. Squinting in the glare, he took several deep breaths, struggling for calm. When he felt more in control, he looked around to make sure nobody was in earshot before he punched a speed dial button on his phone.

"Yes, sir," a hard voice answered.

"She didn't say anything of significance, but she'll have to talk to us. Scoop her up for me."

"Got ya."

He shuddered, hating the man's sloppy speech. And hating that he had sunk so low that he was forced to work with thugs. But he sat on the boards of some of the nation's most important financial institutions, where he kept a low profile. Which meant he couldn't afford to get his own hands dirty. Challenging Dartmoor in that meeting had been a mistake. He wouldn't make another one.

He clicked off, and stood alone among the people going in and out of the overblown hotel, wondering how he had come to such a pass. He was a moral man, sure of his values and sure that Madison Dartmoor was on the wrong side of history. He wanted her to acknowledge that. Perhaps he could persuade her to stop digging into a dung heap if he could just make her understand what was at stake. If not, she would be swept aside like the traitor to her race that she was.

RAMSAY hung back as most of the people who had come to the session filed out of the room, still discussing the strange turn of events. A few approached the podium, but the archaeologist spoke to them only briefly, and he was sure she wasn't giving out any more information than she had to the audience at large.

He had his own questions—and his own disappointment with her abrupt about-face. The academics gathered here might have an intellectual interest in her excavation. His was more personal than that of anyone else—well, except for the guy named Kent Spader. He looked like Dartmoor had stuck a knife in his gut and twisted the blade.

What was this to him?

With no real plan in mind, Ramsay stepped into the hall and waited for Dartmoor to leave the room. She was accompanied by Westfield and a younger man with close-cropped blond hair, dressed in a sports jacket and an open-collared shirt. The three of them were speaking in low voices as they exited the auditorium.

Thinking he'd get a better reception if he didn't break into the conversation, Ramsay followed them through the casino. They stopped at the entrance to the lobby, where the professor patted his former student on the back. She gave him a half smile.

When Westfield and the other guy left, Dr. Dartmoor looked around the lobby as though she had just been beamed down from a hovering spacecraft and wondered where she had landed.

After a few moments' hesitation, she headed for the front of the hotel, and Ramsay followed about fifteen paces behind her, still intending to get a private word with her.

MADISON stood for a moment in the sunlight, letting the desert sun warm her chilled skin. As she started down the curved driveway toward the Strip, anger and disappointment bubbled inside her. Partly, it was anger at herself. She'd been so excited about her discoveries that she hadn't really taken the danger seriously, and now she was paying the price for her naiveté.

Thank God there had been no fatalities in the attack last night. But the raid on the camp had been a wake-up call.

She'd felt sick when she'd heard that some of her security men had been wounded, and she simply couldn't put them in further jeopardy. Yet at the same time, she couldn't ignore her own deep disappointment.

Dominic had promised to hire more men to guard the camp. She'd go back to Italy as soon as possible, never mind the danger to herself. But right now her only goal was to get away from the hotel before anyone else approached her.

RAMSAY watched Dr. Dartmoor start down the curved drive that led to the wide hotel entrance and turn to her right, apparently bound for the Strip. The area was relatively empty of pedestrians, and Ramsay easily followed as she headed toward the casino called New York-New York.

Beside her, a dark blue Ford stopped. When the back door popped open, a man scrambled out.

"Dr. Dartmoor," he called.

She hunched her shoulders and kept walking.

"Dr. Dartmoor," he called again, hurrying toward her.

Without further conversation, he grabbed her arm and yanked her toward the vehicle.

CHAPTER
THREE

AS THE MAN tried to force Dr. Dartmoor into the Ford, Ramsay heard her cry, "No."

"Get in the car, bitch."

She began to struggle with the guy, and Ramsay realized it was one of the characters who'd been watching her the night before in the lobby. Mophead to be exact. Probably Baldy was driving the car.

Obviously stronger than she looked, the archaeologist braced her arms against the doorframe, keeping the man from pushing her into the vehicle. She was waging a pretty good stalling action, but Mophead was bigger and stronger, and it was only a matter of time before he got the better of her. Several people on the sidewalk were watching the scene, but apparently nobody wanted to jump into the struggle and get hurt.

"Let me go! Help! Somebody, help!"

Despite Ramsay's own very sound advice not to get involved in anyone's problems, he sprinted down the sidewalk, covering the distance in a matter of seconds.

"Get off of her."

At the sound of the intrusion, Mophead spun around, his eyes narrowing as he saw the tall man charging toward him.

"Back off, buster. This ain't your business."

"I'm making it my business."

With Mophead distracted, Dr. Dartmoor turned and gave him a kick in the rear.

He yelped, and Ramsay was able to grab the back of his shirt and yank him away.

"Fucker!" The man was obviously furious at the interference, and he wasn't going to give up easily.

As Dartmoor ducked away from the car, Ramsay spared her a quick look. "Get back to the hotel."

She wavered on her feet, bracing her hand against a bus stop bench.

The driver of the Ford had rolled down the front window, and Ramsay saw the glint of a gun barrel protruding. Was the bozo really going to start shooting out here on the Strip?

"He's got a gun. Get back," Ramsay shouted.

The archaeologist gasped, steadied herself on her feet, and dodged around a palm tree in a planter.

The back door of the car was still open. Ducking low, Ramsay shoved Mophead onto the seat. When he tried to push himself up, Ramsay slammed the door shut, bending the man's legs so that he screamed in pain.

For a heart-stopping second, the gun remained pointed through the car window.

But luck was with the good guys. A patrol car was heading in their direction down the Strip. Rather than risk a shot, the driver of the blue Ford sped away.

Turning, Ramsay saw that Dr. Dartmoor was still on the sidewalk.

"Let's get out of here," he said as he hurried toward her.

She nodded and started back the way she'd come.

As they walked, he looked over his shoulder. When the patrol car passed them at a moderate speed, he concluded that the cops hadn't witnessed the scene on the sidewalk. And everybody else was acting like nothing had happened, which was an interesting comment on modern American life.

"Are you okay?" he asked the woman beside him.

She tipped her head toward him. "Yes. Thanks to you." Then she added, "I'll be fine now."

She looked shaken up, and he certainly wasn't going to leave her on her own, not when the men could easily circle the block and come back for her. But he had another motive for sticking with her. He wanted to know what was going on with her, and this was an excellent opportunity to find out.

"You were just attacked. I want to make sure you're going to be safe," he answered, using a hand at her waist to guide her up the sidewalk.

They reached the hotel lobby, and Ramsay escorted her through the casino to the elevators. When a car arrived, he ushered her inside, then pushed the button for the fifteenth floor. As he led her down the hall, he reached into his pocket for his key card. Moments later, they were inside his expensive suite.

As they stepped from the entrance hall into the lounge area, she looked around, apparently realizing for the first time that he hadn't taken her to *her* room.

"Where are we?"

"My suite."

She studied the large room, furnished with a comfortable sofa, easy chairs, a wet bar, and a flat screen TV.

"I can't stay here."

"Nobody's going to look for you in the room of another guest. You'll have a chance to regroup."

She cleared her throat. "But . . . I don't know you."

"I didn't rescue you so I could turn around and attack you," he said in a mild voice.

She looked embarrassed.

"I'm Ramsay Gallagher." He could have held out his

hand to shake hers, but he kept his arm at his side. When he touched her skin to skin, he wanted to focus on the contact.

He'd been attracted to her when he first saw her in the lobby, and he felt the same buzz of awareness now. Or was it just the leftover arousal from his unfulfilled encounter last night?

No, the pull to this woman was stronger than ever.

"Madison Dartmoor," she said in a husky voice, and he wondered if she was feeling the same attraction. And worried about it because she was in a stranger's room. Obviously, that wasn't her style.

"Nice to meet you," they both said politely.

She cleared her throat again. "You're in Las Vegas on a gambling vacation?"

"Actually, I'm attending the New Frontiers in Archaeology conference."

"Oh."

"Are you hurt?"

She flexed her arms and legs. "Just shaken up, thanks to you."

"Sit down and relax. Let me get you something. Do you want a drink?"

She patted her hair, the way women did when they thought it had gotten mussed, then hesitated for a moment. Finally she crossed to the sofa and sat at one end.

"Maybe a little white wine," she allowed.

He walked to the well-stocked bar area and got a bottle of Chablis from the refrigerator, removed the cork, and poured two glasses, which he set on the table. While she sipped at the wine, he also took out some of the cheese and crackers that the hotel provided to guests who rented suites.

"Probably you were too nervous this morning to eat much," he commented as he set the snacks on the coffee table, along with two small plates, napkins, and a small knife.

Her head jerked up. "Why do you think so?"

"I've heard that the two biggest fears are burning alive and public speaking."

She managed a small laugh. "Right."

"And you knew before you walked in that you were going to"—he shrugged—"cut the talk short."

"You were there? Or has word already gotten around?"

"I was there."

He ordered himself to stand casually while she looked him up and down, trying to place him among the men of her world.

"You're a professor? Or are you from a museum?"

He had frequently been asked questions about his background over the years, and he had answers to fit every occasion. "No. But I've been fascinated with archaeology since I was a kid. I'm retired, and I can afford to indulge my interests. So I came to Las Vegas for the meeting."

"Retired?" Her gaze traveled from the top of his dark head, down his well-muscled body. "You're not old enough."

"I inherited family money, then made the right investments and pulled out of the market before the downturn." He grinned. "Luckily, I didn't have any of my capital in Ponzi schemes or anything else questionable."

He could have added that he'd financed several archaeology expeditions over the years, but he didn't want to open up that subject, since he wasn't prepared to go into details about where and when.

"What's your specialty?" she asked, the hint of challenge in her voice.

"I'm interested in civilizations that aren't tied to Western traditions."

"That's pretty broad."

"I've done a lot of reading on the Mayans and visited some of their major cities."

"Chichen Itza?" she asked, naming a prime destination for casual tourists.

"That's always a good starting place. Tikal's more interesting because it was completely covered by the Guatema-
lan jungle until the University of Pennsylvania excavated
some of the temples and other structures. It was sort of the
New York of the Mayan civilization, a city of one hundred
thousand in 500 A.D. You know, the Dark Ages in Europe."

"Right."

He continued to establish his scholarly credentials.
"The Spanish invaders destroyed all but a few of the Mayan
books, and for hundreds of years no one could decipher
their written language. But now scholars have decoded the
pictographs carved into stone. And their calendar is well
known for its accuracy. It has roots that date back to at least
the sixth century B.C."

"I guess you've studied the culture."

"Quite a bit."

She tipped her head to the side, probably still trying to
figure him out. Or decide whether she was really safe in his
room.

Changing the subject abruptly, she asked, "Did you follow me out of the meeting?"

"Yes."

"Why?"

"I wanted to talk about your work, but I didn't want to
interrupt your conversation with Dr. Westfield and that
other guy."

"That was Gavin. My assistant." She pressed her hands
against the sofa cushions. "Thank you for rescuing me, but
I think I should leave now."

FROM his home office on an estate that hugged the northern California coast, Dominic Coleman left a voice mail
for his protégé.

"Madison, this is Dominic. I expected to hear from you
after the presentation. Is everything all right? Call me."

He replaced the receiver in the phone cradle and stared out the window at the artfully designed garden maintained by a squad of Mexicans. Unable to sit still, he pulled on an alpaca sweater and stepped toward the French door, then out onto the patio, listening to the sound of waves breaking on the rocky coastline. He'd bought the Mendocino property years ago, and now he had to fend off offers from real estate developers who saw the potential for multimillion-dollar homes on two- and three-acre lots.

Stone paths wandered through the garden, and he chose one, walking past beds of native and imported plants to the summer house that was perched on the edge of the cliff. It was no ordinary garden structure. The foundation was reinforced to withstand any erosion, and the interior was weather tight so that the small building was furnished much like a club room with comfortable sofas and chairs and an antique Persian rug on the floor. A phone, fax machine, and computer connected the hideaway to the outside world. And a small refrigerator was stocked with beverages and snacks. If he wanted to conduct business from here, he could. Large picture windows faced the ocean, providing a spectacular view of the coastline.

Dominic stood for a few moments looking at the waves rolling in. It was high tide, and the breakers came almost to the base of the cliff. When the tide was out, he could walk down a flight of stairs to the beach.

He glanced at the phone on the desk, willing Madison to call. She was doing exciting, groundbreaking work, and he understood why she wanted to tell the world about it. This was early in her career, and her find in Italy would make her reputation.

But after the attack on the site, she'd made the right decision about calling off her talk. Now he wanted to hear about the fallout.

What if Spader had tried to pull something at the conference?

Like what, exactly? The man was a fanatic, but how far was he prepared to go?

Dominic sniffed. Kent Spader was a wild card that he hadn't figured on when he'd started his quest. But it would be difficult to murder the man, so he had to deal with him as best he could.

Turning away from the ocean, he crossed to the phone and picked up the receiver. This time he dialed Gavin Kaiser, the PhD candidate who had taken the job of Madison's assistant. Gavin was actually working for Dominic, although neither of them had discussed that arrangement with the woman whose grant paid his salary.

"Hello?" the young man answered.

"Gavin, this is Dominic."

"Yes, sir."

"Have you spoken to Madison?"

"Not since right after her session."

"How did it go?"

"People were . . . upset, of course."

"I understand. How did Madison handle it?"

The young man hesitated for a moment. "Pretty well."

"Where is she now?"

"I don't know. She said she wanted some time alone, and I saw her heading toward the hotel entrance."

"See if you can find her for me, and tell her I want to speak to her."

"Yes, of course."

CHAPTER
FOUR

"I DON'T THINK that leaving is a good idea," Ramsay said. "Those men are still out there somewhere."

She made a small sound that he thought signaled her agreement.

"Who are they?" he asked.

She turned one hand palm up. "I don't know."

"They tried to push you into a car. You have no idea who would want to abduct you or why? Is it connected with the attack on your site?"

The look on her face told him that she could at least speculate about that.

"Do you want to call the police?" he asked in an even voice, interested in her answer.

"No."

"Why not?"

"I'd rather not draw any more attention to myself."

"I guess you shouldn't have submitted a proposal to the conference program committee," he pointed out.

"In hindsight, that's right," she snapped.

Moving slowly so as not to alarm her, he sat down on the couch, leaving eighteen inches of space between them. She gave him a nervous glance, then reached for one of the crackers. Anticipating the movement, he reached at the same time, his hand touching hers as he strove to open her mind to his. It was a calculated move, designed to get what he wanted from her. He focused on the lecture she hadn't been willing to give, silently asking her the questions she had decided not to answer in public.

He almost lost his sense of purpose when he felt a zapping sensation, like he'd blundered into an electric fence. It sent a jolt of heat through his body, making it suddenly hard to breathe.

Scrambling to remember what he'd wanted to accomplish, he sent his thoughts toward hers. As sometimes happened when he made mental contact, time seemed to stretch. He could only have touched her for a few seconds, yet his brain was assaulted by a confusing welter of images. A dark room, underground. Someone holding up a powerful light, illuminating ancient images on the wall. They were indistinct, but he was sure he caught images of dragons and men.

Dragons and men. The combination was electrifying.

Was that really what she had discovered? Or was he making it up because he wanted it to be true?

He fought to steady the sudden pounding of his heart. There'd been enough clues to bring him to Las Vegas to hear her talk. Curiosity had just turned to urgency, yet he felt the lack of his powers—the lack of the control he needed. Or perhaps it was his reaction to Madison Dartmoor that was throwing off his abilities.

He had gone stock-still, and it took several moments for him to realize that she was speaking to him.

"Is something wrong?"

"No." He forced a small laugh as he settled on a course of action. "I didn't have anything to eat this morning, either. I guess I need some fuel—after that fight with Mophead."

As he spoke, he sent her an image of his own. Of how the man had tried to push her into the car and how Ramsay Gallagher had fought off the attack.

"Mophead?" she asked in a shaky voice.

"The bozo with the curly hair who tried to abduct you. I didn't know his name, so that's what I called him."

"Oh," she said, and he knew she was recalling the incident in vivid detail—as he'd intended she would.

"I shouldn't have brought that up," he murmured, hating the way he was manipulating her, yet knowing he wasn't going to back off. Not now. Not when he'd seen those images in the underground room.

She had gone pale, and her hand had started to shake.

"I'm so sorry," he said, sliding closer, moving slowly. When he reached for her, she stiffened for a moment, and he sent her calming thoughts.

It's okay. You like me. You trust me. You want me to hold you. You want to be in my arms.

She made a small, sighing sound, then relaxed.

"It feels like we've known each other for a long time," he murmured.

"Yes."

He turned her toward him, stroking his hand over her back and hair, soothing her and at the same time focusing on the sensuality of the moment and on his need for information.

As though familiarity between them was the most natural thing in the world, he pulled her close, flattening her breasts against his chest, letting the intimate contact work on him—and on her.

He had taken her in his arms because he wanted information from her, but holding her was interfering with his ability to think clearly as lust clouded his brain. Or maybe "need" was a more polite word. He'd left himself unfulfilled last night. He knew that was part of the problem. The fragmenting of his abilities was another.

The Ramsay Gallagher of old would have been in complete control of this situation. Now he couldn't even tell exactly what she was feeling.

She raised her head, staring at him, the mixture of intense heat and confusion on her face making his throat tighten.

"What are we doing?" she whispered.

"Getting to know each other better."

"We can't . . . do this."

"Why not?"

"I just met you."

"We won't do anything you don't want to do." How many times had he used that line, knowing he was a master of swaying a woman's decision?

Before she could protest again, he rubbed his lips against hers, back and forth, ready to pull away if she recoiled. When she stayed where she was, he increased the pressure, moving his mouth against hers with all the skill he had acquired over a long lifetime, at the same time caught up in the sensuality as he marveled at the softness of her lips.

Wordlessly, he urged her to open for him. After a moment's hesitation, she did, so that his tongue could slip into her mouth to play with the soft skin inside her lips and sweep along the serrated line of her teeth.

She made a small sound of approval as he deepened the contact, her tongue sliding forward to meet his.

Claiming more of her had suddenly become his main goal. As he stroked one hand down her body, he slid his mouth to her cheek, then found the tender coil of her ear with his tongue.

When she snuggled closer, he wrapped his arms around her and leaned back on the sofa, changing their positions so that she was sprawled on top of him, loving the weight of her small body on top of his and the way she fit against him. He wrapped her closer, increasing the pressure of her breasts against his chest, then slid his hand down her back to her bottom so that he could wedge the cleft at the juncture of her legs more tightly against his erection.

When she moved her hips against his cock, he couldn't hold back a gasp, his body clamoring for release.

Her breath had turned ragged. So had his. If he had ever known anything in his life, he knew she wanted him. Because he had influenced her mind or because the chemistry between them was too volatile to deny?

Totally caught up in the moment, he felt arousal rolling over him with an intensity that shocked him. Yet in some corner of his fevered brain, he dredged up a dim memory of what he was supposed to be doing. He was seducing her for information. He wanted to know what she had found in that dark chamber in Italy and exactly why she'd decided not to talk about it.

Before he could probe her mind, music intruded into the scene, and he recognized "Ode to Joy."

MADISON made a small sound, pushing awkwardly away from the man lying on the couch. "My phone."

"Let it go," he growled.

She might have complied, but her sense of duty was stronger than her . . . she wasn't sure what to call it. Maybe lust. And she certainly wasn't proud of that.

"I have to answer. Nobody knows where I am. People could be worried about me."

She untangled herself from his legs and sat up on the edge of the sofa cushion, then reached for the bag she'd left on the floor beside the couch.

As she pulled out her phone, she saw the man she'd been kissing sit up and run a hand through his hair as he took several deep breaths.

"How are you?" It was Gavin.

Madison swept back her own hair as she spoke into the

phone, glad that her assistant could only hear her—not see her mussed appearance and the flush spreading across her cheeks. Wanting some privacy, she stood and took a few steps away, her back to the sofa, wondering if Ramsay could hear both ends of the conversation. "I'm fine."

"Are you upset about this morning?" Gavin asked.

"I was. But I know it was the right thing to do."

"Dominic called me. He was worried about you."

"Tell him I'm sorry I didn't call. I'm fine," she repeated.

"Where are you?" Gavin asked.

She looked at the man she'd been on the way to making love with. "I'm with Ramsay Gallagher."

"Who is he? Where are you?"

She took a breath. "He's attending the conference. I'm in his room."

She saw Ramsay tense and knew he was wondering who was getting that information.

"You trust this guy?"

"He's . . . okay. I met him after the talk."

"What room?"

She heard her voice turn exasperated as she said, "Gavin, I'll get back to you."

She clicked off and took a few moments longer than she needed to replace the phone in her purse.

Without looking at Ramsay, she straightened her jacket.

She'd never been a creature of impulse. In fact, she'd always thought of herself as being in control, which gave her no frame of reference for what had happened just now. If Gavin hadn't called, she was pretty sure she and Ramsay would be making love by now.

Or it would already be over. She kept her head down as denial flashed through her mind. Ramsay Gallagher was the kind of man who took his time in bed. They'd still be . . .

Ruthlessly, she cut off the thought, astonished at the leaps her mind was taking. He hadn't even taken her to bed. They'd been tangled up on the couch in his hotel sitting room.

When she finally turned to face him, he asked, "What are you thinking?"

"That shouldn't have happened."

"The phone call?" he asked in a soft voice.

"No." She made an exasperated sound. "You know what I'm talking about."

"Yeah."

She wanted him to look away, but he kept his gaze on her, making her feel exposed and vulnerable.

"I'm sorry," he said. "That went too far, too fast."

"It wasn't entirely your fault," she admitted in a low voice. She was off balance—starting with finding out about the attack at the dig site. Then the attack on *her* a while ago. She would have been in a lot of trouble if Ramsay Gallagher hadn't come along.

He changed the subject by asking, "Was that your assistant calling?"

"Yes. He was worried about me when I disappeared after the session."

"And someone else was worried."

She nodded. "I guess you picked up on that."

"Who?"

"Dominic Coleman."

"Who's he?"

"My mentor."

"I thought that was Professor Westfield."

"He is, academically. He taught me everything I know as far as fieldwork goes. But Dominic is financing my expedition." She shook her head. "Why am I telling you all this?"

"Because you want a sounding board."

"What do you mean?"

"You want to know if you did the right thing this morning by standing there in front of two hundred people and refusing to answer questions."

"I did!"

"Okay. But maybe you should tell me who sent those

thugs after you," he said. Last time he'd brought the subject up, it had been a question. This time it was a statement.

Watching his face, she said, "If I had to guess, I'd say it was Kent Spader."

He gave no sign of recognizing the name, but maybe he was a good actor. Maybe this was all some kind of act.

But which part? The rescue? The heated scene?

She didn't think so. Not the last part, for sure. Uncontrolled passion had leaped between them. It hadn't been one-sided.

"Who's he?" Ramsay asked, bringing her mind back to Spader.

"A man with a lot of money who collects ancient artifacts. He wants more information about my work, and he doesn't care how he gets it."

"Would he attack your camp?"

Until that moment, she hadn't connected the two events. "I don't know," she answered. "There are Mafia-like mobs operating in the area. And grave robbers."

BEFORE Ramsay could ask another question, a knock at the door made them both stiffen.

"Are you expecting someone?" she asked.

"No, are you?"

She got up, walked to the door, and looked through the peephole. "It's Gavin."

"You didn't give him my room number."

"I guess he got it by slipping some money to the desk clerk."

"They're not supposed to give out that kind of information. Tell him you'll meet him later."

Ignoring the advice, Madison turned the knob and opened the door.

"What are you doing here?" Gavin asked.

Ramsay stepped forward. "She's with me."

Gavin entered the room and was about to close the door when it flew open and Mophead burst in—followed by Baldy. Both of them were holding guns.

CHAPTER
FIVE

GAVIN WHIRLED TO face the intruders, lunging at Mophead, who fired at point-blank range.

Madison's assistant went down.

Ramsay leaped over him, ducking under Mophead's gun hand as he grabbed the guy and threw him into the hall, where he landed with a thud against the wall.

Madison gasped, but she was already crouching next to Gavin, staring at the red stain spreading across his chest.

Ramsay wanted to get her out of the way, but he was busy dealing with the thugs.

The other one came at him, and he kicked out, smashing the pistol out of his hand as Mophead picked himself up and fired.

The shot went past Ramsay, and he heard Madison yelp.

"Futuo!" He whirled to face her, and saw that she'd gotten a towel from the bathroom and pressed it against Gavin's chest.

While Ramsay was turned toward her, he heard a scrambling sound behind him and whipped back in time to see the two henchmen making for the stairs. He also spotted a piece of Mophead's shirt that had ripped off as he pulled away from a nail sticking out of the baseboard.

He could follow them, but Gavin was wounded and, he assumed, so was Madison. Leaping back into the hotel suite, he slammed the door and turned to the two people on the floor. Gavin's injury seemed by far the more serious.

"Can you keep the pressure on his chest?" he asked Madison.

"Yes."

Crossing to the phone, he dialed zero and got the front desk. "There's been a robbery attempt in room fifteen forty-three," he said. "A man has been shot and needs an ambulance. Call 911."

"Is the assailant still there?"

"No. There were two of them. They fled."

After slamming the phone down again, he turned back to Madison and Gavin. "The medics will be here soon. He needs treatment in the hospital. And maybe you don't."

"Me?"

"You're hit."

She looked down at her arm in shock. "Oh Lord. I didn't even know."

He eased her arm out of her jacket sleeve and examined the wound. As far as he could see, the bullet had passed through her flesh.

"Can you move your arm?"

She tried and winced, but he was pretty sure no bones were broken. He was also pretty sure he could deal with the injury.

"I'll be right back."

Returning to the bathroom, he grabbed another towel and the sash of the hotel bathrobe that was hanging on the back of the door.

When he knelt by Madison again, he wrapped the towel around her arm and tied it in place with the belt from the robe. Then he placed his hands on her cheeks, drawing on the connection he'd already made with her.

She stared at him. "What?"

"We're not going to tell the police you're hurt because it's dangerous for you to go to the hospital. Those thugs could pick you up there. You and I are getting out of here. I'm going to take you somewhere safe." He reinforced the suggestion with his mind, sending her a silent message, telling her that she was better off clearing out of the city than sticking around.

"Will you come with me?" he asked.

"Where?"

"To my house."

"I . . ."

"It's the safest place you can be. Nobody can get to you there." Again, he sent the message on a mental level, holding his breath as he waited for her decision. Once he would have been absolutely confident he'd gotten through to her—not now.

"All right," she breathed.

"Can you get into the bedroom by yourself?"

"Why?"

"Safer if the cops don't know you're here."

"Is that legal?"

"It's the practical way to keep you safe."

When she answered with a little nod, he opened the door to the suite a crack, then took over the pressure on Gavin's chest.

"Get into the bedroom. Hurry, before the police arrive. Close the door."

As she stood, he looked around the room, surveying the scene from the point of view of the officers who would arrive. He saw the two glasses. Hopefully one of them didn't have lipstick.

Madison wove across the room.

"Take your purse."

"Oh, right."

Watching her unsteady gait, he hoped she was going to make it in time. She winced as she bent to pick up her pocketbook, then clenched her teeth as she straightened again. When she closed the bedroom door behind her, he breathed out a small sigh. He had a lot of practice making arrangements that weren't quite legal, but this was going to be dicey.

A loud knock at the door had him calling out, "Come in, I can't get up."

Two uniformed officers rushed in, followed by two EMTs with a stretcher. Both officers were young and fit-looking, with close-cropped hair under their visor caps. One wore a name tag that said Edwards. The other was Columbus.

"What happened?"

"We were having a meeting," Ramsay said as he got out of the EMTs' way. "There was a knock at the door, and when Mr. Kaiser opened it, two men forced their way in."

Both cops looked around, surveying the scene, trying to figure out if Ramsay was lying about the unknown assailants. He was lying, but not about that.

"Where are the men who broke in?" Edwards asked.

"I fought them off."

"They were armed?"

"Yeah."

"You could have gotten hurt."

"What was I supposed to do, let them rob us?"

"Of what?"

"This is a deluxe suite. Maybe they thought I scored at the casino last night. At any rate, while I was tending to Mr. Kaiser's wounds, they disappeared. But one of them hit the wall out there and left a piece of his shirt."

Columbus stepped out of the room. He was back a few

moments later with a piece of fabric in an evidence bag. Ramsay hoped the guy didn't think he'd planted it to cover up an attempted murder of his friend, Mr. Kaiser.

The EMTs were working feverishly on Gavin. Ramsay heard them calling out blood pressure numbers, saw them start a bottle of what he assumed was Ringer's lactate solution as they gave a status report to their base.

As the EMTs prepared to wheel Gavin out, he asked, "What hospital?"

"Las Vegas General."

"Is he going to make it?" Ramsay didn't know Gavin, but it would be strange if it didn't seem like he cared.

"Hope so. Good work with that compress."

He nodded as the EMTs wheeled Kaiser out of the room.

When they had left, Edwards said, "We're going to want a statement from you."

"Sure," Ramsay answered, when he wanted to get the cops out of there as fast as possible. But he knew they wouldn't simply leave. "As I said, I was having a meeting with Mr. Kaiser, when we answered the door and two men with guns burst in."

"You were unarmed?" Columbus said.

"Yes."

"What happened to Kaiser?" Edwards asked.

"He tried to fend them off, and one of them shot him."

"Can you describe the assailants?" Edwards asked.

Ramsay gave a detailed description of Mophead and Baldy.

"You're observant."

"I try to be."

"Which one shot Kaiser?" Columbus asked.

"The one with the mop of hair."

Edwards looked around the room, focusing on the two wineglasses and the plate of cheese and crackers. "What kind of meeting were you having with"—he consulted his notebook—"Mr. Kaiser."

Did the guy think they were a couple of homosexuals who had met in the casino? Maybe.

What was the best thing to say about their supposed get-together? As he considered his options, he knew he had already made a decision. When Kaiser came to, he wouldn't back up Ramsay's story, but by that time, he would have left town. Too bad he'd checked in under his own name.

"We're attending the same archaeology conference. Mr. Kaiser is the assistant to Dr. Madison Dartmoor. I was, uh, pumping him for information."

"About what?"

"Why she cut her talk short. Anybody who attended can tell you that she walked out when she'd barely begun."

"You're a professor?"

"Just an enthusiastic amateur."

He could see his stock drop as the cops took in his hanger-on status. Maybe he should get a PhD from one of those companies that kept offering diplomas over the Internet. Then he could claim better credentials.

"Okay," Edwards said. "Can you add anything else about the incident?"

"That's about it."

Edwards nodded. "How long have you been in town?"

"Since yesterday."

"And how long will you be here?"

"Until tomorrow," Ramsay lied.

"If we find the men, we'll need you to come down to the station house and identify them."

"Of course."

The cop looked around again, taking in more details. "This suite has a bedroom?"

"The bedroom's empty," Ramsay said in a loud voice, hoping the cop was going to take his word for it, and at the same time trying to warn Madison what was happening. *Stay out of the bedroom. Stay out of the bedroom.* He sent the admonition to the officers. But he didn't have the connection with them that he had with Madison, and apparently they didn't get the message.

"I'd just like to have a look at the clothes in your closet," Edwards said as he strode toward the bedroom.

CARL Portland, also known as Mophead, dragged in a breath and let it out. His score wasn't so hot today, and he had more bad news to report. He pulled out his cell phone and punched in a speed dial number.

Kent Spader picked up. "Do you have her?"

"No."

"What do you mean, no?"

"A guy named Ramsay Gallagher stuck his big nose in where it doesn't belong."

Spader's voice took on a dangerously quiet edge. "Where is Dartmoor?"

"We heard Gavin Kaiser get Gallagher's name from a desk clerk and followed Kaiser to Gallagher's room." He paused and looked at his partner, John Trainer, also known as Baldy. Trainer shrugged.

Portland took a breath and expelled it before saying, "Gavin got shot, and we cut our losses."

"That's just wonderful. Did anything go right? Did you get the artifact?"

"We searched her room. It's not there."

Spader's angry exclamation had Portland holding the phone away from his ear. When they'd first met, the guy had seemed mild, soft-spoken. Polite. With manicured fingernails and high-priced suits.

Now Carl was finding out that there was another side to Kent Spader. A very dangerous side.

"I want Gallagher out of the picture. Do you take my meaning?"

"Got ya."

"Then make Dartmoor tell you what she did with the artifact."

Before Carl could answer, the connection snapped off.

CHAPTER
SIX

OFFICER EDWARDS STRODE toward the bedroom and threw open the door.

Ramsay clenched his fists, frustrated again by the absence of abilities that he'd taken for granted. He should have been able to keep the cop in the living room, but the man obviously hadn't heard him at all.

Both men stepped through the door, and Ramsay followed, his gaze immediately zinging to the bed. It was empty, and the thick comforter and blanket were piled in a messy heap at the end.

When Edwards walked to the clothes closet, Ramsay's breath caught. But the closet was empty except for the ironing board and iron provided by the management and the clothing Ramsay had hung up. Edwards riffled through the shirts and slacks. Columbus checked the trash cans. Neither found any fabric that matched what was in the evidence bag.

Finally, they checked the bathroom.

Also empty.

"We'll be in touch."

Ramsay followed the officers back into the living room and closed the door behind them. Then he ran back to the bedroom.

Madison was lying across the bed, breathing hard.

"Where were you?"

"Under the pile of covers."

"Good thinking."

"You said you didn't want them to know I was here," she said in a barely audible voice.

"Yeah." He sat down beside her and unwrapped the towel he'd tied around her arm. There was no fresh blood, so he retied the makeshift bandage, then started unbuttoning her shirt.

"What are you doing?" she asked, her voice going high and thin.

"Getting rid of your bloody jacket and blouse. Can you sit up?"

She pushed herself up, and he continued to unbutton the blouse, trying not to touch her as he worked. But he couldn't drag his gaze away from the rounded curves of her breasts above the cups of her bra, and his fingers burned when they brushed her skin. From the shallow sound of her breathing, he knew she was reacting to the intimacy, despite her wound.

He clenched his teeth and got the blouse and jacket off, then reversed the process, helping her into one of his dress shirts. When he'd gotten it buttoned, he rolled up the sleeves so they didn't hang over her hands.

"That should do," he said in a husky voice.

He had just stuffed her jacket and blouse into his suitcase when the phone rang, and they both turned to the instrument.

"Who is that?" she whispered.

"Probably the hotel," Ramsay answered, then picked up the receiver. "Hello."

"Mr. Gallagher?"

"Yes."

"This is the manager, Shari Chisholm."

He looked at Madison and nodded.

"The police have informed us there was an attempted robbery and a shooting in your room."

"Yes."

"We deeply apologize. Your bill will be taken care of by the hotel. Is there anything else we can do for you?"

He thought for a moment. Ms. Chisholm was handing him an opportunity he hadn't considered. "Yes, thanks," he answered, then glanced at Madison. "My girlfriend is pretty shaken up."

He saw her face wrinkle. "Girlfriend?" she mouthed.

He shrugged and continued speaking. "We're leaving early, and we'd like an escort down to the lobby. Can you send some security men to my room to accompany us?"

"Of course, sir," Ms. Chisholm answered. "They'll be at your door momentarily."

"Give me fifteen minutes to pack."

When he'd hung up, Madison gave him a hard look. "I'm not your girlfriend."

"Yes, but it avoids a lot of other questions about what you're doing here."

"I guess," she whispered, then said, "but it won't take care of Gavin."

"In what way?"

"He'll tell the police I was with you. He's always very . . . precise."

"And we'll be gone."

"If I'm going to your house, you'd better tell me something about yourself."

Sure. Like maybe about the time he'd ruled a small kingdom? Or when he'd escaped from African headhunters? Or about the years he'd spent in a Buddhist monastery? Instead, he said, "I'm a nice guy."

"I hope," she murmured, then asked, "Why were the cops in the bedroom?"

"One of the bad guys left a piece of his shirt in the hallway. They wanted to make sure it didn't match something of mine."

She sucked in a sharp breath as she took in the implications. "They think you were fighting with Gavin and shot him?"

"They have to consider every angle. But hopefully, he'll back me up on that part—if he's precise."

She gave him a questioning look. "When I got shot, you shouted something. It sounded like '*Futuo*.'"

"Yeah."

"You made it sound like a curse, but I never heard it before."

"You picked that up? In the middle of an emergency?"

She laughed. "It stood out."

"It's Latin. Doesn't translate well to modern English." In fact the Romans had considered it a vile epithet, although it simply meant the man's role in sexual intercourse.

"You curse in classic Latin? Where did you pick that up?"

He grinned. "In school a long time ago. If people can't understand your swear words, you don't offend them."

She nodded, but the conversation had exhausted her, and she lay back, closing her eyes. Her breath was shallow, her skin was pale and clammy, and he knew she was going to need some treatment soon.

"How are you?"

"Not too bad."

Sitting on the side of the bed, he cupped her face again and spoke to her in a low voice. "You're going to be all right. But you need to relax. Just let yourself drift. I'll take care of everything. You don't have to worry about a thing." Again, he reinforced his words with a mental suggestion.

"How do you feel now?"

"I feel good. What did you do to me?"

"A kind of hypnotic technique." He added, "We're getting out of here."

Her eyes snapped open. "I can't leave!"

"Why not?"

"I have something in my room . . . ." Her voice trailed off.

"The thing in the trunk?"

She made a small sound. "How do you know about that?"

"I was in the lobby when you arrived last night. I saw the way you were hovering around the luggage cart."

Her voice turned sharp. "You already knew who I was. What have you been doing—stalking me?"

"I did not know who you were!" he said, punching out the words. "I saw you with the bellman. I was attracted to you, so I paid attention to you."

She held his gaze for a moment longer, but the effort was apparently too much, and she closed her eyes. "Okay."

He turned to the closet, grabbed the rest of the hanging clothing from the rack and folded it into his suit bag, then swept his toilet articles into his Dopp kit.

While he was waiting for hotel security, he went into the living room and called Ufly, the private air carrier he used, and told them to be waiting for him and another passenger. By the time he was finished, a knock sounded at the door.

When he looked through the peephole he saw two men holding security badges.

After opening the door, he ushered them in.

"You have the hotel's apologies for what happened," one of them said. They both looked around and spotted the bloodstain on the carpet.

"Jesus," the other one muttered.

"Sorry for the mess."

"Not your fault."

"I appreciate your coming, but there's been a slight change of plans. We need to get some things from my girl-friend's room. Can you escort us?"

"Certainly."

"She was very unnerved by the incident. And she took something to settle herself down. She's a little out of it."

"Yes, sir."

Ramsay called the bell captain and arranged to have his luggage collected and stored until they came downstairs. Then he went into the bedroom.

"What room?" he asked Madison.

"Six twenty."

He helped her up and slung his arm around her waist as they stepped into the living room.

In the hall, one security man walked in front of them. The other in back. Still, all Ramsay's senses were on alert, because he knew that getting out of the hotel could be dangerous.

Although neither of the assailants appeared in the hallway or in the elevator, Ramsay did see a stairwell door close as they walked with their escort from the elevator to her room. But there were no problems until they stepped inside Madison's room.

AFTER watching the party of four come down the corridor, Carl Portland eased the stairwell door closed. He was wearing a straw sun hat and keeping his head tipped down so his face wouldn't get caught on candid camera.

"They've got company. Two security guards."

"Can we take them?" John Trainer asked. A baseball cap covered his bald head, and he also kept his face turned down.

"Maybe. But then we have to get rid of three dead bodies. You want to deal with that?"

"Not fuckin' likely."

"You're sure she got shot?"

"I can't be positive, but I'm pretty sure. And she wasn't too steady on her feet when she came down the hall just now."

Trainer shifted his weight from one foot to the other. "How often do they check the video from the guest floors?"

"Not as often as they should." Portland thought for a moment. "There are only two ways out of this place. Either the guy's got his own car, or they take a taxi. I'll go to the lobby. You go to the garage and get into the car we rented. Whichever way they leave, we'll be able to follow them."

They both turned and walked down the stairs to the next floor, where they pushed the elevator button.

BESIDE Ramsay, Madison gasped as she took in the state of her belongings. Someone, probably the same two guys who'd pushed their way into Ramsay's room, had been there, searching for the trunk, because the room was utter chaos.

"Jesus," one of the security guys swore again, then looked at Madison apologetically. "Can we help you clean this up?"

"No need. I want the two of you guarding the hall," Ramsay answered. "We'll take care of this."

The men stepped into the hall, and Ramsay figured they were wondering what was really going on. First a robbery attempt in his room. Then the search of Madison's.

After shutting them out, he turned toward Madison. "Did they get your case?"

"I don't know yet."

She wobbled to the bathroom on unsteady legs, where she looked up at the drop ceiling, then pointed to one of the tiles. "I put it up there."

"Good thinking." He looked at her with concern. "Sit down."

She closed the lid on the toilet seat and sat.

Ramsay was tall enough to reach up and push the ceiling tile aside, then he began to feel around.

At first he found nothing, and he thought with a stab of

disappointment that Madison's trick hadn't worked. Then his fingers brushed against something rectangular.

Grasping the object, he lifted it down and saw it was the trunk that Madison had been worried about on her arrival.

"What's inside?"

"Something valuable," she answered, but didn't elaborate.

After he'd retrieved the box, they returned to the bedroom, where Madison dropped into the easy chair.

"Are you all right?" he asked her.

"I've been better."

He nodded, then glanced toward the door and lowered his voice. "The wound's not bleeding—or anything?"

She gingerly felt her arm. "No. It's the same."

"Good. We'll take care of it soon." He looked at the mess in the room again. "Is it okay for me to scoop everything into your bags?"

She shrugged. "I'm not going to sit here straightening it up."

"It will be a jumble, but you can sort it out later."

He moved around the bedroom, picking up belongings that had been tossed about like used tissues. When he came to a pile of silky panties and bras, she made a small sound, and he looked quickly toward her.

"Those goons touched my . . . underwear."

"Yeah. Sorry."

He stuffed them into her suitcase. Then he folded up the items strewn on the closet floor and put them in her hanging bag. She'd left her cosmetics in a travel kit, which made it easier to clear the bathroom.

In ten minutes, he had everything squared away. Next he called the bell desk and arranged to have his luggage brought up on the cart that came to Madison's room. After calling the garage, he informed the security guards that they were ready to leave.

"You look like you've made a few quick getaways," Madison murmured.

"I have."

"Care to tell me about it?"

"Later."

A knock at the door announced the bellman, who'd brought Ramsay's luggage as requested. Still with their armed escort, they took the elevator to the garage.

Ramsay breathed out a small sigh as he saw that his rental car was already waiting. After settling Madison into the passenger seat, he tipped the bellman. It looked like they were making a clean getaway, but as soon as he pulled out of the garage, he saw that another car was right behind him.

CHAPTER
SEVEN

IN THE REARVIEW mirror, Ramsay studied the vehicle following them. It could be someone simply leaving the garage. Or perhaps not.

He headed down the Strip, then pulled into the parking lot surrounding another one of the large hotels.

The other car did the same.

Madison had been sitting with her eyes closed. When she felt the car suddenly turn, her eyes blinked open, and she looked around. "What are you doing?"

"Taking evasive action. Someone's following us."

She tried to crane around in her seat to look out the back window, then sucked in a sharp breath at the effect of the twisting movement.

"Sit still. I assume it's the same guys who've been after you. In a different car."

He drove too rapidly through the parking lot, dodging a Cadillac that was just pulling out. In the rearview mirror, he saw that the big car had cut off the pursuers. As horns blared behind him, he turned the corner, zipped down another row, then headed for the exit.

Looking back again, he didn't spot the pursuing vehicle. But he didn't take any chances. Instead of heading west toward the airport, he made a right and wound through the type of inner-city neighborhood where he'd picked up the working girl the night before.

After a dozen minutes, he made for the highway, knowing the men might assume he was going to the airport. But he didn't want to delay treating Madison's wound. As he drove, he kept glancing behind him during the ten-minute ride, turning in at the general aviation part of the terminal.

"Where are we going?" she asked.

"I've booked a private flight."

They pulled up at the Ufly office. Inside, he asked if they could turn in his car for him.

"That will cost you extra," the blond behind the counter said.

"That's fine. My girlfriend isn't feeling well, and I'd like to get out of here as soon as possible."

"I believe your plane is ready."

The pilot, who introduced himself as Larry Warren, led them to the small jet.

"There's a refrigerator stocked with drinks and sandwiches," Warren said.

"Thanks."

The copilot, Avery McDuffie, was already on board.

The luxury jet had plenty of leg room. Ramsay settled Madison in a bulkhead seat in the back and buckled her in. He took the aisle seat next to her.

The pilot closed a curtain between themselves and the main cabin, then spoke over the intercom, saying they were cleared for takeoff and advising them of safety procedures.

"Our flying time to Rodeo Mountain Airport is just under two hours. Keep your seat backs upright and your seat belts fastened until I give the all clear," he said.

Once they were airborne, and the pilot had told them they could move about the cabin, Ramsay went into the head at the back of the plane where he washed his hands and the blade of the penknife in his pocket, then grabbed some paper towels.

"Let's have a look at your wound," he said when he returned. "You need to unbutton your shirt and slip your arm out."

She glanced toward the cockpit.

"They're busy flying the plane."

"Okay."

When she fumbled with her shirt buttons, he helped her get them open, then gingerly eased her arm out of the sleeve, watching her clench her teeth in pain.

"Sorry."

"What are you going to do?"

"Taking a look." He unwound the makeshift bandage from the entrance and exit wounds. It bled a little as he pulled off the towel, but as far as he could tell, it wasn't infected.

"How is it?"

"Better," he answered.

"Oh sure."

"Let's put your seat back so you can rest," he murmured, as he used the controls to make the chair into a recliner.

"Comfortable?"

"Um-hum."

He continued speaking to her in a low, soothing voice as he mentally prepared himself to treat her.

"Just relax. I'm going to make you feel better. You're just going to drift away and let me take care of everything," he said aloud, reinforcing the words with mental suggestions.

Her eyelids fluttered closed.

"How are you feeling now?" he asked.

A small smile curved her lips. "You're doing that hypnosis thing again?"

"Um-hum. Do you like the mountains?"

"Um-hum."

"That's where we are. You're lying on a chaise in the sun. You can feel the heat on your skin. It feels good."

"Yes," she murmured.

Lifting his head, he glanced toward the cockpit and made sure that the curtain was still closed. Then he cupped his left hand. With his right, he used the penknife to make a slash across his palm, squeezing so that blood welled up.

His blood had healing properties. Or it had, the last time he'd needed them. But what if that had gotten screwed up in the battle with Vandar?

When he'd collected a small pool of blood, he leaned over Madison, making sure his body blocked her view of the wound as he let some of his blood drip onto the place where the bullet had entered her arm.

"The sun feels good on your face," he whispered. "And the mountain breeze is putting you to sleep."

This time she didn't answer.

Lowering his hand, he pressed the side of his palm to her flesh, making a dam so that he held a small pool of his blood over the entrance wound. He kept it there for five minutes, watching the liquid thicken, wondering if he was doing any good.

He sat with his heart pounding, waiting for the verdict, knowing he had to give the treatment some time.

He could see Madison's face, see the flush spreading across her cheeks. Side effects. But was he also getting the main effect? Sweat broke out on her brow. And on his, as well.

After five minutes, with a hand that wasn't quite steady, he wiped the blood away from her arm with the paper towels he'd dampened and looked at the wound. He was elated to see that it was starting to close.

Breathing out a small sigh, he turned Madison's arm over, cupping his hand over the exit wound as he'd done with the place where the bullet had entered, again letting blood pool over the small hole. When he'd given it another five minutes, he wiped the blood away again and also wiped his hand, seeing that the slash where he'd cut himself was also healing.

Madison was sleeping, which he took as a good sign. Hopefully, she'd stay that way for most of the remaining hour of the flight, because he wasn't sure how he would deal with her on the plane if she woke up. Or with himself.

He looked down at her open shirt front, watching the rise and fall of her breasts. He wanted to reach out and stroke the tender skin at the edge of her bra, but he ordered himself not to touch her.

Because he didn't want to disturb her, he left her arm out of her sleeve and covered her with a blanket, in case the pilot or the copilot came back to use the head.

Pressing the controls on his own seat, he reclined himself to a comfortable angle and tried to relax. But his blood was humming now because he'd made a mental connection with her, and the side effects were transmitting themselves to him. Unfortunately.

When the pilot announced that they were making their descent into Rodeo Mountain Airport, Madison's eyes fluttered open. For a moment, she looked confused. Then she focused on Ramsay.

"How are you?" he asked.

Her face tensed as she flexed her arm. When it didn't hurt, she looked surprised.

Turning her head, she scanned the wound, then carefully poked at it with her finger. "It's almost gone. What did you do?"

"I've developed a special treatment," he said, hearing the husky quality of his own voice. "It works with the hypnotic suggestion."

"Oh," she answered, and he wondered what she was really thinking.

"You should put your shirt back on."

She flushed. "You didn't do it?"

"You were sleeping, and I didn't want to disturb you."

She tugged her arm back into the sleeve, then quickly dealt with the buttons, but he saw her hands were unsteady. He could have explained what she was feeling, but then he'd have to explain why, and he wasn't prepared to do that.

It was late afternoon when they landed at the small Colorado airport near his home. As soon as they'd taxied to the general aviation terminal, he thanked the pilots, then helped Madison down the short flight of stairs to the ground. He knew he was in a vulnerable position at that moment, and he looked around carefully for signs that anyone had figured out their destination and arranged for a reception committee. But no one seemed interested in their arrival.

Madison studied the small facility, which seemed entirely out of place among the towering mountains. *Like an intrusion*, he thought. But it served its purpose. It had allowed them to get back here quickly. And speed had been of the essence.

"Your house is near here?" Madison asked.

"About an hour away," he said, carrying their luggage to the SUV that he'd left in the terminal parking area.

As they drove into the pine-covered mountains, he saw her shift restlessly in her seat.

He switched on the headlights as they turned off the highway, onto a two-lane road. At this time of year, the sun was already setting behind the mountains. There was hardly any traffic, but he was starting to think that they weren't going to get home fast enough.

Madison was sitting with her lower lip between her teeth. As he watched from the corner of his eye, she slid him an unsettled look. "What did you do to me?" she asked in a barely audible voice.

"Just what I told you."

She turned her head toward him, her eyes piercing. "I feel like you gave me some kind of drug. Did you?"

"Like when? Did you drink anything? Eat anything?"

"I don't think so. My memory is fuzzy."

"What you're feeling is a side effect of the medical treatment I used."

"Then you shouldn't have used it!"

"Maybe. But you needed to mend. The wound is healing faster than normal. That's because your metabolism has speeded up."

He didn't tell her that he hadn't counted on the side effect being so strong. Or that, unfortunately, he was trapped by the same intensity she felt. It wouldn't have happened if he wasn't already attuned to her. Or if they hadn't been close to making love in his hotel room.

When she lifted her arm and grasped the handle above the door, he saw her fingers clench around the U-shaped grip. As they had been earlier, her cheeks were flushed, and he saw a sheen of perspiration on her brow.

His own hands were clenched on the wheel, and he knew he wasn't going to be driving much farther.

He had lived in this area for more than thirty years, and he'd watched civilization creep into the wilderness, but he knew there were still places where the forest reigned supreme.

Making a quick decision, he turned off the secondary road, onto a gravel track that was used mostly by fisherman heading for the lake a few miles ahead. But it was early in the year for fishing.

He pulled to a stop behind a rock outcropping, and Madison looked around. "This is where you live?"

"It's still a half hour ride."

"Then why are we stopping?"

"I think you know why."

He unbuckled his seat belt, then reached across the console and unhooked hers.

She shrank against the door, looking at him helplessly as he pushed back his seat, adjusting it to the reclining position.

Before he could question the wisdom of what he was doing, he reached for her and lifted her onto his lap. Wrapping his arms around her, he pulled her down so that she was sprawled on top of him the way she'd been on the hotel sofa.

"Don't."

"Do you really mean that?" he asked, just before he melded her mouth with his for a kiss that turned frantic the moment their lips touched. Not just for him. He felt her need, too. And her confusion.

He fought to control the impulse to conquer, an old impulse that ran deep in his soul. He'd enjoyed great powers during his long life—and one of those powers was his sexual magnetism. But with this woman, he sensed that communication was more important than conquest.

Deliberately slowing himself down, he slid his lips against hers, then turned his head to nibble at her ear, talking to her in a low, seductive voice.

"You need this. We both need it. It's not just the treatment. It's because we mean something to each other. I knew that the moment I saw you. You feel it, don't you?"

"I . . ."

"Don't fight it. Let it happen."

"I . . . don't do this . . . with men I don't know."

"I know," he murmured.

In the gathering dusk, with the aroma of the pine forest all around them, he gathered her closer, marveling at how perfectly her body fit against his. Swaying her in his arms, he reveled in the way he could slide her breasts against his chest.

Claiming more of her, he sucked her lower lip into his mouth, entranced by the taste and textures of her.

He knew she tried to hang on to her sense of propriety, but he felt the moment of her surrender. She made a small sound and opened for him, so that he could kiss her deeply, drinking from her essence.

The intensity of his need for her made his head spin. Because he had been unfulfilled the night before, and then in his suite at the hotel, he had started something that they hadn't been able to finish.

But in this place and time there would be no interruptions. Or, to put it another way, he was prepared to tear any man limb from limb who interfered with him now.

His hands went to her bottom, cupping her sweet curves so that he could press her center to the erection straining at the front of his slacks.

She moved against him, shooting him to another level of madness.

Thank the heavens she didn't have on pants.

He pulled up her skirt, then tore at her panty hose and panties, ripping the delicate fabric apart, then tossing them onto the floor.

Free to explore her now, he stroked the enticing curve of her bottom, then reached lower, into the folds of her sex. She was wet and swollen for him, and she cried out as he slipped two fingers into her.

Need made his voice low and rough. "Help me out of these damn pants."

When she hesitated, he begged, "Please."

She searched his face. Maybe his desperate expression convinced her, because her hand went to his belt buckle, opening it and then the hook at the top of his slacks.

As she lowered his zipper and reached inside, he couldn't hold back a cry of gratitude.

He knew she had gone past any semblance of modesty when she freed his cock from his shorts and wrapped her hand around him.

"You're huge," she whispered.

Fighting for control, he moved her hand away, then lifted her up, bringing her down again so that she sheathed him.

They both cried out at the joining, and he sensed that this would be a wild, frantic ride.

She looked at him, her eyes dazed as she took him deeper inside her. When she began to move in a jerky rhythm, he found her clit with his fingers, circling the head while he teased one taut nipple with his other hand, watching her face as her inner muscles clenched around him. He wanted to tear off her shirt so that he could lap at her breasts and suck one of her nipples into his mouth, but he was too far gone to do more than touch her through the fabric.

"Ramsay. Oh Lord, Ramsay!"

As he felt her coming, he let himself go, his shout of satisfaction mingling with her cry. He might have extended the pleasure, finding her neck with his feeding teeth and drawing blood from her. But she'd already lost some blood when she'd gotten shot. Taking more would be a bad idea, for more than one reason. He couldn't risk her finding out that he wasn't human.

CHAPTER
EIGHT

MADISON COLLAPSED AGAINST Ramsay, and he cradled her in his arms, marveling at the intensity of his response to her. At the same time, he knew that making love with her hadn't been the smartest decision he'd ever made. But he'd wanted her—fiercely—and he wanted to savor the aftermath. When she raised her head, he stroked the damp hair back from her forehead.

The words she whispered weren't what he wanted to hear. "That was . . . outrageous."

"Yeah." He kept his gaze on her, and she was the one who looked away, then down at the floor by his feet, where he'd thrown the clothing he'd shredded.

Untangling herself from him, she levered herself back into the passenger seat and yanked her skirt down.

"I must look like I've been . . . caught in a hurricane." She flapped her hand in exasperation.

"Nobody's going to know about it," he said as he put himself back together.

"*I* know about it. And I don't like it."

Reaching down, he swept her ruined underwear into the side pocket in the door and hoped that she wasn't watching him.

Perhaps she was, because she snapped, "I need to get cleaned up—then get back to the airport."

He kept his gaze straight ahead as he started the car and circled the rock, heading back toward the two-lane highway. "Not a good idea."

"I'll be the judge of that."

"You want those guys to find you?"

"How do they know where I've gone?"

"I don't know. But I'm not willing to take a chance on their detective skills. And where *would* you go? Not back home or to your office, certainly. What would stop them from looking for you *there*?"

While she thought that over, he started the car and pointed it toward his own home, then asked, "How did you get hooked up with Dominic Coleman?"

"Why are you bringing him up *now*?"

"Because you don't want to talk about us at the moment."

"There is no *us*."

"I think there is, but we can save that for later. Tell me about Coleman."

"What do you know about him?"

"Not much."

She sighed. "He was a friend of my parents. He's known me since I was little." She paused for a moment, then went on. "Mom and Dad were killed in a car accident while I was still in college. Dominic stepped in and offered to pay my tuition. He'd always encouraged my interest in archaeology. He was delighted when I wanted to go on to graduate school. While I was still working on my PhD at Santa Barbara, he told me he was investigating a local legend about an Italian tomb. When he found evidence that it actually existed, he asked if I wanted to be in charge of the project, and I jumped at the chance."

"Pretty heady for a new PhD. I'll bet there was some talk in the department."

"Of course!" she snapped. "But I ignore it."

"You're on the faculty at Santa Barbara?"

"Yes."

"Did Westfield recommend you?"

"Of course. He knew my skills. And he knew my dedication."

He nodded, and they both lapsed into silence. He'd impulsively decided to bring her to his house. Now he was thinking about the practicalities. There was no real need for him to keep human food in the house—beyond a few luxuries like good coffee. But he liked to be prepared for the occasional visitor.

MADISON wanted to fold her arms across her chest, but she forced herself to sit with her hands in her lap. She was still coping with her own out-of-kilter behavior. She longed to blame it on whatever drug Ramsay had given her, but she hadn't actually felt drugged. It was something else. She'd wanted *him*, and even when she'd denied it, she knew there was an attraction between them that she couldn't explain.

More than that, he'd brought out an uncharacteristic wildness in her, and she wanted to think about what had happened.

She tried not to tense as the SUV turned off the highway, then started climbing a steep gravel road with no guardrail. Mercifully, she couldn't really see the drop-off on the driver's side.

As they pulled to a halt in the middle of blackness, she was startled by an overhead light clicking on. It shone on the car and on a metal gate that blocked the road. Ramsay rolled down the window and punched the security code into the keypad, reading the display, which apparently gave him a status report.

"Nobody's been here since I left."

"You like your privacy," she murmured as the gate swung open.

"Yeah. And I like knowing nobody's tried to burglarize the house."

He drove through, then up the steep road, watching her catch her breath as she took in the chalet he'd built on a mountaintop. It was illuminated by floodlights which he'd installed for security, but they also created a dramatic effect.

"How did you get the supplies up here to build this place?"

"Donkey."

"You're kidding."

He laughed. "Yeah."

"They really do that in the hills of Italy. There are houses you can only get to up steep, narrow pathways—with endless steps."

"I know. And the houses up there can be hundreds of years old."

"What made you pick this isolated location? Did you defraud a bunch of investors? And now you want to make sure they can't get to you?"

"Is that what you really think of me?"

"Well, probably not that, exactly. You're more the type for physical crimes."

He shrugged. "I've just become security conscious over the years."

More lights clicked on as they approached the house. After opening the garage door with the remote, he drove inside and parked between another SUV and a sporty little Bentley convertible. Although she knew the luxury car cost as much as a lot of houses, she made no comment as he led her to a sitting room.

But she was unable to hold back a shocked exclamation as she looked around at the objects in the room.

A painting that was certainly a Monet hung on the wall over a comfortable sofa. On the side table was what she would swear was an authentic Greek amphora. The sideboard held a collection of Roman coins. An ancient Chinese trunk topped with a thick slab of glass served as the coffee table. And the marble fireplace looked like it had come from a French chateau.

"You have a fortune in antiques here," she breathed. "I see why you'd worry about burglars. You like attending auctions?"

"Or garage sales."

She laughed. "Right."

He turned toward the hallway. "Let me show you one of the guest bedrooms. When you're rested, we'll talk about our next move."

"Our?"

"You think you're better off without me?"

After a moment's thought, she answered, "Probably not."

"How about something to eat first. Something light."

"Chicken soup?" she asked, wondering if he could produce it.

"I've got some cans. Then you should get some sleep," he answered in that soothing voice that made her a little nervous.

They stopped in a spacious modern kitchen, where he opened a can of soup and poured most of it into a mug, which he put in the microwave.

When it was heated, he made another mug of tea. "Sugar?"

"Yes, thanks."

He added a packet, then put both mugs on a tray, along with a spoon, a napkin, and some crackers. Apparently he didn't want to stay with her while she ate, because he carried the meal down the hall to the guest room he'd mentioned and set it on a seventeenth-century writing desk.

Like the sitting room, the bedroom was full of antiques—
in this case, mostly furnishings that probably came from an
English manor house. And the rugs were genuine Persian,
she was sure.

"Get some sleep. We'll talk when you get up."

"Yes. Thanks," she answered, annoyed with herself for
going along with him so easily, but he seemed to be an
expert in having things go his way.

When he'd closed the door, she waited for a few
moments, then clicked the lock. Not that she didn't trust
him, she told herself. She just wanted to feel secure.

With a sigh, she wandered into the luxurious bathroom.
Deciding to indulge herself, she drew a bath in the huge
tub, then brought her soup and tea into the bathroom. After
undressing and slipping into the hot water, she used a bath
pillow she'd found to prop up her back. As she sipped the
soup, she tried to process everything that had happened
since the night before.

It occurred to her belatedly that she shouldn't be in the
tub. Not when she'd been shot in the arm. But when she
looked at the wound, all she could find was a red place that
looked like a healing scar.

Whatever he'd done to fix it had apparently worked.

She'd have to ask him about that again. And a lot of
other things. Although he talked a good game when it
came to archaeology, she really didn't know his background. Where he'd gotten his education, or even how he'd
built this house and transported so many rare treasures to
such a remote location.

But at the moment, her brain wouldn't even provide the
right questions. Finally she admitted defeat, dried off, and
slipped into the robe draped over the dressing table chair.

She was still wearing it when she pulled back the cover
and climbed into bed.

Almost as soon as her head hit the pillow, she was
asleep.

* * *

IN the library that functioned as a control center for the house, Ramsay pressed a button that slid back a section of the wall to reveal a bank of monitors. *Modern technology!* He couldn't take it for granted. Not after the primitive conditions he'd lived through.

From the control panel, he turned on the camera that gave him a view of the guest room and watched Madison sleeping. He hated to spy on her, but he had his own private business to take care of, and he didn't want her watching him.

She tempted him as no other woman had in ages. The intensity of their sexual encounter shocked him, yet he knew that getting too close to her could be a mistake— for both of them. There was no way a relationship with her could end well, for either of them. But he'd thrown caution to the wind and brought her here.

Unable to account for his own behavior, and feeling guilty about the camera, he looked over his shoulder, then closed the panel again.

After changing into jeans and a T-shirt, he used his secure phone line to call the Las Vegas hospital where her assistant had been taken.

He was relieved to find out that the young man was out of surgery and in recovery. Not that he cared about Gavin. But he knew Madison would.

Satisfied that he could give her some good news when she woke up, he walked down a flight of steps that gave him access to the hillside below the house.

It was dark outside, but his night vision was excellent. He stood for a moment breathing in the clean mountain air, so different from the smoke-clogged Las Vegas casino.

He started down a winding trail, then came to a narrow wooden bridge that crossed a ravine where a cataract of water cascaded over weathered granite rock. On the far side of the bridge, he rounded an outcropping of rock and whistled softly into the wind. When he heard a rustling in the vegetation, he looked up to see two graceful caramel-colored deer walking toward him. The lead animal nuzzled its head against his hand, and he scratched behind its ears. More of the herd appeared, and he greeted them warmly, moving easily among them. When he sat down on a large rock, they crowded in closer, warming him with the heat of their bodies. He put his arm over the shoulder of a buck, then bent to find the animal's neck. He sank his feeding teeth into the gamy flesh and drank—but not too much.

When he lifted his head, the buck stepped away, and a doe took his place. He drank from her, too. Then from another buck. When he was feeling recharged, he stood and looked back at the house.

He'd left Madison sleeping. She shouldn't awaken for several hours. Still, he walked around an outcropping of rock to a high mountain meadow before taking off his clothes and standing naked in the darkness, feeling the wind on his skin.

He'd gotten back some of his old powers, but they were minor compared to what he most wanted—to transform into his other self. A dragon. He wanted to spread his wings and leap into the air, circling the house, roaring his triumph. This was why he lived so far from the abodes of men. Where he was free to change into a winged beast whenever he wanted.

Until a few months ago, he had taken the dragon for granted. After long months of failure, he understood what the loss meant.

Eyes closed, he went deep into himself, trying to summon the other part of his being—the part that had eluded him since the fight with Vandar, who came from another universe and planned to conquer this one.

They'd fought as dragons, two beasts wheeling in the

air, spewing flames and slashing at each other with talons and teeth.

They'd both known it was a fight to the death. And he had emerged victorious. He wasn't sure whether it had been through luck or skill, but he'd used the last of his strength flying away from the field of battle. Burned, clawed, and weak from loss of blood, he changed to his human form, and he'd been stuck in this frail body ever since.

Unwilling to accept that he was damaged forever, he struggled to summon the dragon that had been his to command for so long. But he felt no stirring in his flesh. No stirring in his brain. The ability to change simply didn't exist for him, and he was afraid that it would never return.

"Futuo!" His curse rang out across the meadow. He should have let humanity take its chances with Vandar. *Yeah, right.* That wouldn't have worked out, either. Because as soon as he'd found out about the other dragon's plans to conquer this world, he'd known that only one of them could survive.

He made a rough sound. Right now his problem was getting his full powers back.

Caught between depression and anger, he pulled on his clothing and stood in the darkness for long moments, ordering himself not to give up. As he approached the house, he remembered the luggage he'd thrown into the trunk. Unloading it, he carried his bags to his room; then he set Madison's suitcases outside her door.

But he kept looking at the mysterious trunk.

The defeat in the meadow had put him in a reckless mood. Leaving her suitcase, he picked up the trunk again and carried it to the living room, putting it on the coffee table. As he sat down on the sofa, he contemplated invading her privacy again.

Was this worse than looking at her in her bedroom? He wouldn't know until he opened the case.

It was locked, of course. But it was a simple matter to use a piece of wire to spring the catch.

Feeling a thrill of anticipation mixed with guilt, he lifted the lid and found soft packing material cushioning some sort of artifact.

When he lifted the thing out and unwrapped it, it moved in his hand, and he almost dropped it. Then he saw what he was holding, and the breath froze in his lungs.

CHAPTER
NINE

IT WAS AN eighteen-inch-high figure that looked like it was made out of a gray blue stone. But as he hefted it in his hand, he suspected that it might really be synthetic.

A shiver went through him. Gingerly, he set the figure down before he dropped it. If he had to try and explain what he had pulled from the trunk, he might have compared it to a toy that changed shape when you twisted the moving parts. But this was no mere plaything.

The statue looked like it was a man. But when he pushed up one of the arms, it elongated and changed into a wing.

As he moved both arms, the figure shifted. The body bulked up, a tail spiked from the rear, scales formed down the back, and the figure changed from a man standing on his feet to a crouching dragon.

Man to dragon!

A few minutes ago, he'd been trying to effect that trick himself. And here was a little figure that did what he could not.

What did it mean?

Carefully, he picked it up again, moving the wings, folding them downward so that they became arms again, and the whole figure changed from dragon to man once more. He was so absorbed in playing with the statue that he didn't hear footsteps coming down the hall.

"What the hell are you doing?"

His head jerked up as he confronted Madison, who stood in the doorway wearing a pair of pants and a long-sleeved shirt that had been in her luggage. The outraged expression on her face was as fierce as that of a dragon.

He strove to meet her angry gaze with equanimity when his heart was pounding so hard that it felt like it was going to break through the wall of his chest.

"I opened the trunk," he said in a voice so steady that it surprised him.

Her hands went to her hips. "I see that. You're overstepping the bounds again. But why should I be surprised?"

"You claim you found this in an ancient tomb."

She shrugged.

"This is a phony," he said, punching out the words. "It's not made of any material available to the ancients. It's a hoax. Like Piltdown Man. Or . . . a fake Picasso."

"A hoax! How dare you."

"So what is this thing, if you're not trying to pass it off as real?"

"You don't think I'd bring a valuable artifact to a Las Vegas conference without an armed guard, do you?"

"Sit down and tell me about it."

She remained standing. "Why should I?"

"Because I've proved to be your friend."

"I'm not so sure of that."

They stared at each other across six feet of charged space. Finally she said, "All right. I found an object like this in the tomb I've been excavating in Italy."

"A tomb dating from when?"

"At least the first century B.C."

He sucked in a breath, then said, "You might as well sit down while we talk."

After hesitating for a moment, she took an easy chair opposite him.

"Dominic had this copy made. I had no intention of claiming it was anything besides a re-creation, and I intended to show it at my lecture. That was before the attack in Calabria. Gavin supported my decision to cancel the talk."

"You trust Gavin?"

Outrage bloomed on her face. "Of course I trust him."

"He led those thugs to my room."

"By accident."

"If you say so."

"I do. I know his motives. But I don't know yours!" She stopped and ran a hand through her hair. "Oh Lord, what am I thinking. I don't even know if he's all right."

"He is."

Her eyes narrowed. "What—are you telepathic?"

"No. I called the hospital while you were sleeping. He's out of surgery and in recovery."

"Thank you."

"I thought you'd want to know."

"Yes. But let's get back to your motives. What's your interest in my discovery?"

Of course he couldn't tell her the truth. But he had to give her an explanation. Watching her carefully, he said, "I'm a student of extraterrestrial archaeology."

He saw her struggling to keep her expression neutral. "What do you mean by 'extraterrestrial archaeology'?"

"Forty years ago when I first saw *2001: A Space Odyssey*, I was fascinated by the concept of mankind being visited by space travelers. I started reading about the subject, and the more I read, the more sense it made to me," he said, skirting the truth, yet coming close enough. There was no way he could convey his shock when he'd first seen that movie. He'd done a lot of research on the director, Stanley

Kubrick, and he'd finally concluded that the man was simply sharing a private vision with the public.

"When I heard about your lecture, I wondered if it might have something to do with extraterrestrials, since you weren't lecturing on any known civilization."

Her breath had turned shallow.

Pressing ahead, he asked, "And now you've told me the statue is a copy of something you found at the site."

"Why should I believe your story? Maybe you learned about me, and you've been spying on me all along."

The word "spying" must have registered on his face, because he saw her expression change.

"Do I have to walk back to the highway? Oh wait—I can't, can I? Not with that gate of yours."

"Why don't you just walk down the hall to my library?"

"So you can come up with a plan to keep me here."

"If you still want to leave after you've looked at some of my books and other materials, you can do it."

"What difference will any of that make?"

"I think I can give you an idea about the depth of my interest in the subject we've been discussing."

Without waiting for her to agree, he got up and headed back down the hall, thankful that he'd remembered to close the panel in front of the television screens.

For a tense moment, he wondered if she was going to accept his invitation. Then he heard her soft footsteps behind him.

In the library, he gestured toward a wall of books. "These are some of the materials I've acquired—some at considerable expense."

MADISON walked to the shelves and pulled down a nineteenth-century translation of an ancient Greek text on beings who had challenged the gods and goddesses of their pantheon. After thumbing through the pages, she replaced the book and went on to another, this one Roman in origin. Again it was a translation of a long-ago manuscript, speculating on how certain artifacts had ended up in the Italian hills.

When she reached for a fragile volume, he cautioned, "Careful with that one. It was damaged in a flood."

She pulled her hand back. "Where did you get it?"

"From a dealer in Amsterdam."

"Okay. What's it about?"

"Speculation on alien visits to Latin America before Westerners crossed the ocean. I've got a lot more books on ancient visitors, but you might like to see some pictures."

He walked to the shelves, opened a wide drawer, and withdrew some folders and portfolios with drawings and photographs.

She shuffled through the contents, slowing as she compared dragons from various ancient cultures. Many were from China and Japan.

Another series of photographs showed stone disks with lines inscribed in concentric circles. There were close-ups of the lines, revealing that they were actually tiny hieroglyphics.

"Where did you get these?"

"I took a lot of the photos myself. On location."

She pointed to the disks and the hieroglyphics. "These were locked up at Beijing University in the late 1950s."

He shrugged.

"You couldn't have gotten in there. No Westerner could."

He said something in a language she couldn't understand.

"Are you speaking Chinese?"

"Mandarin. Yeah."

"Where did you learn it?"

"In my travels."

"Wait a minute. We're talking about the late 1950s."

"They may have been locked up then, but you can get into any closed facility—if you have the right approach."

"How?"

He laughed. "Money often works. I mean, think about the Chinese pandas. They rent them out to U.S. zoos for a million dollars a year. And any offspring must go back to China."

She switched back to the photos of the disks. "A Dr. Tsum claimed he translated the hieroglyphics, but the Chinese thought he was faking and kicked him out."

"I'm not judging his account. I'm interested that stones like these were found in a remote area of the Himalayan Mountains. Where there were caves with tombs nearby. Tombs that wouldn't be large enough for a normal human."

She felt a shiver go over her skin. "You were there, too?"

"Yeah."

Hard to believe. But somehow she didn't doubt it.

He pulled out another folder, with photos of ancient statues and medieval paintings. "The artwork is mostly from various galleries. Some original, some reproduction," he was saying.

She looked at a painting of Saint George dressed as a knight slaying a fierce-looking dragon.

"Interesting how many cultures have myths about dragons, isn't it?" he remarked. "In the West, they breathe fire and destruction. In Asia, they breathe cool mist and protect mankind."

Carefully, she replaced the portfolios and folders in the drawer and moved to the modern section of the bookshelves, scanning titles that ranged from science fiction novels by Arthur C. Clarke to speculations by Carl Sagan and Erich Von Daniken and accounts of people who claimed to have been abducted by aliens and taken aboard their ships for medical experimentation.

"There are so many clues, even references in the Bible. And it's startling how many cultures have space traveler mythologies—I mean from India to Brazil, from China to North America.

"In some stories, visitors who came from the sky are credited with teaching mankind agriculture, astronomy, medicine, and a lot of other things that they needed to know."

When he saw her slight nod of agreement, he went on. "Believers in alien visitations to Earth cite all kinds of evidence. Statues from the Dogu period in ancient Japan. Stonehenge in England. The Nazca Lines in Peru. I don't have to give you all the examples. You know them as well as I do."

CARL Portland paused outside the small Ufly office and dragged in a draft of the desert air. At least he had something positive to report—not just the bad news that Gallagher had gotten Dartmoor out of town.

Turning, he walked to the car where his partner, John Trainer, was waiting. Trainer had followed Gallagher from the garage, but the bastard had taken evasive maneuvers.

The guy could have driven out of the city and headed for Lake Tahoe or even Los Angeles. But his license plate had been for a rental car. Desperation had them checking the airport rental lots. When the car wasn't in any of the lots at the major rental companies, they'd kept driving around, and found the vehicle outside a small general aviation company called Ufly.

"Did you find out where they went?" Trainer asked.

"The woman behind the counter decided she could use some extra bread. One of their planes flew Gallagher and Dartmoor to Rodeo Mountain Airport in Colorado."

"Where the hell is that?"

"In the middle of nowhere—the mountains. The plane's not back yet."

He pulled out his cell phone and pressed the speed dial.

Spader picked up on the first ring.

"You got them?"

"They left the city."

"And where did they go?" Spader asked in the quiet voice that Carl had come to fear.

"A place called Rodeo Mountain Airport, Colorado. He chartered a small plane from a general aviation company called Ufly."

"That's something."

"The clerk is under the impression that's his home base."

"Why does she think so?"

"She looked up his records. He's used the company before, and he usually leaves from that location."

"That's excellent information."

Carl glanced back at the car where his partner waited. He could explain that losing the couple was John's fault, but he didn't think that would buy him any brownie points. Instead, he asked, "You want us to fly there?"

"Yes. And while you're in the air, I'll check on his location. By the time you land, I should be able to tell you where he lives."

"Okay. You want we should charter a plane?"

"Obviously. But use a different company."

"It'll be expensive."

"Money is no object." Without waiting for an answer, he kept speaking. "And this time I want results. I want Dartmoor. And I want Gallagher out of the picture."

The phone clicked off, and he was left feeling a trickle of sweat drip down the back of his neck.

He'd gone to work for Spader because the pay was great, but now he was wondering what his life expectancy was if he screwed up this assignment. Or anything else that Spader considered important. The guy was *intense*.

A couple of days ago it had seemed like a no-brainer to

scoop up Madison Dartmoor and her carry case. That was before Ramsay Gallagher had entered the picture. Spader was a dangerous man, if crossed. But Ramsay Gallagher had proved to be equally dangerous.

CHAPTER
TEN

AS SHE CLOSED the portfolio, Madison kept her back to the man who had brought her to this refuge. She didn't know him well, but she understood that he was more complicated than he appeared to be on the surface.

Every time she was sure she wanted to get away from him, he came up with a reason to make her change her mind. She took a deep breath and let it out before turning to face him, caught by the wary expression on his face. He'd showed her a book and art collection that was worth a fortune, but she still sensed he was hiding something.

Was that part of her motivation? She wanted to know his secrets?

"All right. I see your interest is serious."

"Thank you," Ramsay answered, visibly relaxing. He cleared his throat. "How far have you gotten in the excavation of the tomb?"

And how much should she tell him? "Far enough to find that dragon-man."

"Where's the original?"

"Dominic has it for safekeeping."

"Have you found any other artifacts?"

"No. I'm still trying to figure out the best place to keep digging—without creating any damage to the area."

"Maybe I can help."

She gave him a studied look. "You haven't even seen the place."

He gestured toward his collection again. "But I have a pretty good knowledge of ancient cultures. Particularly ones that don't follow what we think of as Western traditions. What if the two of us shared a Native American vision quest? That might bring out something that you haven't thought of."

She tried to wrap her head around the suggestion, which had come from left field as far as she was concerned. "You're serious? How would that help?"

"You're trained in modern archaeology techniques. I gather you're very left-brained. Very logical."

"Is that a fault?"

"Of course not. Logic is important. So is intuition."

"What is a vision quest going to do for me?"

"It's going to let us blend the traditional and the nontraditional. And open you to the spirit of the universe."

"God?"

"I prefer to think in terms of spirituality. Not just one belief system. There are many forces in the universe. Unfortunately, modern culture has chosen to block most of them out. Too many people have closed their minds to the invisible world."

"But you haven't, because you've studied ancient beliefs?"

"It's been a lifelong . . . obsession."

"Why?"

"I want there to be more than the obvious. More than what anyone can glean with his five senses. Modern man skims the surface of reality. I want to prove there's more."

There was deep conviction in his voice and also a kind of yearning that tugged at her heart.

"And the healing technique and the hypnosis stuff you use are part of it?"

"Yes."

She studied his face, trying to pin down what she sensed about him. It was almost as if he were speaking from personal ancient knowledge. But that was impossible, of course.

Curiosity and caution warred within her. "A Native American ceremony would be a . . . strange step for me. I'd like to think about it."

"I'm not pressuring you, simply making a suggestion." He looked at her arm. "But speaking of healing techniques, I'd like to see your wound."

The thought of his touching her again made her words come out more sharply than she'd intended. "It's almost good as new. You don't need to look at it."

He waited.

"Sorry. I'm on edge."

"We both are, but I really would like to take a look at your arm."

She gave a small nod. He'd healed her in some unorthodox way, and she was acting like he didn't have a right to find out the results.

Her shirtsleeve was loose enough for her to push it up so that he could see the red place where the bullet had entered her flesh.

He looked at it but kept his hands at his sides. "It's a lot better."

"What did you put on it, exactly?"

"It's an ancient remedy."

She laughed. "That works better than modern medicine?"

"Yes."

"But you're not going to tell me what it is?"

He took a breath before answering. "You could say there's an . . . element of faith healing. It doesn't work unless you believe."

"I . . . don't."

"But I do." He shoved his hands into his pockets. "Why don't we have something to eat while you're considering the vision quest."

"All right," she answered.

As he started back to the kitchen, he said, "You should probably keep it light. More soup."

"Are you keeping me on a liquid diet?"

He laughed.

"What's funny?"

"I was just thinking about my own diet," he answered, then turned away and opened a pantry. "What about split pea? That's got a little more body than chicken soup."

She agreed, and he got down two more mugs and more crackers.

He poured the larger portion of the soup into her mug, then took a little for himself.

"You're not hungry?"

"I ate while you were sleeping," he said, his back toward her as he put her mug in the microwave. "How about some herb tea?"

"To go with the vision quest?"

"Yeah."

He took down a sampler pack of teas, and she selected mint. He chose ginger.

As she sipped the soup and the tea, he asked, "Where's the tomb?"

"In a pretty inaccessible area."

"How was it discovered?"

"The entrance was unsealed in a landslide."

"Can you describe it?"

"It's dug into a hillside. There's a main chamber, with faded paintings on the walls. But there has to be an inner chamber that we haven't found yet."

He took a swallow of tea, and she could see that he was trying to maintain his cool while excitement was bubbling inside him. "How did Coleman get onto it?"

"I think he keeps his ear to the ground for information about . . . ancient astronauts."

"You mean that's his primary interest?"

She felt her jaw clench. "I didn't mean to say that."

"I'm not going to call up CNN."

"Sorry. I'm used to keeping my mouth shut. Going to that conference was a wild leap for me, and see where it got me."

They ate in silence for several minutes.

Finally, he set down his mug and asked, "Have you decided to try the vision quest?"

"Are there drugs involved? I mean, I've read about Native Americans burning herbs for the purpose of . . . freeing their minds from . . . reality."

"Yeah."

"And what are they going to do to me?"

"Like I said, open your mind—to possibilities you haven't considered."

"Is it dangerous?"

"I've done it dozens of times."

"And look where it got you," she quipped, hearing the nervous quaver in her voice. Before she could change her mind, she said, "Okay, let's do it."

"I'm sure you'll find it enlightening."

While he carried his mug to the sink, she retrieved the tray from the bedroom, then helped him load the dishwasher.

"You use the fireplace?" she asked.

"I have an authentic ceremonial chamber downstairs."

Curious but still wondering why she was willing to try something so out of her realm, she followed him down a flight of stairs into a lounge area. There were no windows.

"This could be a bomb shelter."

"It is."

"You're kidding."

He shrugged. "I've always considered that it's better to

be safe than sorry." Turning away, he opened a door in the far wall, and held an animal skin aside. When she looked in, she drew in a quick breath.

Apparently he'd blasted a chamber out of solid rock. There was a fire pit in the middle and a chimney hole that must vent to the outside. The floor was covered with what she thought must be buffalo robes.

"Where did you get those?"

"They're old—but they're in excellent condition," he answered, then turned toward the lounge again where he crossed to a rough antique chest and opened a drawer. He rummaged inside and took out a leather shift decorated with elaborate beadwork.

"What's that for?"

"We should dress for the part. There's a bathroom down the hall where you can change."

"What if I don't want to?"

"Then you've got less chance of success."

"You just happen to have a Native American dress that fits me?"

"I had a chance to buy it, and I did."

"Has any woman shared this ceremony with you?"

"No."

She studied his face, sure that he spoke the truth. "Why me?"

"Are you thinking of reasons to back out?"

"No."

"You have a combination of qualities few people possess."

"Like what?"

"Fishing for compliments?"

"Maybe."

"You're smart. Brave . . ."

"If I'm so brave, why did I cancel my talk?"

"To protect your workers. If it was only you taking a risk, you would have gone ahead."

She nodded.

"And you're not bound by conventional wisdom. Your agreeing to the ceremony proves it. Change your clothes before you talk yourself out of it."

She took the dress from him, surprised at the softness of the leather.

For a moment, she stood running her fingers over the beadwork, then she turned and hurried down the hall to the bathroom. After closing and locking the door, she stared at her pale face in the mirror.

What was she getting herself into?

With a shake of her head, she began to undress. When she had stripped to her bra and panties, she hesitated, then unhooked the bra and laid it with the rest of the clothing. But she kept her panties on for modesty's sake. The dress was a little snug, but it would do.

When she raised her eyes to the mirror again, she caught her breath. She didn't look like Dr. Madison Dartmoor. She looked like a combination of herself and . . . what? Pocahontas with short blond hair.

Barefoot, she walked back to the lounge area and stopped short as she saw Ramsay Gallagher, dressed in only a leather loincloth.

He'd been wearing his dark hair in a short ponytail. Now he had shaken it out so that it hung around his shoulders.

She caught her breath as she took in his magnificent body with its well-defined muscles. Wearing the loincloth, with his hair loose, he looked like he could have stepped out of a primitive cave.

A long slash of scars ran down from his chest into his ribs, like some great animal had dug its claws into his flesh.

"What happened to you?" she murmured.

"I was in a fight."

"With a bear?"

"Something like that."

Apparently he didn't want to talk about it. Before she could ask any more questions, he turned and stepped through the doorway to the ceremonial chamber.

Fighting the impulse to turn and run before this went any further, she followed him inside, where he had already lit the fire. Wood smoke drifted upward toward the chimney hole, and she wondered if some modern exhaust system was serving the ancient-looking chamber. Perhaps because she wanted to stall for time, she walked to one of the walls and ran her hand against the rough surface.

"It's real," he said.

"How did you do it?"

"Blasting. Then with a chisel."

"That must have taken some time."

"It's more interesting than sitting and watching television."

"Why?"

"It gives you time to think—instead of mindlessly sucking up what's presented to you. Sit down and get comfortable."

She sat on one of the thick buffalo robes. He settled on the other side of the fire pit, then took a small leather bag from under the edge of the robe where he sat.

"Did you do anything yet?"

"It's just wood smoke. Are you ready for the ceremony?"

Her mouth was dry, and she wasn't sure she was ready for this, but she wasn't going to end up being a coward, so she nodded.

He poured some of the contents of the bag into the palm of his hand, and even across the fire from him, she could smell their potency.

"What is that?"

"Leaves, bark, and berries."

"Where did you get it?" she asked, hearing the nerves in her voice.

"I gathered the ingredients myself. I learned about the ceremony from a tribal elder."

"They let you . . . join them?"

"Yes." He gave her a long look. "We should start, unless you've changed your mind."

"Do it."

He sprinkled some of the herbs onto the fire, and immediately the smoke took on a pungent smell.

When he leaned over and took several deep breaths, she hung back. Still, she began to feel light-headed.

"You're going to feel dizzy if you stay sitting up. You should lie down."

She stretched out on the robe as Ramsay began chanting in a low voice. She couldn't understand any of the words, but they drew her into the smoke in some mysterious way.

He switched from the words she couldn't understand to English.

"We are here to explore the past. Ramsay Gallagher and Madison Dartmoor. She has discovered an ancient burial place. We want to know more about that place. We want to know more about the people who created it."

She lay with her head swimming, bright colors dancing behind her closed lids. She hadn't expected a light show, and she wasn't sure what would come next, but fear had vanished, replaced by acceptance, and she let herself drift with the strange sensations.

Was Ramsay feeling the same things, or was it different for him because he was more experienced?

SLOWLY, so as not to jar his swimming senses, Ramsay moved to the other side of the fire pit and lay down beside Madison.

"What?"

"It's okay. I want to share this with you." When she felt his fingers close over hers, she made a small sound.

"You said . . ."

She didn't finish the thought. Probably she couldn't.

When he felt his mind drifting away from the modern world, he pressed his shoulder to Madison's. He'd been betting he could control this process, the way he'd silently bet at the craps tables in Las Vegas. But as the smoke overwhelmed his senses, he scrabbled to maintain any sense of control, and finally lost the battle.

CHAPTER
ELEVEN

RAMSAY'S MIND WAS no longer fixed in the twenty-first century. Time was fluid. Usually it flowed one way. But now he had drifted back into the past. He had wanted to know about the tomb, but it wasn't part of the scene. He was walking through a forest, toward a low, primitive building.

Beside him Madison moaned.

"Sorry," he managed to say while he was still Ramsay Gallagher.

Still Ramsay?

That made no sense, yet he understood that he had taken on a different persona.

Vandar? Fear and disgust leaped inside him. He wouldn't be that monster who had lived to make humans his slaves.

Yet he was someone else. Another being. Not a man. One of *them*. He had come to this primitive planet from a world far away. He had been here for a long time, and at first he and his people had been masters of the world, but now something had happened to change everything.

He turned his head, looking at the woman who walked beside him. She had Madison's face, and she wore the dress that he had given her for the ceremony, but her hair was much longer and hung around her shoulders in graceful golden strands.

Somehow he knew that she was human. Not one of the dragon people, but she was his lover.

"Where are we?" she asked, and he knew it was Madison's question.

He couldn't answer, because he didn't know the name of the place. But he knew the time was long ago.

Uncertainty contorted her features, and then she relaxed and he knew that Madison had fallen away and the other woman had taken over her body. Or was that the right way to think about it?

Another question he couldn't answer. He could only let the vision sweep him along.

She spoke his name, but he didn't catch what it was. Late afternoon sunshine filtered down on them as they stepped from the shade of a grove of trees.

He wanted to enjoy the day. Enjoy the escape from a harsh reality he didn't entirely understand, but he knew it was his duty to protect her.

"We shouldn't have gone out," he said.

She raised her face to the sun. "I can't stay in the shelter all the time," she answered, reaching down to pick up a stalk of tall grass and run it through her fingers.

"You love natural things," he murmured.

"So do you," she answered, giving him the smile that he loved so much.

He had been lonely for a long time, then he had found his soul mate. Her. "I'll go out and gather anything you want."

"I know. And I thank you for the offer. But I need to get them for myself. I need to feel the wind in my hair and the sun on my face. I need to know that I have . . . freedom."

"Nobody has freedom."

"Our child must."

Their child. The son who might stop this terrible war. The knowledge gave him hope, but his nerves were buzzing. Far away, he sensed a presence in the sky, winging toward them.

"Come back inside. Now."

She turned and started to run, then stopped when she saw he was still there—facing the threat.

"I'm not leaving you."

"You must."

The thing in the sky was closer. Above them, the shadow of giant wings blocked out the sun.

He tore off his loincloth, willing his body to change. For a terrible moment, he was afraid he couldn't do it. Then he felt the transformation grab him, as his limbs and the shape of his body morphed from human to dragon.

Even as he recognized the danger of the fight, he felt a spurt of elation. He had done it!

With a cry of triumph, he leaped into the sky and arrowed toward the monster bearing down on them.

Fire shot from the beast's mouth. Far below him the woman screamed.

He dodged the blast, then churned up his own flame-thrower and hurled a blast at the enemy.

The woman screamed again. And he realized he was no longer in the sky and Madison wasn't on the ground below him.

She was lying next to him, clutching his arm.

"The dragon," she gasped. "It was going to kill you. And then you . . . changed."

His eyes blinked open, and he stared into her terrified face.

"What happened?" she gasped.

"I think we went back . . ." he managed to say. He was still trying to cope with his own feelings. He had *transformed*. It hadn't been *him*. He had been someone else, from long ago, but maybe that would make a difference for Ramsay Gallagher.

He wanted to think about that, but he had dragged Madison into a vision with him, and he had to deal with the fallout.

Her hand tightened on his bare arm, her fingers digging into his muscles. "Was it real?"

He was pretty sure it had been, depending on your definition of reality, but he didn't want to admit that. Instead he said, "I don't know."

"If it wasn't real, where did it come from?"

"From what we know. From what we've studied. From what you've speculated about that shape-shifting figure."

"You're saying it came from *me*?"

"From both of us."

"It was so vivid."

"That's the nature of a vision quest," he answered, even while he was still hoping that he'd gotten a glimpse of his ancestors. He'd had visions of the dragon people before, but they had never been this clear—this real. He'd always been an observer. It had taken Madison Dartmoor in the equation to make him a participant.

"They were fighting with each other," she whispered.

"It seemed like it."

She stared at him. "I saw you change into a dragon. I saw you leap into the air and go after the other one."

"Yes."

"Was I a dragon, too?"

"I don't think so."

"But we were lovers."

"Yes. Because we belonged together," he answered, wondering if it was true. *Back then? Now? Both?*

At the moment, "now" filled his consciousness. He and Madison were lying on a buffalo robe in the re-creation of a primitive cave. And he felt as though something within himself had shattered. He was vulnerable to this woman as he had almost never been vulnerable.

"You were a dragon," she said again, drawing back a little, her eyes searching his.

"I didn't make it happen."

When she started to pull farther away, he kept her close. The scent of the herb-filled smoke lingered in the air.

Wordlessly, he reached to brush back her hair so his lips could find the tender place where her jawline met her neck.

Her hair was short now. In the vision, it had been long. But she was the same woman.

When she stayed where she was, his finger moved to her mouth, where he touched her with a featherlight stroke.

Her lips parted, and she nibbled at his fingers, sending darts of sensation along his nerve endings.

He played with the line of her teeth, then moved his finger so that he could stroke the sensitive tissue of her inner lips.

When her breath caught, he eased far enough away to meet her eyes.

Her gaze collided with his, robbing him of breath.

In the car, he'd been in too much of a hurry to show her any finesse as a lover. He ached to remedy that now.

The front of her doeskin dress was held together with laces. He unknotted the ends of the cord, then eased the placket wide, pulling away the leather strings so that he could part the bodice of the dress, baring her breasts to him.

Her nipples were beaded to beautiful coral points, tightening his own body. Leaning down, he stiffened his tongue and delicately circled one firm crest, feeling her body arch in invitation. He did the same with the other, then sucked it into his mouth, drawing on her while he used his thumb and finger on its mate, pulling and twisting, bringing little cries to her lips.

Needing more, he gathered her close, rocking her in his arms, dragging her breasts against his hair-roughened chest.

"Ramsay," she gasped.

"Your shift is in the way."

He helped her sit up, then pulled the doeskin dress over her head and tossed it aside. When he saw that she still wore her panties, he dragged them over her hips and flung them to join the dress.

"You are so beautiful," he whispered.

"So are you." She reached to touch his chest, sliding her hand downward until she reached the loincloth. It was standing straight out, barely covering his rigid cock.

Her gaze locked with his, she reached underneath and closed her hand around him.

When she tightened her grip, he let himself enjoy her caress for a few moments, then lifted her hand away.

"You're going to push me over the edge," he managed to say, then brought her hand to his lips, folding her fingers inward so he could kiss her knuckles and nibble at them.

"What are we to each other?" she asked in a throaty voice.

"I don't know, but I want to find out. Do you?"

"Yes. Is this the way to do it?"

"One way." His other hand slid down her body, pausing to play with the curly hair between her legs before slipping lower into her feminine folds.

He made a hungry sound when he found her wet and slippery for him. He bent his head, nipping at her breasts, then soothing her with his tongue.

Hot currents surged through him as he stoked her pleasure, sucking on one of her nipples while he glided two fingers from her clit to just inside her vagina and back again.

He was rewarded with the frantic movement of her hips.

"I'm going to come."

"Oh, yeah."

"I want you inside me." Her fingers plucked at the leather cord that held his loincloth in place. When she couldn't figure out how to remove it, he did it for her, his own hands clumsy.

"Yes." Feeling slightly dizzy, he covered her body with his, then claimed her.

Gripping her shoulders and hips, he rolled to his side, taking her with him, then reached between, working his fingers against her clit, giving her the jolt of sensation she needed. When he felt her inner muscles clench around him, he let himself go, shouting his satisfaction as he poured himself into her—while her orgasm swept over her.

He held her close, shocked by the depth of his response to her and gratified to find that she seemed as dazed as he felt.

She settled against him, her hand stroking over his shoulder and down his arm.

"Was it like that for them?" she asked in a dreamy voice.

He knew who she was talking about. The dragon-shifter and the woman. "I hope so."

"How did we share the vision?"

He wasn't going to tell her that had been his plan.

"If you go back in time and inhabit someone else's body, it doesn't have to be a human body," he murmured, not really answering the question.

"Have you done that before? Gone into a vision and been some other . . . life-form?"

"Yes."

"What?"

"I've been a wolf," he said. "And a bear."

When she opened her mouth to ask another question, he pressed his fingers against her lips.

"My brain's too foggy to stay coherent," he whispered, ducking away from the conversation.

"Yes. Sorry."

"I want to drift off to sleep holding you in my arms," he said. It had been a long time since he'd had the pleasure of sleeping beside a woman.

"Okay," she whispered as she snuggled down next to him.

He must have slept, because the sound of a bell ringing
brought him back to awareness.

Beside him, Madison tensed.

"What's that?"

"My alarm."

CHAPTER
TWELVE

NAKED, RAMSAY STOOD and strode to the animal skin that blocked the doorway. In the lounge area, he pressed a button that slid aside a panel, giving him access to the security system.

Behind him, he was aware that Madison had pulled on her doeskin dress and followed him out of the ceremonial chamber.

He switched on the monitor screens, scanning the area around the house and then farther away. Several hundred feet from the gate, he saw a car pulled to the side of the road. Another screen gave him a view of the path where he'd gone to mingle with his deer herd. Two men were moving through the meadow, heading for the house. The approach was a recent weakness of his defense system. If he'd been able to transform into a dragon, it would have been no problem at all. He would have simply blasted them off the mountainside. But that was not an option. And even if it had been, there was the problem of doing it in front of Madison.

As she studied the invaders, she gasped. "It's them. The men from Las Vegas."

"Yeah."

"How did they get here?"

"My best guess is that they checked out the airlines, then the general aviation companies. Someone at Ufly must have told them where we flew to."

"It's a big area."

"But I get my mail from a post office thirty miles away. I should have checked into the Versailles under an alias. Once you know you're looking for Ramsay Gallagher around here, you can get a line on me."

"It's my fault. They're after me." She gasped. "Like in the vision."

"The attacking dragon was after you?"

"Yes. I know he was."

She'd understood something that he hadn't, he realized with a start. But there was no time to ponder that now.

"We're not going to let them get you."

"You're not a dragon," she whispered.

His face hardened at the insight.

"I've still got options. I could wait until they get here, then blow up the house."

She made a strangled sound. "You're not serious."

"I've got the charges in place. But I'd like to save that for a last resort."

"You can't blow up all the artifacts here."

"They're just *things*."

She stared at him. "Things you love. Things that mean something to you."

"They're not the main problem. There's too much personal information on me. Plus that artifact you don't want them to get."

"Then what are we going to do?"

He considered the irony of the situation. Anyone else living in a fortified stronghold would have guns to defend himself. The old Ramsay Gallagher hadn't needed guns. Which put him in a vulnerable position.

"What's the plan?"

"I'm going to stop them."

"Naked?"

He'd forgotten he hadn't bothered to get dressed and answered with a bark of a laugh, then quickly sobered.

"I'm going to need a little time. Can you stall them?"

Her face paled.

"They want to interrogate you. They're not going to kill you."

"We hope," she whispered, then raised her chin. "What do you want me to do?"

He looked at her Native American dress. "Put on your clothes. Then I'll show you where to stand."

They both sprang into action. Madison dashed down the hall to the bathroom where she'd changed and came back in record time.

Meanwhile, he climbed into his own clothing, then led her upstairs to the main living level. "Can you see the bridge down there?"

Madison stared down the mountain, following the direction where Ramsay was pointing.

"Yes."

"Wait until they're about halfway across, then step out onto the deck."

She knew he caught the little shiver that traveled over her skin.

"Then what?" she asked.

"When you've got their attention, tell them you're willing to give them the artifact—if they'll stop following you."

"Okay."

"And if I yell at you to duck, hit the deck."

She caught her breath. "Where will you be?"

"Between you and them."

"That's too dangerous."

"It's my call, and we don't have time to argue now. Just consider that I've got a lot more self-defense experience than you do."

She wanted to argue. Before she could, Ramsay pulled her close and hugged her tightly for several heartbeats. Then he turned and hurried out of the sitting room.

With no other choice, she moved to the sliding glass door, staying in the shadows as she kept her eyes trained on the bridge.

She could hear him running down the hall, pounding down a flight of steps.

Then she was alone in the silence, except for the drumming in her ears. She'd gotten Ramsay Gallagher into a hell of a mess, and she was going to do what she could to get him out of it.

Hands balled into fists, she kept her eyes trained on the wooden bridge he'd pointed out. She and Ramsay had come here at night. Now the sun had come up over one of the snowcapped mountain peaks, and the meadow below the house was lush with different shades of green. It would have been a beautiful scene, if she'd been able to focus on anything besides their desperate situation.

One of the men came into view, testing the surface of the bridge before venturing any farther. It was the guy that Ramsay had called Mophead. His friend was behind him. Both of them were holding guns.

She dragged in a breath and let it out before stepping onto the deck.

They stopped in their tracks. "She's up there," the one in the lead called, pointing toward her, and she stiffened as they both zeroed in on her.

"Why are you following me?" she called.

"You have something we need." As he spoke, he raised his gun and pointed it at her.

She felt her heart start to beat like a jackhammer, but she stayed where she was, betting her life on Ramsay's assertion that they wouldn't kill her.

"You—or Kent Spader?" she asked.

"That's for us to know."

"I'll give it to you."

"You could have done that in Las Vegas."

"I've had time to think. I want you to leave me alone. I'll do whatever it takes."

"Where's Gallagher?"

"He's not here."

The thug gave her an assessing look. "You're saying he left you alone? I guess we'll see about that."

As he spoke, a flicker of motion to his right caught his attention.

His gun swung away from her as Ramsay stepped out from behind an outcropping of rock.

"Leave, and you won't get hurt," he said.

"You're kidding, right?"

"I'm giving you a chance to back out gracefully."

For an answer, the man aimed and fired.

CHAPTER
THIRTEEN

MADISON SCREAMED, BUT Ramsay dodged back so quickly that all she saw was a blur of motion. In the next second, the bridge exploded. One second it was there; in the next, wooden pieces were flying into the air amid a cloud of smoke. The shock wave propelled her backward through the doorway into the living room where she landed on the Oriental rug as pieces of wood hit the sliding glass door. But the glass must have been strong, because it didn't shatter.

When the debris stopped falling she picked herself up and cautiously made her way to the window. Only a shred of the bridge remained on the near side of the chasm. The rest had disappeared, along with the men.

And Ramsay? What had happened to Ramsay?

Struggling to speak around the clogging of her throat, she called his name, and he stepped out from behind the boulder where she'd last seen him.

He gave her a long look, then walked toward the chasm where the bridge had been.

"Come back!" she called out.

Ignoring her, he peering over the edge.

"What happened?" she choked out.

"I blew it up."

"And them."

"I assume so," he said, then continued in a flat tone. "As you noticed, I gave them an opportunity to leave. Instead, they shot at me. Sorry I didn't get a chance to tell you to duck."

He disappeared under the overhang of the balcony, and she stood staring at the remains of the bridge until he stepped to her side.

Mutely, she turned toward him, and he folded her into his arms. As she clung to him, he murmured, "That was very brave to keep their attention focused on you."

"Braver of you. You could have gotten shot."

"My reflexes are good."

She nodded against his shoulder, thinking that he'd moved in a blur of motion. Could he have dodged a bullet like some kind of superhero?

He held her for a long moment, and she was comforted by his strong arms.

"I've gotten you into a lot of trouble," she whispered.

"I can handle it." He cleared his throat. "But sometimes the best offense is avoiding more trouble. We'd better get out of here, in case Spader sends someone else."

"Where are we going?"

"Away. And maybe it's time we get some help," he suggested.

"From whom?"

"How about Dominic Coleman? I think he's got a big stake in this."

She breathed out a small sigh. "I hate involving him."

"Isn't he the one who got you into the project?"

"Yes."

"We should leave soon."

She was still trying to absorb what had happened. "You're not going to call the police?"

"I'm not sure what that would buy us."

She didn't like the flat way he said it, but she understood the wisdom of not making any kind of report. They'd have to stay around—and answer a lot of questions.

"What about their car?" she asked.

"It's a rental parked along the public road. They could have left it there and gone hiking or camping. There's nothing to tie it to us."

She nodded. She'd never gotten involved in criminal activity—or the cover-up of murder.

Was it murder?

"Self-defense," he said.

Her head jerked toward him. "How did you know what I was thinking?"

"Deductive reasoning. I know you're a moral person. Unfortunately, you've gotten in with the wrong crowd."

"Those men?"

"And Spader." He paused for a moment. "And your friend Dominic."

Outrage bubbled inside her. Pushing away from Ramsay, she said, "How can you include him in your assessment— if you're planning to ask for his help?"

"He left you hanging out to dry."

"No!"

Ramsay continued to stare at her. "Are you sure of that? Are you going to tell me that Spader just came out of the woodwork this week?"

She looked away. Actually, she suspected that Spader and Dominic had been at odds for years, each of them wedded to a point of view that the other could never accept or understand. But loyalty kept her from admitting that to Ramsay. Finally, she said, "Perhaps you should ask him."

"That's what I'm hoping to do."

She wanted to start enumerating all of Dominic's good qualities. She wanted to tell Ramsay Gallagher everything Dominic had done for her, starting with the way he'd stepped in as a surrogate father after her parents had died. Instead she said, "I'm sure he'll want to meet you."

"Where?"

"He's frail. He doesn't travel much. We'll have to go to his house. *El Bigote*."

He laughed. "He calls his house 'the mustache'?"

"Yes. Because it's perched on the bluffs above the ocean in Mendocino."

"I guess he's got a sense of humor."

"Yes," she answered, thinking that it hadn't been much in evidence over the past few years. He'd grown more intense as he'd aged.

Ramsay nodded. "And I guess we'd better not take Ufly. Or Spader's going to be on our tail before we get to California. He could have guys waiting on the ground for us at the airport."

She winced. "What's your alternate plan?"

"We'll drive to Denver—then pick a different general aviation service."

"They'll take you on short notice?"

"I'll call ahead. If they have a plane and pilots available—and I've got the honey."

"The what?"

"The money." He laughed. "Sorry. Cockney rhyming slang."

They separated, each of them taking a shower. When Madison had dressed again, she found Ramsay in his office, making copies of portfolio items he'd shown her.

"Can I lock the man-dragon thing in the safe?" he asked. "Or do you want to bring it?"

She debated. "I guess you can lock it up here."

After he'd taken care of the artifact, he pulled down a

few of his books and added them to the safe, along with a portfolio of illustrations.

Before they left, he closed metal shutters over the windows and secured the house.

AS Ramsay drove down the mountain, he handed Madison his cell phone. "Call Coleman and make sure he doesn't mind company."

"Okay."

She made the call, obviously relieved when her benefactor answered. Ramsay's hearing was excellent, and in the confines of the car, he could pick up both sides of the conversation.

"Madison, I've been trying to reach you. Where are you? Your phone's off."

"Yes. It's lost its charge. I'm in Colorado with Ramsay Gallagher."

"Who?"

"Ramsay Gallagher. He was attending the conference." She pictured Dominic Googling him.

"Perhaps you should fill me in."

She kept her eyes fixed on the road. "He thought I'd be safer away from Las Vegas. We went to his house, but . . . Spader's men followed us."

"I don't like the sound of that."

"Ramsay took care of them."

"Thank the Lord."

"I'll give you the details later."

"It sounds like you're lucky to be with Gallagher," Coleman said.

"Yes. He'd like to meet you. I'm bringing him to *El Bigote*, if that's all right with you."

"You trust him?"

She continued to look straight ahead. "Mostly," she answered in a small voice.

"All right. I'll see what I think when I meet him."

"He doesn't have a degree in archaeology," she said, then looked at Ramsay for confirmation.

He nodded.

"But he's collected books and other materials from all over the world, and he's got an interest in some of the same subjects you do," she said, deliberately keeping the comment general.

"Intriguing."

"We'll call you when we land in San Francisco."

"Or Oakland," Ramsay supplied.

When she clicked off, she said, "He's anxious to meet you."

Which wasn't exactly what the man had said, but Ramsay wasn't going to explain that he'd heard Coleman's side of the conversation.

As they drove to Denver, he mentally threw a dart at a board and picked a different carrier. AirTranspo had a plane, pilot, and copilot available. He booked a flight, then stayed on the alert as they waited in the terminal building. He didn't think Spader would have someone covering every airport in the area, but he wasn't going to take any chances.

Once they boarded the plane, Madison sank into a seat near the back, and he gave her a critical look.

"You're exhausted, and probably hungry," he said. "Let's have a snack."

She ate an egg salad sandwich. He sipped tomato juice, thinking it might look like blood, but it didn't have the same kick.

"Dominic took care of you after your parents died?"

"I took care of myself. I lived in Chicago on my own. I had an apartment there, but I came to *El Bigote* every summer. Well, until graduate school. Then I took classes all year long."

"You're close to Dominic?"

"Very."

He wanted to ask about her other relationships, but he figured that was going too far.

"How did you pick Santa Barbara?"

"It has an excellent archaeology program. And a fun campus," she added.

He studied her, wondering how much fun she'd had. "But you spent most of your time studying?"

"I wanted to get a good job after the PhD program." She kept her gaze on him. "You were going to tell me more about yourself."

"I told you, I inherited money. I'm very lucky that it gave me the luxury of traveling, studying anything I wanted. I love digging into the past. And seeing new places. And learning new languages."

It was all true, as far as it went. But he didn't want to elaborate, so he sent her messages designed to help her sleep.

When she reclined her seat and closed her eyes, he relaxed.

He watched her for a while, marveling that she was here with him. He knew that if he wasn't careful, he could care too much about her. He should pull back his emotions, but he didn't know if he could take his own advice.

As she slept, he took in sweet little details. Her slightly parted lips. The graceful way her lashes lay against her cheek. The way her bottom lip pouted out more than her upper one. Finally, he tore his gaze away. Trying to relax, he reclined his seat. Since his battle with Vandar, his energy level had been much lower, and he needed to recharge after the confrontation with Spader's thugs. He wished he'd been able to bring a pint of blood on the plane with him. But he'd have to make do with human food until he could find a blood supply.

His gaze shot to Madison again, this time to the creamy column of her neck. It was tempting to consider putting her into a trance and drinking from her, but that would be a bad idea, for a lot of reasons.

With a sigh, he closed his eyes and was able to sleep until shortly before they reached Oakland.

After they landed, he rented a car, and they headed north past wineries and redwoods. This was beautiful country, sometimes compared to Cornwall in England because of the sweeping fields and ragged cliffs along the ocean.

As they drove north, he wondered if she'd put too much trust in Coleman. But there was no point in arguing about it. He'd get a chance to form his own opinion.

Five hours after they'd left his house, they were driving up to the gates of *El Bigote*.

He announced himself to an intercom, and they were buzzed through, onto the grounds of an estate that could have been an arboretum. Narrow roads wound through lush landscaping, and as they rounded a curve, he could see they were on a high cliff overlooking the ocean. Coleman's house was a sprawling Spanish hacienda that appeared to have been built early in the previous century.

Ramsay pulled up under a sheltered portico, and a gentleman with a mane of thick white hair, wearing dark slacks and a cream-colored sports coat, came out to greet them. The guy looked to be in his late fifties or early sixties and also looked totally at ease in his own environment.

Madison scrambled out of the car, and they hugged warmly.

Stepping back, he gave her a critical inspection. "Are you all right, my dear?"

"Yes. What about you?"

"I'm tolerable," he allowed. Switching his attention, he said, "And you must be the very competent Ramsay Gallagher. I'm so grateful that you kept Madison safe, but you're quite a mystery man."

As they shook hands, Ramsay was aware that Coleman was evaluating him with keen blue eyes.

"You looked me up?" he asked, wondering what Coleman would have found out.

"There's not much information on you. How do you manage to be so private?"

"It's an art."

Coleman nodded. "Madison indicated that you have considerable archaeology experience."

"None of it official. Over the years, I've studied sites that interested me."

"I get the feeling you're too modest about your academic background and your bodyguard skills."

He shrugged.

"How was the trip?"

"Fine," he and Madison both answered, and he could tell from her voice that she wasn't entirely at ease. Why not? She and this guy were supposed to be like father and daughter.

"Are you hungry?"

"We ate on the plane," Madison answered.

Coleman led them into a grand entrance hall, filled with antiques and artifacts that would have been right at home in a museum.

"Quite a collection," Ramsay murmured, stopping to admire an eight-foot-tall stained glass window mounted on the wall with a light behind it. Is that a Tiffany?"

"Yes. I was lucky to get it at auction several years ago."

Beside it was a bust of a young Greek man. And a few feet beyond were bronzes by Frederick Remington and Daniel Chester French. Obviously Coleman had plenty of money to indulge his love of art.

They settled in a library with floor-to-ceiling shelves. Some of the books were quite old, others were clearly modern—on a wide range of topics from space exploration to native plants of northern California. The exterior wall was all windows, giving them a view of the ocean crashing against rocks at the foot of the cliff.

When Ramsay caught his host watching him, he smiled. "You have a very impressive library—with a spectacular view." *And your wealth must be measured in the billions*, he silently added.

"I've always sought knowledge—and the serenity of nature."

"An interesting combination," Ramsay commented.

They settled into comfortable leather chairs that were grouped around an ornate stone fireplace held up by caryatids, pillars that were figures of women.

Ramsay got right to the point. "Tell me about the tomb that Madison's excavating in Italy."

"You don't beat around the bush," Coleman remarked.

"No. I prefer the direct approach." When it suited him. He wanted information from this man, but he wasn't going to start off offering any kind of exchange.

Still, it seemed that Coleman wouldn't open up without knowing more about his guest.

"Tell me how you dealt with Spader's men when they showed up at your place."

"I gave them a chance to leave. When they shot at me, I blew them up."

Before the statement could hang in the air for more than a second, Madison jumped in. "It was self-defense."

Coleman nodded. "But it must have taken nerve—and cunning. And a certain ruthlessness."

Ramsay shrugged. "It was more a matter of pragmatism."

"Did you call the police?"

"No. What's done is done, and I didn't want to answer a bunch of questions."

"You've proved you're resourceful," Coleman said, telling Ramsay that he wasn't overly concerned about legalities.

"I'd like to understand your interest in Madison's project," her mentor went on.

Ramsay pulled the pages he'd brought from his briefcase. "These are copies. For obvious reasons, I locked up the originals before I left home."

When he handed the papers over, Coleman began to shuffle through them.

"As I told Madison, the idea that mankind wasn't alone captured my imagination when I was young. And I've welcomed evidence that our world was visited by extraterrestrials. It's hard to believe it's not true, but most of the evidence is circumstantial. I'd like to uncover something nobody could refute."

Coleman nodded. "That's why we're so excited about Madison's find in Italy." He glanced at her. "I understand why you wanted to tell the world about it. I'm sorry it didn't work out that way."

"In retrospect, it was a mistake," she said in a small voice.

"You think her dig site was attacked by this Spader guy?"

"Not necessarily," Coleman answered. "It's a lawless area with local gangs looking for tombs to rob. They could have gotten wind of the discovery."

Still digging for information, Ramsay said, "But we do know Spader tried to steal the copy. And he was willing to kidnap Madison to get it."

He saw the two other people in the room exchange a look.

"What are you keeping from me?" he snapped.

They both remained silent.

Ramsay stood, his gaze flicking between them. "Spader's men tried to kill me in Las Vegas—then hunted me down and tried again in Colorado. If you can't tell me the real reason for the attacks, I think it's time for me to leave."

As he turned and started for the door, Coleman called out, "Wait."

Ramsay pivoted, eyeing the billionaire questioningly.

"It's complicated," Coleman allowed.

"I've got as much time as you'd like to take."

"I guess you've figured out Spader isn't simply a collector of antiquities," Madison said.

CHAPTER
FOURTEEN

"WHAT ELSE IS Spader?" Ramsay asked in a danger-ously quiet voice.

Coleman answered, "He's a power in the U.S. financial community. He's also the executive director of the Kush-ing Society, which is dedicated to the nobility of man and maintaining the primary place of mankind in the universe. They keep a low profile, but they loathe the possibility that humanity received any help in its development from an outside source. Madison's excavation, with its suggestions of human–extraterrestrial contact are a serious threat to his value system. He considers her research vile, and he's prepared to stop it at all costs."

Ramsay sat back down, his gaze fixed on Coleman. "And you have just the opposite view. You want to discover a connection between mankind and visitors from the stars."

"Yes." The billionaire's voice rang with conviction.

"Why?"

"Because I take the long view. Humanity must join the peoples of the universe. I think we've already made the connection. I think they're just waiting for us to prove that we can get off this planet now and join them. Not just to the moon. Mars and then Alpha Centauri. And farther."

"And you're sure they'll welcome us?"

"I think they already did. I think they came here to set us on the road to membership in their community of planets. And I think that if we can prove they made contact with us long ago, others will work toward funneling money and manpower into space exploration. I'm willing to put a lot of my own fortune into it, once I get others on board. That will be my legacy."

Ramsay nodded. But he wasn't focused on the future at the moment.

"Madison's camp's already been attacked. Won't she be at risk if she goes back to the tomb site in Italy?"

"I've hired more guards. We've got a virtual army there now."

"And you're prepared to guarantee Madison's safety?" Ramsay pressed.

The woman in question leaned forward, her expression fierce. "Stop talking about me like I'm not here."

"Sorry," Ramsay answered. "We're both concerned about you."

"Let Kent Spader or anyone else try and chase me away."

Ramsay took in the look of conviction on her face. "If you're determined to put yourself at risk, then I'm going with you."

"It's not your fight," Coleman said.

"You're wrong," he answered.

When the room went silent, Ramsay wondered if he'd given too much away by the impulsive exclamation.

"What kind of personal stake do you have in it?" Coleman asked.

Ramsay scrambled for an explanation that would make sense but wouldn't give too much away.

"When Madison was at my house, I invited her to share a vision quest. I was thinking that it would help her infuse intuition into her logical mind," he said in an even voice. "But it swept the two of us back to a long ago time—when humans and aliens were interacting with each other."

Madison shifted in her seat, and he gave her a reassuring look. He wasn't going to reveal any personal details from the encounter. For her sake—and for his.

The silence in the room stretched.

Finally, Coleman asked, "Are you saying you believe it was real?"

"I'm not sure," he answered. "If it wasn't, it was a sign that I should help Madison with her work in Italy."

"A sign from whom?" Coleman asked.

"You can call it the cosmos. Or perhaps the universal consciousness."

"You believe in that?" Coleman pressed.

"I've studied many spiritual teachings. The universal consciousness is as good a guide as any."

"What happened in the vision?" Coleman pressed.

"It was confusing," Ramsay answered. "Madison might have seen it differently," he added, although he was sure from her reaction and their frantic lovemaking afterward that her experience had been exactly the same as his. "But when we talked about it later, we both shared the conviction that humankind had mingled with aliens."

Coleman looked from one of them to the other.

"That's fantastic, if it's true. Or was it what you wanted to believe?" Coleman pressed, his gaze fixed on Ramsay.

"That's possible," he acknowledged. "The only proof may be in that tomb."

To cut off the conversation, he stood. "It's been a stressful twenty-four hours. I'd like to get some rest."

"Of course," Coleman answered. "I've had a guest room prepared for you. Dinner will be at seven."

"If I don't show up, don't wait for me," Ramsay said.

Madison and Coleman both stood. The older man led them to a wing of the house that stretched along the cliff. Ramsay's room was at the end of the hallway, which suited him perfectly. He wasn't planning to join Madison and her mentor for dinner, but he knew he'd have to go out later.

He thanked Coleman for his hospitality, then closed the door. As soon as he was alone, he made a thorough inspection of the room. As far as he could tell, there were no video or audio recording devices.

Then he lay down, thinking about everything that had happened over the past thirty-six hours.

He waited until long after dark before he slipped out the sliding glass door onto a small patio. The night was chilled and cloudless, and above him, a sky full of stars twinkled. They were bright and numerous out here along the coast, but still he was conscious of how much the display had dimmed over the years. Once the Milky Way had stood out against the darkness. Now modern pollution had dimmed it to near invisibility.

There were no lights on the grounds, and most of the windows in the house were dark. After waiting a few minutes for his eyes to adjust to the low light, he took a path into the estate grounds, listening to the rustling of the foliage and casting his mind outward. As he wandered down the trail, he hummed softly, signaling his presence.

He'd walked only a few hundred feet when a doe glided onto the trail and stared at him with large, questioning eyes.

"It's all right," he murmured. "I'm a friend."

She didn't understand the words, but his tone of voice and the mental signals he was sending soothed her. He'd dealt with deer so often over the years that he had a good rapport with them. When he slowly reached out a hand, she came to him. And after a few minutes she allowed him to drink from her while he stroked her head.

It was a relief to feel the fresh blood hit his system,

spreading warmth and well-being through the cells of his body. It was always a temptation to keep drinking his fill, but he'd taught himself restraint long ago. He took only what he judged to be a half pint from her, then silently called to the rest of the herd. Another doe stepped out of the foliage, and he repeated the process with her. When he was finished, he wiped his mouth and started back toward the house. He was almost to his patio when a figure stepped out of the shadows. It was Coleman, and he was holding a gun.

"What are you doing out here?" the man asked in a harsh voice.

"I often have trouble sleeping when I've had too much excitement."

"Excitement. Yes."

"It helps to walk," Ramsay answered, wondering if he'd really gotten all the blood off his mouth.

"This is unfamiliar territory for you. Or have you been here before, scouting out the area?"

Ramsay tried not to stiffen. Keeping his voice even, he said, "Of course I haven't been here before."

"I guess you can't prove that."

"How would I?" he snapped, then warned himself to keep his temper. He might be dealing with a paranoid nut—with a gun. Or a man with good reasons to be suspicious.

"It's quite dark," Coleman said in a milder voice. "You could get hurt. There are steep cliffs at the edge of the ocean."

"I stayed on the paths." Ramsay cleared his throat. "This conversation might be more friendly if you weren't pointing a weapon at me."

He stood with his hands hanging easily at his sides while the billionaire considered the request for a few long seconds before lowering his arm.

"Thank you."

"Madison's important to me. What are your intentions toward her?"

It was a question Ramsay had asked himself more than once, and he still didn't have a good answer. He'd started off wanting information from her. Along the way, things had taken a turn toward the personal. "I just met her."

"But I get the feeling you've become close in a very short time."

"Danger can be a powerful shortcut to friendship."

"Or intimacy."

When Ramsay didn't rise to the bait, Coleman continued.

"If you hurt her, you'll be sorry."

"I wasn't planning on hurting her," Ramsay answered automatically, but he was thinking that things didn't always work out the way he expected.

Although he didn't particularly like this turn in the conversation, he could understand where Coleman was coming from. A guy named Ramsay Gallagher had blundered into Madison's life and taken charge, at least temporarily.

"She's vulnerable," her mentor said.

"She's a strong woman," Ramsay countered.

"She was young when she lost her family. I've watched out for her, but she's been focused on her work. She's not the best judge of men."

"And you are?" Ramsay asked.

"I'm old enough to have met a lot of con artists."

"Is that what you think I am?"

"No. But I sense that you're not telling us everything about yourself."

"I can say the same for you. Experience has taught us both to be cautious."

Coleman shrugged. "Did you come to the Las Vegas conference to make contact with Madison?"

"I came because the topic of her talk interested me." He laughed. "If you're thinking I was planning to seduce

Dr. Dartmoor, I was surprised to find out she was a woman! And I'd never heard of Kent Spader until two of his men tried to abduct her."

"But you were right there to rescue her."

"Like everyone else, I was disappointed that she didn't give her talk. I was hoping to speak to her, and I'd followed her outside. Which put me in the right place at the right time."

"Yes. I should thank you for getting her away from Spader's men. But that still doesn't clear up why you're so hot to join the expedition."

Ramsay shifted his weight from one foot to the other. "I'm like you. I'm fascinated with the idea that man's not alone in the universe. I'd like to help prove it."

"Spader could have sent you as a plant."

The paranoia was back, and Ramsay fought the urge to sling a sarcastic retort. Instead, he remarked, "That would require a lot of devious and intricate planning, don't you think?"

"He's capable of being devious."

"So you think he'd send men after us—so that I could kill them to prove my bona fides?"

Coleman made a snorting sound. "He doesn't care much about human life, but he also doesn't waste resources."

"You know him better than I do. Like I said, I wasn't aware of him at all until his men went after Madison."

Coleman nodded. "I'm still taking a lot on faith—with regard to the way you got involved in her life."

Ramsay waited quietly, thinking that this was one of the oddest conversations he'd had in his long life. He wanted to resolve it by reaching out and touching the man, to make physical contact, to wrap him in a soothing, reassuring buzz. In the old days, that would have worked. But he couldn't be sure of the effect now, even if he gave the guy a bear hug. And he didn't want to do anything else that would arouse Coleman's suspicions. Keeping his hands at his sides, he sent his interrogator a silent message. *You like me. You want to trust me. You know I'm on your side. You know I'll be an asset to the expedition. I can help guard the camp. Help guard Madison.* He repeated the silent words several times, sending them toward Coleman, wishing he knew they were effective. Maybe he could get through to the man. Maybe not. And maybe it wouldn't even be the deciding factor.

CHAPTER
FIFTEEN

RAMSAY WAITED AS the seconds ticked by.

Finally Coleman nodded. "You may be an asset to the expedition. I'm going to book you a seat on the plane with Madison. But I'm also going to have her keep me fully informed of your activities."

"You could come with us."

"That's one of the annoyances of my situation. I'm not in good enough health to travel the way I used to."

"That must be frustrating."

"I've learned to deal with it. I was lucky that Madison was interested in furthering my research."

Ramsay wanted to ask if she'd thought of that herself. Or had her mentor made it impossible for her to refuse? he wondered with sudden insight. She'd seemed passionate about her work. But perhaps Coleman had put in a lot of time cultivating that passion.

While Ramsay was still contemplating the question, Coleman turned and left the patio.

Ramsay stared at the man's stooped shoulders, thinking

that he might have had a sense of humor when he'd named his house, but he'd apparently lost it in his later years.

The conversation wasn't exactly finished. The billionaire had asked a lot of questions and provided little opportunity for Ramsay to satisfy his own curiosity. But he'd learned patience over the years.

EVEN though Madison was up early, she knew Dominic would be waiting for her. She'd pleaded fatigue the night before to avoid any serious discussion, but now she was in for an interrogation.

Dressing quickly, she made her way to the small dining room. As she'd anticipated, her mentor was sitting at the table with a cup of coffee and a plate of sliced melons and berries in front of him. His laptop was also on the table, along with some notes, indicating that this was going to be a business meeting. *Good.*

"Help yourself to breakfast," he said, gesturing toward the food laid out on the sideboard.

She took a helping of scrambled eggs, a chocolate-filled croissant, and some fruit before pouring coffee and adding cream and sugar. Cream was a luxury she wouldn't get when she went back to the dig site.

Not that she was really hungry, but she knew Dominic would be watching her, judging her readiness to return to the site after getting shot. She didn't want to give the impression that she was less than fit.

When she sat down at the antique hexagonal table, he said, "You've had a rough couple of days."

"I survived."

"Last night you told me you were shot. I'd like to see the wound."

She rolled up her sleeve and showed him the red marks where the bullet had entered and exited.

Dominic ran his thumb over one red circle. "It hardly looks like you were injured."

"I know. Ramsay put something on it."

"What?"

"I don't know. He said it had a faith-healing component."

"You think he's learned to do that?"

She shrugged. "He did *something*."

"It looks like he could make a living at it, if he wanted to."

She took a sip of coffee. "I think he only uses it when it suits him."

"Do you trust him?" Dominic asked the question he'd asked over the phone.

"I think so."

"But you're not absolutely sure."

"He's mysterious." She forked up some eggs before asking, "Do *you* trust him?"

"I found him wandering the grounds last night."

"With a signal device in his hand?"

"No. But it was odd that he was tramping around strange territory."

"He's an odd man."

Coleman gave her a direct look. "Did you get personally involved with him?"

Of course she'd been prepared for that question. And she'd spent a good portion of the night thinking about her relationship with Ramsay Gallagher. She'd acted wildly out of character with him. She simply *did not* make love with men she barely knew. Of course, she could tell herself that it hadn't been a normal reaction—either time. First he'd given her something that had made her aroused. Then there was the Native American vision quest. Was that how he got women—by drugging them?

Even as she asked the question, she silently admitted there was more to it. He was a very attractive man, with a magnetic personality that drew her to him. It wasn't just physical. It was his mind—the way he thought and the things he thought about. He knew her subject so well that she didn't have to explain any background to him. He was already keyed in.

She vowed not to let her attraction affect her judgment, but the deliberations were private.

She wasn't going to discuss any of that with Dominic. Her relationship with him was close, but that didn't include discussing her sex life.

"That's my business," she said, keeping her voice as even as possible.

He reached out and laid a hand over hers. "I'm just looking out for your welfare. I'd be cautious of getting too close until you know him a lot better."

"I'm aware of that."

"It could affect the project."

"It won't!" she answered, wondering if she was telling the truth.

To her relief, her mentor changed the subject. "There's hardly any information on him. What could you tell about him—from his house? His lifestyle."

"He's rich. Money's no object. He's a collector of antiquities—the way you are, but not on quite so grand a scale. He doesn't have any servants, but his cooking skills are confined to the microwave."

"I guess he doesn't care about fine dining."

"Not at home, anyway."

"Is he serious about the theory of early alien contact?"

"I think so. He gets excited when he talks about it."

"Yes."

"I can't find any record of his having formal training in the field."

"He said he was self-taught."

"There should be *something*."

"Maybe he was using another name."

"What's he got to hide?"

A noise in the doorway made her look up to see Ramsay watching them. She felt a flush spread across her face. "I didn't hear you coming."

"You were too caught up in your conversation."

Yes. Talking about you. The flush deepened, and she felt like a kid who'd gotten caught shoplifting.

Dominic showed only his usual cool control. As he had with Madison, he gestured toward the sideboard. "Help yourself to breakfast."

RAMSAY crossed the room, picked up a plate, and filled it with food he wasn't going to eat much of—eggs, fruit, and a blueberry muffin. Setting it down, he poured himself a mug of black coffee.

From the corner of his eye, he watched Madison. Her hair fell over her temple, and she reached to sweep it back, revealing her delicate profile.

She looked guilty, and Ramsay had the feeling her mentor had warned her not to get too friendly with their new team member.

Coleman glanced up. The man had a smug look on his face, confirming Ramsay's impression, but was there something else operating here besides his concern for his protégé's welfare? Was he also out to make sure that her primary relationship was with him and not this new man who had come charging into her life?

Actually, either possibility suited Ramsay pretty well. He'd been worried that the relationship with Madison was heating up too fast, and Coleman had practically ordered him to take a step back.

That was as good an excuse as any.

"Are you having a planning session?" he asked in a neutral voice.

"Yes," Coleman answered. "Why don't you join us."

"What did I miss?"

"Not too much."

Ramsay walked toward a chair, then stopped short. He could see a laptop on the table, and a scatter of papers. But the table had hidden something sitting beside one of the chairs. A box about eighteen inches square. As he studied it, his pulse began to pound.

"Is that what I think it is?" he asked, wondering if his voice sounded as strained to them as it did to him.

Coleman's expression grew more smug. "The original of the artifact."

"Can I see it?"

Coleman waited a full thirty seconds before answering. "I suppose that won't do any harm." He turned to Madison. "Would you bring it up, my dear?"

Madison nodded and pushed back her chair, then stooped down and picked up the box, which she held close to her body as she transferred it to the table.

Ramsay's breath turned shallow as he watched her unfasten the catch and lift the lid. Inside was the same kind of foam packing material that had cushioned the copy she'd brought to the conference.

When she removed it, he saw the gleam of polished stone. Or was it ceramic? He couldn't be sure which. He'd seen ancient pottery that looked like it had just been made. The object in the box had the same newly minted quality.

As he bent down to have a better look, he saw that both Madison and Coleman were watching him.

Madison glanced at her mentor.

"Go ahead and pick it up," the old man said.

Gingerly, Ramsay reached into the box and cupped his fingers around the statue. Carefully, he extracted it from the packing material and held it up. In its current form, it looked like a man.

It was very much like the replica that he'd already seen except that the surface had a more lustrous green sheen, and it wasn't as heavy as the copy. "What's it made of?" he asked.

"We're not sure. We didn't want to damage the surface by taking a scraping. We also didn't want to take it to a laboratory. So we're just accepting it at face value for the moment."

Ramsay nodded. He would have wanted a scientific evaluation to confirm that it was genuine, but he could understand the other point of view.

He cleared his throat. "And it . . . shifts?"

"Yes," Madison answered. "We discovered that by accident." She gave a nervous laugh. "At first we thought we'd broken it, but then we realized it was supposed to move." He could hear the reverence in her voice.

Carefully he lifted the man's arms so that the figure shifted into the dragon configuration.

"How old was the tomb?" he asked.

"At least two thousand years."

His chest was so tight he could barely breathe. Had his people made this thing? Struggling to keep his tone normal, he asked, "Have you figured out how it works?"

Coleman answered, "We're being careful with it, so we haven't done any testing."

"Understood."

"I'd like to put it back into the safe now," the owner said.

"Yes," Ramsay answered. He wanted to give the artifact a closer inspection, but he wouldn't insist. "Nobody can get into the safe?" he asked.

"It's quite secure here." The billionaire turned to Madison. "Would you take it back and lock it up now?"

"Yes."

Ramsay reluctantly put the statue back in the carry case. When he'd closed the cover, Madison picked up the box and left the room.

"I'd want to authenticate it," Ramsay said.

"We're hoping to do that through our examination of the tomb."

"Right."

"I've got some pictures from the site, if you'd like to see."

When he nodded, Coleman pulled the laptop over and went to a file of photographs. Ramsay scrolled through them slowly. The first ones showed a mountainous location, which was obviously along a seacoast. Then there were close-ups of the site where the tomb had been discovered and finally views of the interior, which had been brightly lighted.

"How was this discovered?" he asked.

"Apparently, there were old tunnels that lead down from the mountains to the Ionian Sea. They were used for smuggling, and about a year ago, some young men were poking around in the area, maybe looking for something valuable that had been left behind. There was a landslide, and the tomb entrance was uncovered."

Coleman switched to another shot, which showed a rectangular room.

"The tomb?"

"Well, not the tomb proper. There were no bodies. This is the antechamber, we think. We haven't found the actual entrance."

Ramsay listened, fascinated. On the far wall of the chamber he could see a mural, but unlike the man/dragon artifact, the picture had faded.

"What's that?" he said, pointing to the picture.

"We haven't been able to make it out," Madison answered as she came back into the room.

He looked up, working to conceal his excitement. Maybe they couldn't figure out what was on the wall, but he was pretty sure he knew what it was.

CHAPTER
SIXTEEN

"DO YOU HAVE a close-up of the wall?" he asked.

"Sorry. We were in a hurry to send the photos," Madison said.

"But you can see it in person in a few days."

"Why not now?"

"I want a security report first, and you need to go down to San Francisco and do some shopping. I assume you're buying your own clothing."

"Of course."

"Then why don't you drive down now, and Madison will meet you at the airport the day after tomorrow. I've already booked your flight."

Ramsay nodded. It wasn't the way he would have done things, but he wasn't going to complain about it as long as he was going with the team to the site.

He longed to be there now. But he could wait a couple of days.

"I'd better do some packing," Madison said and disappeared again. If she was trying to avoid him, that wouldn't be possible on the two long plane flights ahead of them. He could ask questions then. Or maybe it was better simply to see the site and make up his own mind.

AFTER a frustrating twenty-four hours, Kent Spader was left to pace his office and wait for news. Madison Dartmoor had escaped from him again. He knew she had gone to Coleman's estate. How long would she stay there?

When the phone rang, he stopped in midstride and hurried back to the broad desk.

"I have some information," the harsh voice on the other end of the phone line said.

Spader's hand tightened on the phone. "Which is?"

"Madison Dartmoor is booked on a flight to New York. Then to Italy. Do you want me to nab her?"

He thought about that for a moment, considering all the angles. He didn't want any more failures. Time to change tactics. Madison was going back to the site. That was a much more controlled environment where it would be easier to corner her. "No. She might as well get back to work. I want to know if there are any new developments."

"The Ramsay Gallagher guy went to *El Bigote* with her."

"That buttinsky! If you can find a way to get rid of him, do it."

He hung up and walked to the window, looking out at the Los Angeles skyline. He'd prospered by making the right decisions at the right time. For years he'd fit himself into upper-crust society. But long ago he'd been in the Marines, where you got things done in a very pragmatic way. Perhaps it was time for him to stop hanging back and let those old instincts take over.

ONCE again Ramsay was astonished at how quickly the world moved today. One minute he'd been in California. In the next, he'd stepped off a plane in Rome, then transferred to a flight to Crotone, where three cars met him and Madison. They were riding in one. The other two were filled with security guards Coleman had hired for their protection. Behind them was a truck with their luggage and other supplies going to the site. Apparently Coleman hadn't been kidding about the precautions he was taking.

Which was good, because Ramsay's senses were tingling as they drove south through rugged mountains thick with pine forests. When he'd been in this area before, exploring, he hadn't found anything he could tie to his heritage. Still, being here energized him in a way he couldn't articulate.

They passed vineyards and citrus orchards that gave way to scrub land with prickly pear cactus and other vegetation that thrived in dry conditions. As the roads grew narrow and winding, he tried to spot anyone following them and saw no other vehicles, yet he couldn't shake the conviction that they were being watched.

He glanced at Madison. She had gotten some sleep on the plane, but she still looked worn-out. Also excited. She'd spent the past three months at this site, and it was obvious that she was eager to get back to work. The dig was important to her. She had a lot riding on her discoveries here.

In Las Vegas she'd looked sleek and professional. She still looked professional, but in a different way. For her appearance at the conference, she'd been dressed like a business executive. Out here she was wearing a comfortable shirt, khaki pants, and light boots.

They had carefully avoided any personal discussion on the trip. She'd given him more photos of the site as well as the notes she'd taken. He'd spent the time alternating reading them and thinking about taking her into the bathroom and finding out if he'd imagined the spark that had previously leaped between them. He had the feeling that all he had to do was pull her into his arms to feel the passion spring up between them again. But he knew that following his impulses was a mistake. Staying on good terms with her was more important than his desire for her. So he kept his hands to himself.

His breath caught as they rounded a rocky curve and came out on a promontory facing the Ionian Sea.

He'd found on previous visits to Italy that the country was densely populated. But this area was too rocky, too dry, and too hilly for intensive development. In other words, worthless real estate. Which might be why the tomb hadn't been discovered until recently.

THEY angled away from the coast, putting jagged brown hills between themselves and the ocean. As they rounded another curve, he could see a group of one-story stone houses nestled in a small valley. Apparently someone had tried to make a home here, then abandoned the habitation. Had he been in any of those huts? He could imagine himself here, yet he knew the place looked like a thousand primitive villages where stone was abundantly available for building material.

Trucks and other vehicles were pulled up around the buildings, making it clear that this was the expedition's base camp.

"Nice that you could take over this place," he observed.

"Yes," Madison answered. "It's convenient to the site. We just had to clean out the debris and fix the roofs."

"How did the people make a living here?"

"They were goat and sheep herders."

"Do you know why they abandoned it?" he asked.

"I believe the wells failed."

He looked at the rocks and the scrubby vegetation. Probably it had been a marginal existence, even for the sheep, but he hoped there were still some wild ones around. Or perhaps shepherds used the area.

Before they reached the buildings, they came to a

roadblock where men armed with machine guns inspected their credentials before letting them pass. It was heavy security for an archaeological site, but Ramsay was glad of it. He already knew that Kent Spader could be ruthless.

A few hundred feet beyond the barrier, the car came to a stop. Without waiting for him, Madison climbed out and walked toward a man who was leaning against the side of a building. When he looked more closely, he saw it was Gavin Kaiser. He'd been wounded by Spader's men at the hotel, and Ramsay hadn't expected to see him again, but here he was—looking somewhat the worse for wear.

As Madison hurried toward him, Ramsay followed.

"What are you doing out of bed?" she called.

"I wasn't going to let you leave me behind, not when . . ." As he glanced at Ramsay, his voice trailed off.

"But you're not well yet."

He shrugged. "I can manage."

Ramsay took in his pale face and the way he leaned forward. It looked like he was on massive doses of painkillers. "You should be recuperating," he said.

They eyed each other. Gavin had gotten shot by Spader's goons because he'd come to Ramsay's room. Now he was doing something stupid again.

"I'll be the judge of my fitness," he said in a tight voice.

"Suit yourself," Ramsay answered, unwilling to waste any effort in arguing with this guy. If he wanted to risk infection or worse, that was his problem.

One of the armed men came up to Madison and began speaking rapidly in Italian. Apparently he was the security chief.

She answered in the same language, maybe assuming that neither Ramsay nor Gavin could follow the conversation, but Ramsay was perfectly able to keep up with the rapid-fire exchange.

He was seeing her in an entirely new light. This was her dig, and she was totally in charge.

She asked about the attack. The security man assured her they'd sent the would-be invaders running, and now they had extra men on duty.

When she called over another guy to discuss the work in progress, Ramsay kept listening. He gathered that they'd been in a holding pattern since she'd left. Apparently the archaeologists on staff didn't want to make any mistakes while the boss was away.

"Can we go right to the site?" He couldn't stop himself from asking.

"We've been traveling for fourteen hours. Don't you want to . . . freshen up?"

"I'm fine," he answered. "I'd like to see the entrance to the tomb."

"Well, you'll have to wait," she muttered. "I want to check the supplies."

Was she making it clear that she was in charge here? He wanted to tell her that someone else could show him the tomb. Instead, he waited while she introduced him to some of the staff, including Dr. Calvin Collins and Dr. Harold Martin, both Americans with scraggly beards. One dark and the other blond.

All of the security men were dark-haired Italians dressed in rough pants and T-shirts. He met Raphael, who was the head guy, Ambrose, Giovanni, Guido, and Marco. The latter two were new hires. Coleman had said there was a virtual army here. Too bad the numbers didn't look quite so impressive on the ground.

After the introductions, Marco led him to a stone hut, furnished with a narrow cot and a stand for his suitcase. The floor was dirt. There was no electricity and no running water, but a heavy-duty battery light sat on a small table.

He sank down on the cot, figuring he might as well get some rest until Madison deigned to send for him.

As he sat looking around the rough interior, memories flooded over him. This place wasn't all that different from the house where he'd lived for the first few years of his life with the old couple who'd found him up in the mountains not too far from here. They'd been poor, but they'd treated him like a son until the harvest had failed two years in a row and they'd been forced to sell him for enough money to buy themselves a little food. The man who'd bought him had been cruel, and worked Ramsay until he was ready to drop. He'd finally turned on the man, not physically but with an arrow of hate rising up from the depths of his soul. To his shock, it had felled the man, and that had been the start of a life he'd like to forget. He wasn't proud of what he'd been. A thief and a murderer. An opportunist who had used his powers to make a comfortable life for himself. But he knew that he could have come out a lot worse. He could have turned into Vandar—the dragon-shifter he'd defeated.

Vandar's life had soured him on humanity, but Ramsay had fared better. He'd had some rewarding relationships, and he'd found a woman named Bethany who gave him a faith in humanity that he'd never felt before. He'd fallen in love with her, and she'd changed him for the better. When he'd shared his secret with her as he'd never done before, she'd accepted him for what he was. The tragedy was that his life was so much longer than hers.

Now he was back in the part of the world where the old couple had found him—hoping he could figure out who he really was.

A shadow fell across the doorway, and he looked up to see a woman staring down at him. For a startled moment he thought it was Bethany, come back to him. Then he realized it was Madison and saw for the first time how much she looked like his lost love. He hadn't picked up on that before. Not consciously. Now he realized it could have been part of what had drawn him to her.

Their eyes met, and neither of them spoke. It looked like she might be going to say something personal; instead she asked, "Ready?"

"As ready as you are," he answered, trying to slow the pounding of his heart. He could have asked about the two of them, but the personal relationship had receded into the background. His focus must be this unique place. This unique situation. Had he come home? Or was this simply another dead end in his search for his origins?

No. He wouldn't believe that. It couldn't be a dead end. Not after he'd seen the movable artifact Coleman was keeping locked up at his estate.

Or was that part of an elaborate scheme to scam Ramsay Gallagher? Coleman said he'd known a lot of con men. Could he be out to turn the tables?

Even as that thought surfaced, Ramsay dismissed it. It couldn't be true, not after everything that had happened.

Coleman hadn't known anything about him. Or was that another lie?

He hated questioning everything, but that was one of his survival mechanisms.

"Where's the tomb?" he asked.

"Up in the hills. Bring a flashlight."

Madison turned without speaking, and he followed her across the dusty ground toward the back of the small village.

They walked through a narrow opening between two hills into a passageway that led farther into the rough terrain.

He saw that a pile of rubble had been swept out of the way, and crude steps cut into the side of one hill, leading upward to a narrow ledge. There was no railing, but Madison climbed confidently. He followed in her wake, his heart still pounding.

Stopping on a ledge about twenty feet from the ground, she waited for him.

When he joined her, he saw nothing that could be the opening to the tomb. Without speaking she kept going around a curve, stepping onto a wider ledge that gave way to a narrow opening in the rock.

"In there?"

"Yes," she answered, turning on her flashlight as she disappeared inside. As he followed her, he felt like his heart would burst through the wall of his chest.

They were in a rectangular room about fifteen feet long and ten feet wide, the walls hewn out of the rock of the mountainside. The ceiling was about ten feet above their heads. It had been left rough. But the floor beneath his boots was smooth, as were the walls. He played his light over the floor first, seeing the grid that Madison and her team had laid out. Then he moved the beam to the walls, staring at faded images that must be a couple of thousand years old. They seemed to be murals as opposed to individual pictures. He imagined that the colors had once been bright and the lines sharp, but time had not been kind to the artwork. It wasn't like the artifact, which had been bright and shiny, as though it had been made the day before.

He'd seen these walls in the pictures on Coleman's computer. Now he was viewing them in person. Once again he wondered if it was for the first time. Or had he actually been here? In this secret place. That possibility had circled in his mind all the way to Italy. Now that he was here, he couldn't bring any real feeling of familiarity into focus. But he'd been so young when the old couple had found him wandering these hills. A child might not remember.

"Do you know what they are?" he asked Madison.

"They're too faded," she answered. "Can you make anything out?"

CHAPTER
SEVENTEEN

AS MADISON LOOKED at Ramsay expectantly, he played his light over the murals. It should have been impossible to see anything specific in the faded images, but his brain filled in the missing pieces. The scenes were much like the ones from the vision he had shared with Madison in the vision quest ceremony.

He saw men and women together, in a flower-filled valley. At one end of the mural the sun shone brightly in a brilliant blue sky. Below it, the people were going about their business. All was calm and peaceful. Some of the men and women were even making love. Dragon men and human women? There was no way to tell for sure.

He kept walking along the wall, playing his powerful flashlight across the images, intent on discovering more. At the other end of the scene, everything changed. The sky darkened with storm clouds. Lightning flashed, and in the midst of the storm, a dragon flew above the valley, raining fire down on people who ran for their lives. And as they fled, some of the people were changing to dragon form—like the figure that he'd held in his hand at Coleman's house.

In the last panel, some of the transformed figures were rising into the sky to challenge the dragon attacking them.

What did it mean? That his people had broken into factions? And why? Maybe some of them had wanted to join with the humans and others had been opposed. Perhaps they'd even been repulsed by the very idea.

He didn't know. Not from this cryptic picture. But he did know that something bad had happened. Maybe something catastrophic.

"What do you see?"

When Madison asked the question, he realized that he'd been standing stock-still, staring at the wall.

"It's hard to tell," he answered. What was he going to say? That these images confirmed the vision they'd shared? He wasn't prepared to go that far with her because she'd want to know where he got his insights—particularly since nobody else had gotten much out of the faded mural.

"You look like you're seeing something I can't."

He shrugged. "I wouldn't want to make guesses."

"Of course not!" she snapped.

"You want me to make something up so you can put it in your notes?" he asked.

"No."

He started back in the direction from which he'd come, moving slowly, letting the ground tell him what was below his feet.

"What are you doing?" Madison asked.

"Trying to figure this place out. Why do you think it's the antechamber to a tomb?"

"Because it was well hidden."

"Where did you find the artifact?"

She walked to a place along the wall and pressed

against the stone. A small section rotated inward, revealing a secret compartment.

"There."

He joined her, knelt down, and examined the hiding place. "It moved that easily when you first pressed?"

"No. But I could see a faint line in the stone, and I started trying to see if the block came out. When I pressed at this corner, it opened up."

He looked at the spot she'd indicated and saw a man standing at that section of the wall. His foot had a wing at the back. Something like the feet of the Roman god Mercury. That had been an indication of what might lie behind the rock. But Madison hadn't seen it. She'd only been checking out the condition of the wall and found the crack.

"Good going," he murmured. "Were there any other hiding places behind the wall?"

"Not that I found."

He looked back at the mural and saw something else that he hadn't noticed before. There was a woman standing beside the man with the winged feet. Her arm was outstretched and pointing downward, toward a particular section of the floor.

Excitement coursed through him, but he couldn't tell Madison that he saw an arrow drawn toward a spot a few feet away.

"Let me walk around some more," he murmured.

She backed off, keeping her eyes on him as he paced around the chamber. He covered the whole room, then started over again. When he glanced up and caught Madison's eye, she pressed her lips together, obviously struggling not to interrupt him.

Finally, he stopped at the area where the woman's arm was pointing. He stood very still, his eyes closed, breathing deeply and swaying slightly.

When he opened his eyes, Madison was staring at him. "I think this might be the right place to dig."

She came over, looking down at the floor. "I don't see anything. Why do you think so?"

"I can't explain it. But I'm getting a strong feeling that there's something below the floor—here."

"And you want me to start digging because you have a flash of mumbo jumbo?"

He shrugged. "It's near the spot where the stone moved."

"A lot of other places are near there, too."

"I wish I could give you something more concrete. I can't. It's just an impression I have," he answered, knowing that the explanation sounded lame.

He was tempted to start talking about the mural, but he had the gut feeling that was a mistake. It would give too much away.

Her expression hardened. "As a matter of fact, we've done 3-D X-ray scans of the floor. That was one of the spots where we were going to start digging."

He stared at her, feeling trapped. He'd been careful to hide his reasoning, and now it turned out that his "impression" confirmed what she'd already discovered.

"What are you dancing around?" she asked in a cold voice.

"Are you trying to imply that I have inside information about this site?"

"Do you?"

"No. Where would I get it?"

"You tell me."

"I've trained myself to use more than my five senses, and I got some kind of impression from this area of the floor. I'm sorry I can't tell you where it came from. But over the years, I've had psychic insights. That's why I was open to the Native American herbs that I used in the ceremony. They heighten those powers."

"You didn't tell me that," she accused.

"I figured you'd think it was odd. You think it's odd now, don't you?"

Before she could answer, the light in the room changed,

and they both turned to the door to see a figure blocking the entrance.

Ramsay tensed until he saw that it was Madison's assistant.

"Gavin?" she asked. "What are you doing here?"

"Dominic wanted to make sure you'd arrived safely. Have you called him?"

"Not yet."

"You'd better do it."

Was her assistant giving her orders? Ramsay watched the body language of each of them.

She sighed. "You're right. I was too caught up in getting back here to think of anything else. But I know he's concerned about me." Without waiting for Ramsay she followed her assistant out of the antechamber.

Ramsay stared after her. He'd underestimated her, and that had been a mistake. He'd thought he could fake her out, and all he'd done was make her suspicious.

But at least she hadn't dragged him out of the antechamber as she should have done. Instead, she'd been too focused on phoning Coleman. Which was insightful in itself. Was her mentor calling the shots because he was the money man? And maybe also because he'd assumed a father's role in Madison's life?

For the moment, that wasn't Ramsay's problem. Alone in the light from his power torch, he walked to the wall again, pressing the flat of his hand against part of the mural where he wasn't going to damage anything important. He stood there for a long moment, connecting with the rock and trying to get beyond the surface, to the picture and to the artist who had painted it.

Did he feel some sort of kinship with his people? Or was he just making that up because he so desperately *wanted* to feel something?

He couldn't answer the question; he could only stand in awe, absorbing the feel of the ancient place.

Once again, the light shifted, and a harsh voice asked, "What the hell are you doing?"

It was Gavin again, come back to check on the man he considered an interloper.

CHAPTER
EIGHTEEN

RAMSAY MOVED SLOWLY away from the wall. "I was just absorbing the atmosphere of the place."

"You don't have any formal training. You could damage something."

"I hope not," he answered, keeping his voice even.

"It will be sunset soon. You don't want to be on the ledge in the dark."

"Thanks for warning me," he said without bothering to explain that his night vision was excellent.

"We've got enough problems without someone getting hurt," the assistant added brusquely.

Ramsay followed him out of the excavation area and onto the ledge.

Gavin moved close to him, and Ramsay wondered if the guy was thinking about pushing him off. If he tried he was in for a surprise.

But the other man kept his hands to himself as they walked back to the corner, then down the stone steps.

"Coleman said there are caves in the area."

"Yes."

"Where?"

"There's an entrance farther along the mountain. I wouldn't go in there if I were you. They're like a maze. You could get lost, and then we'd have to waste the manpower to find you."

"Is there a map that shows their location?"

"Yes, but I'd stay away from them."

"Thanks for the warning."

The light was dimming as they approached the stone buildings. In the open area, a fire crackled, and he could smell lamb roasting on a grill.

Madison came out of her cottage and joined the group. Marco, Giovanni, and Ambrose had gone off to stand guard duty, and Ramsay met the men who had come off shift, Paolo, Emilio, and Edoardo. All of them were new to the job.

They sat around the campfire with plates of meat and spaghetti, speaking among themselves in Italian. Again, Ramsay was able to follow the conversation, although it was pretty mundane—mostly about the working conditions, the food, and the living quarters.

As he watched and listened, he evaluated each of the men. One or more of them could be a spy for Spader, feeding him information about the camp and the progress of the excavation. For that matter, Gavin could be playing that role, since he'd been so anxious to get back here. Or did he have some private reason? Madison trusted him, but Ramsay wasn't taking his loyalty for granted.

Ramsay turned in early, using the long trip as an excuse. In his hut, he waited until two in the morning before getting up. If anyone asked, he could say he was going to the latrine. Really, he wanted to explore the camp and make sure he knew his way out if trouble developed. And if he happened to discover the caves Coleman had mentioned, so much the better. There was supposed to be a passage down to the sea, and he'd like to know exactly where it was. Could he find it in the dark, or should he wait until morning?

He slipped out of his quarters, standing in the darkness, absorbing the feel of the place.

He'd learned from listening to the conversation of the guards that they didn't patrol inside the camp, only the perimeters. Up on the hill, he saw a man with a machine gun. He knew another two had to be down by the road. Although there were others in the hills, that still left a lot of territory open to invaders. It also made for trigger-happy guards, which meant he might be better off exploring during the day.

A light shone through the window of a hut to his left, and he took a step in that direction. He knew it was Madison's quarters. The temptation to join her was almost overwhelming. She was working late. He was sure he could persuade her that there were more rewarding nighttime activities. But he checked his steps before he'd gotten more than a few feet.

Not a good idea. It was hard to keep anything private in a small community like this one. If he made love with her, everyone in camp would know about it pretty soon, which was an excellent reason for not starting anything. An excellent reason among many.

He eased back into his own hut, pulled off his boots, and lay down. He had learned to sleep lightly, so that no one could come upon him by surprise. Tonight, dreams grabbed him. Dreams of the past. Of his people. The pictures he'd seen on the mural played through his mind, only he was part of the scene—going about his daily business and then turning to challenge the attacking dragon as it rained fire down on the community of shifters and humans. It was like the battle with Vandar, and he struggled to yank himself out of the nightmare.

He woke in a sweat, his heart pounding, struggling to bring himself back to this reality.

The camp stirred at the first light of dawn, and he joined the men, making himself useful by adding wood to the fire. The stockpile was getting low, which gave him an idea. If he was caught out in the surrounding area and challenged, he could always say he was hunting up fuel.

When Madison came out of her hut, she gave him a long look. As she stared at him, he could almost hear her saying, "I expected you to come to my room last night."

But instead she remarked, "We're going to be busy today, investigating that area of the floor."

"Fine."

"You'd probably just be in the way."

He resisted the urge to protest. He'd given her the clue about where to dig. He'd like to be there. Instead he said, "I'm going to be investigating the other caves in the area. Gavin says there's a map that shows their location."

"Marco told me they're dangerous."

"Gavin told me the same thing. I'll be careful. Do you have the map?"

"Yes." She walked back to her tent, then reappeared a few minutes later with a folded sheet of paper, which she held out. He was tempted to see what she'd do if he reached for her hand. Instead he simply took the paper, wondering about his own responses. Was he reacting to her deliberate aloofness, or was his male ego bruised because a woman was rejecting him?

He ate a quick breakfast of bread and cheese while he looked at the crudely drawn map.

By whom? Marco or someone from the local area? But the abandoned village was clearly marked, and there were enough other landmarks that he thought he could find the entrance to the caves.

As soon as he'd eaten, he got his knapsack and flashlight

and took a bottle of water from the pallet sitting in the shade of one of the buildings.

Madison was still talking to the men when he started off. He gave her a little wave as he headed into the hills.

The first landmark was an animal skull—probably a donkey. He found it easily and continued into the scrubby brush, toward an outcropping of rock about an eighth of a mile from the antechamber to the tomb. But he could see that he wouldn't be climbing as far up the hill, which was good because the ground was dry and unstable. More than once he kicked up little rock and dirt slides as he climbed.

He stopped and looked back. A couple of off-duty guards were watching him. They turned away when they saw him staring at them.

He was glad when he disappeared from sight around a massive rock. Following a crude trail that hugged the side of the hill, he kept walking until he came to the conclusion that he had gone too far.

Reversing direction, he walked more slowly, scanning the side of the hill, and finally came to a natural crevice that he'd missed the first time. It was almost invisible in the rocky landscape, even when he looked closer and saw that someone had enlarged the opening so that a man could slip inside.

He stared into the darkness, then shone his light inside, but he didn't see anything immediately threatening.

His shoulders were broad and he had to turn sideways to get through. Inside, the temperature dropped ten degrees.

As he waited for his eyes to adjust to the dim light, he saw that he was in a natural tunnel. Well, mostly natural. He could spot where areas had been chipped away to make the passage wider. Still, the ceiling barely cleared his head.

After his vision had adjusted to the darkness, he moved cautiously into the opening in the hill.

There were animal droppings on the floor, and he guessed

that someone had tethered donkeys in here. Probably to carry away smuggled goods.

The cave branched out into several tunnels, and he could see why it would be easy to get disoriented and lost. But his spatial memory was excellent, and he knew he could find his way back to the crevice where he'd entered.

He turned right, walking first on an inclined floor and then down a series of uneven steps hewn into the rock. As he descended, he could hear the sound of waves breaking far below. They became louder the farther he went, until it was a roaring ebb and flow.

The stairs grew damp, and he came out on a landing cut into the rock. A ring fixed to the stone could be used for a mooring. But at the moment, the waves rushed in and out with force, so that any boat would be in danger of getting smashed. Perhaps a landing here would be safer when the sea was calmer.

The stone staircase had the feel of antiquity, like the steps at the Great Wall of China or Machu Picchu, built back when nobody demanded that each one be a certain thickness or a certain distance apart. Who had carved them? His ancestors? Or were they constructed after the battle that he'd seen depicted on the cave wall?

He breathed in the salt air, marveling that the sea was so close to the campsite where he'd left Madison and her team.

After watching the waves for several moments, he turned and started back the way he'd come. This time he went to the left, again seeing side passages along the route.

He took one, moving slowly in case he encountered something unexpected. The passageway led about fifty feet into the cave, and at the end he found a small room that someone had been using for a shelter. A pile of blankets on the floor was spread into a crude bed. There was also trash scattered around that was left over from what looked like several meals. Shuffling through the debris, he decided it could have been there for a few weeks or a few years.

He'd like to know who'd been here, and why. But that would take a more thorough search.

For now, he wanted the big picture, so he continued down the main passage, sensing that there was something interesting ahead.

He wasn't disappointed. After a five-minute walk, he stopped abruptly. Ahead of him was a vast space where the cave opened out into an enormous cavern.

On the far wall, his light glinted against something. He steadied the beam and tried to figure out what he was seeing. It appeared to be a drawing where no drawing could exist, because there was no way to get there and nowhere for the artist to stand—unless he could fly.

His breath caught when he realized it hadn't been scratched or drawn on the rocky surface. It looked like it had been blasted into the rock with heat. As though a dragon had shot fire at the wall.

He stared at the symbol. It was something like the letter "M"—only the side pieces slanted outward like wings. Was it a symbol for a dragon? And what had happened to the artist? Had he blasted this message onto the rock wall, then plunged to his death?

The notion was fanciful, yet Ramsay couldn't banish it from his mind.

Perhaps there had been a great battle in this cave. Perhaps the two factions had fought, and some of the winged warriors had died.

If he climbed down, would he find dragon bones? Could anybody but a dragon get down there?

He shone his light toward the bottom of the cavern. It was too far down to see. And as he played the beam over the walls, he found that there were few handholds. Maybe a team with ropes could make it, but the best way would be to fly.

Automatically, he fumbled for the buttons of his shirt, thinking that he would try to transform. But just as he opened the top button, he heard a loose stone rattle behind him.

Quickly he redid the shirt and hurried back toward the main tunnel.

NINETEEN

GAVIN KAISER WAS standing in the passageway, looking uncertain.

Gavin again.

"What are you doing here?" Ramsay asked.

"Madison was worried about you. She sent me over here."

"I'm fine."

"Did you take the steps down to the water?"

"Yeah. Someone could come up that way."

"I take it you noticed the sea is kind of rough?" Gavin commented.

"Now. What about low tide?"

"At this time of year, the waves are always a problem."

Ramsay nodded, wondering if it was really true. He wasn't going to argue the point because he didn't know much about this region.

"Are you finished exploring?"

"Yes."

"Find anything?" Gavin asked in a casual voice. So

casual that Ramsay wondered if the other man had hidden something in this place. Or found something significant that he was keeping to himself.

Yeah, I found a secret sign on the wall that only a dragon could have put there. He didn't bother with that observation, either. Instead he asked, "How's the work going at the tomb?"

"Madison's proceeding with caution."

Ramsay understood where she was coming from. If she worked too fast, she could hit some priceless object and ruin it. Still, he was impatient to find out what was down there.

IN the mountains above the encampment, Kent Spader felt an exhilaration he hadn't experienced in years. Finally, he'd come here to see the place for himself, and as he watched men scurrying around, he knew it was the right move. The work here was wicked. There was no valid reason to believe that mankind had gotten help from any outside influences. That theory was an affront to the nobility of the human race. Anyone who was trying to prove otherwise must be stopped, and any false evidence to the contrary must be destroyed before the evil could spread.

He smoothed his hair across his head, watching through binoculars as the two men descended toward the camp. One was Ramsay Gallagher. The other was Gavin Kaiser. Gallagher must have been poking around in the network of caves and tunnels that connected the land side of the mountain to the sea, for all the good that was going to do him. And Gavin had come to bring him back, probably on Madison's orders.

Kent hated the little twerp, but he had his uses. He was also expendable. And so was Gallagher, for that matter. The two of them were going to end up dead—very soon. Along with all those guards strutting around with machine guns like they were Mafia wise guys or something.

Once he got rid of them and everybody else, he'd have a free hand with Dr. Dartmoor. She was going to tell him exactly what she'd discovered since she'd gotten back to camp and where to find the original of that statue she'd found here. He was certain it existed. He was pretty sure he knew where it was, but he wanted confirmation. After he was finished here, he'd destroy the statue. And then this whole travesty would be over.

MADISON was talking to her crew when Ramsay and Gavin walked back into camp.

"Find anything?" she asked.

"I think that's my line," Ramsay countered.

"We've taken off a foot-deep layer of the cave floor."

"No artifacts?"

"Just packed dirt."

"Okay."

He wanted to tell her that if he went up there, he might pick up some sense of how to proceed, but then he'd be stuck trying to explain another psychic impression. The last time hadn't gone so well.

"We'll eat soon. I want to get an early start in the morning," she said.

He couldn't stop himself from asking, "Can I come up there with you?"

She hesitated for a moment, then nodded.

"Thanks. I want to be helpful."

"You already have," she answered.

He could see Gavin watching them, looking like he'd sucked on a lemon.

"I'm going to wash up," Ramsay said, leaving the scene so Gavin could speak to Madison in private if he wanted to. Probably the less the new guy interfered with their relationship, the better. But he was going to keep an eye on her assistant, because he didn't trust the bastard.

The tension in the little group continued through dinner, and Ramsay excused himself early. The reconstituted freeze-dried food filled his belly, but he could feel his energy level dropping. He needed blood, and he was going to have to go out and look for it.

Could he use one of the guards—the way he'd used the prostitute in Vegas? It was tempting to consider slurping down a pint of human blood. But he'd used a sexual fantasy to make the prostitute forget what he was doing. He wasn't prepared to kill the guy if it didn't work out. Better to search for an animal whose mind he could control a lot more easily.

He filled some of the time by using the crude shower facilities set up behind one of the huts. Then he changed his clothes and lay down on his bunk fully dressed.

At two on the morning, when he got up, he was relieved to see no lights on in camp. Not even in Madison's quarters.

Firmly turning his mind away from her, he slipped out of his hut and waited for a few moments in the moonlight, absorbing the sense of the place. It was peaceful, but he felt something at the edge of his awareness. Something that didn't feel right.

He waited, hoping for some other clue, but he couldn't discern anything more. Should he go back to bed? He was too restless for that. He waited until the guard on top of a nearby hill was looking in the other direction, then slipped from hut to hut until he was clear of the little village.

As he walked, he sent his senses before him, scanning for danger and also for the scent of blood. The countryside was barren, and he wondered if he was going to find anything. He needed to feed, and he could conjure up a very seductive alternative. What if he went back to Madison? What if he clouded her mind, shared a fantasy with her while he drank? No problem reaching her. They were already tuned to each other.

He made a rough sound deep in his throat. He kept

picturing himself sinking his teeth into her when he knew it was a bad idea. His sexual gratification didn't depend on drinking the blood of his partner. It was just an additional pleasure he'd enjoyed from time to time, and Madison was the wrong woman to enjoy it with.

Doggedly he kept walking, and he was rewarded with success. Apparently, someone was still using the area for grazing. Or a sheep had gotten lost from its flock.

The animal had fallen into a narrow channel that probably ran with water when it rained. Now it was dry. When the sheep saw him, it galloped away until it came to a place where the sides of the channel were too narrow for it to keep going.

Ramsay jumped down, sending it calming thoughts as he approached. The animal was shivering as he reached it, but he extended his hand and his mind, holding it still while he soothed it.

After a few minutes, he was able to raise its head and find its neck, where he sank in his feeding teeth.

It was tempting to drain the animal. It was just a sheep, but he held back, taking enough to give himself more energy.

When he was finished, he lifted the sheep in his arms, boosting it out of the channel where it had been trapped. Without a backward look, it bounded away, and he watched it disappear into the darkness, hoping it would find the rest of the herd before it encountered a predator.

Alone again, he stood for a few minutes in the darkness, absorbing the power of this place. It was no illusion. There was something ancient in the very rocks that he could almost grasp with his mind. His people had lived here. Did that give him more of a chance to recover his true nature?

Although he was far from the encampment, he wasn't going to take a chance on being discovered. Stepping behind a rock, he began pulling off his clothing. When he was naked, he raised his face to the stars and focused his mind, trying to find the potency within himself and within this place to change his form. He willed his cells to transmute, his limbs and his body to change the way the artifact had changed, struggling to find the magic formula that he had taken for granted until after his battle with Vandar. But once again, the effort was wasted. He was stuck in his man form.

Finally, he gave up.

"*Futuo*," he muttered, wanting to shout the curse so that it echoed from the hilltops, but he kept the exclamation low in case one of the guards heard him.

Bubbling with frustration, he pulled on his clothing. He'd been sure he could make the change here—of all places.

But what did "here" mean? He was standing outside on a barren hillside. What if he went to the tomb? Would that give him the extra push he needed?

Willing it to be true, he hurried back toward the camp. He stopped short when a figure stepped into his path, and he saw the glint of a gun in the moonlight.

"What are you doing?" a cold voice asked.

It was Madison.

"I was out for a walk."

"I don't think so."

"What do you *think* I was doing?"

"I don't know, but we're going to find out."

"Madison . . ."

"Don't try to talk your way out of this. You're up to something. You've been up to something from the moment we met."

He could easily take the gun away from her, but maybe not before she pulled the trigger and woke everyone up. Instead he turned and walked past her, down the hill.

He was conscious of her keeping pace close behind him.

"What are you planning?" he asked.

"I don't know."

"We need to talk."

"You mean, you're going to tell me some kind of story? Like you always do?"

He didn't answer, because he had no idea what he was going to say. He couldn't tell her the truth, and he couldn't allow her to keep him captive. Was he going to end up fleeing into the countryside? And then what?

They were about to round an outcropping of rock when a flicker of movement made him glance up toward the tomb entrance.

What he saw made him stop short. When Madison started to speak, he whipped behind her, covering her mouth with his hand and lifting the gun out of her grasp.

Before she had time to struggle, he pulled her close and lowered his mouth to her ear. "Don't speak. Look up there."

She lifted her head, following his gaze. He heard her indrawn breath.

"Gavin," she whispered.

"Yeah. I guess he didn't expect us to be out at this time of night."

Madison's assistant was walking up the steps toward the tomb, and he wasn't alone. Another man was with him. He was dressed like one of the guards, but it was no one Ramsay had seen before.

The two figures disappeared into the antechamber.

"I've got to go up there," Madison whispered.

When she started toward the stairway, he grabbed her arm. "Not until you know what's going on."

"I won't find out unless I do."

"I'll do it."

"You think I'm crazy! For all I know you're working with them."

"Doing what?"

"We'll see, won't we." Again she started forward, but

this time his supertuned senses told him it was the exact wrong move.

Without even thinking, he threw her to the ground and came down on top of her, just as a massive explosion above them shook the ground and rained down rocks around them.

CHAPTER

TWENTY

MADISON FELT A couple of direct hits vibrate through Ramsay, but his body kept the impact from affecting her.

"Are you all right?" she called out urgently.

He didn't answer, and all she could do was lie still as more rocks and dust pelted down around them. A few chunks landed beside her, but Ramsay's large body shielded her from the worst of it.

It seemed to go on forever. Finally, the debris stopped falling, and she tried to move.

"Ramsay?"

He didn't answer, and his weight held her in place.

"Ramsay?" she called again, panic gripping her when he failed to respond. He must be hurt—because he'd protected her.

She reached up to touch his face and froze. His cheek was wet. Bringing her hand down, she saw blood.

God no!

As quickly as she could, she wiggled out from under

him, turning him over as she did. In the moonlight, she could see a place just above his hairline where blood oozed.

"Ramsay."

His eyes blinked open, but they had lost their usual brightness.

"We have to get you to a doctor."

She could see him making an effort to focus on her. "No doctor."

"What?"

"Like in . . . Las Vegas. Dangerous. You can take care of me."

She was about to protest, when his fingers closed around her arm, and she felt a light-headedness steal over her.

"No doctor. Too dangerous," he whispered. "We've got to hide."

She nodded, but her brain wasn't functioning with any kind of efficiency. *Hide? Where?*

She looked up, focusing on the entrance to the antechamber and gasped. It was no longer there. Instead, a pile of huge rocks covered the place where the opening had been.

"It's gone," she gasped, hardly able to take in what had happened. She'd put her blood, sweat, and tears into this place. Was it all for nothing?

"They were inside," Ramsay whispered. "One of them must have been carrying explosives."

"But why?"

"To destroy the tomb," he ground out.

She was still grappling with reality. "I have to . . ."

"We have to get out of here," he answered, and her attention snapped back to him. He was covered with debris from the explosion, and he was hurt—because of her. She hadn't trusted him. When she'd gone to check up on him, he'd been missing from his hut. Then she'd brought him back to camp at gunpoint, but as soon as he'd known she was in danger, he'd acted instantly to protect her.

She winced. She might not know everything about him, but she knew he hadn't hesitated to shield her from the explosion. He'd risked his life to save hers.

While those thoughts were spinning around in her head, he pushed himself up and stood swaying on his feet.

"Dangerous here," he repeated. "Have to get away."

"Where?"

He looked toward the hills. "The caves."

"The ones that lead down to the sea?"

He started to nod, but the movement obviously made his head hurt, and he grimaced.

She swallowed. She had briefly explored the caves, when she had thought they might contain more artifacts. She'd dismissed them as a dead end. Now she wasn't sure she could find her way through the maze of passageways.

Still uncertain, she looked up and froze. Four men were walking rapidly from the direction of the road toward the camp, and one of them looked like Kent Spader.

Spader? He'd come here himself? How long had he been in the area?

Dominic had obviously miscalculated the lengths to which the man would go to shut down her dig.

Ramsay followed her gaze. Even in his weakened state, he took in the situation instantly. With surprising strength, he pulled her around an outcropping of rock.

"Hurry."

When he started in the direction of the caves, her only alternative was to follow.

KENT Spader strode up the road toward the camp, his machine gun in firing position. It was sleek and lightweight. Perfect for this mission. He'd watched the explosion through binoculars, and he had no doubt that the antechamber to the tomb was filled with a mountain of rock. Thanks to that little worm, Gavin Kaiser.

His only loyalty had been to himself. After Gavin had gotten out of the hospital, Kent had contacted him and offered him a deal. Money to spy on the camp. Of course Kent hadn't needed another spy at the site, but Gavin hadn't known that. He'd played hard to get, then agreed. He hadn't a clue he'd been designated to play a much more important role than spying. He'd had the honor of leading one of Kent's men to the work site, and he hadn't realized he was doing more than taking one of the enemy into the heart of Madison's dig. The man who'd followed him inside had been carrying explosives, but he had thought he was going to set the charges and get out before the fireworks started. Instead Kent had detonated the payload by remote control.

Too bad for both of them. But it had been the most expedient way to make sure that whatever was in that tomb never saw the light of day.

The next job was to find Madison Dartmoor and make her tell what she knew about this evil project and about Coleman's plans for the future. This was obviously just the beginning for him, but he'd be stopped in his tracks now.

Dartmoor could join Gavin and the guards, who were also dead—their throats slit while they slept or guarded the camp. A few of them had gotten away, but they were a bunch of cowards who had already fled into the hills rather than stay and fight. Maybe some of them would try to contact Coleman. It wouldn't do them any good. Kent would be long gone before then—with this place in ruins.

He waited in satisfaction while four of his men entered the two huts they hadn't previously visited. A few minutes later, they came back with news he didn't want to hear.

"Dartmoor's not there. Neither is Gallagher."

"How the hell did that happen?"

"Maybe they slipped out for a little hanky-panky among the rocks."

"Find her," he ordered. "And kill him."

* * *

AS they trudged up the hill, Madison remembered being annoyed that Ramsay had gone off to explore this area yesterday. Now she was grateful because he seemed to know where he was going. Still, as he led her up a narrow trail into the hills, his steps faltered. When she glanced at him, she saw that blood was still dripping from the wound in his head.

He stumbled, and she caught him, then wrapped her arm around his waist.

"Lean on me."

She knew he didn't want to do it, but he allowed her to take some of his weight as they staggered along.

His breathing had turned ragged, and she stopped to let him catch his breath.

"Got to get out of the open," he whispered, starting up again. "If they come this way, they'll see us."

Knowing he was right, she kept pace with him, amazed at his stamina—or his iron will. Maybe both.

When he slowed, she looked back, relieved that she didn't see Spader or his men. But it was only a matter of time before they took this route, and in the moonlight, they'd see a trail of blood.

Ramsay stopped as they reached the side of a rock outcropping, and she thought he was going to finally give up. Then she saw he was inspecting the rocks to their right.

"Look for the entrance," he ordered. "Hard to see."

She joined him in the search, but she would have missed the opening if he hadn't stopped and pointed.

"In there."

They both slipped inside. She watched him close his eyes as he leaned back, pressing his shoulders against the wall as he struggled for breath.

When she touched his arm, his eyes snapped open, and he focused on her. "Don't know how long we've got before they . . . come this way. Better if you slip out and brush the path with some branches. Quick."

Her heart was in her throat as she moved to the opening and looked out. How much time did she have?

She didn't want to go out, but she could see their footprints in the sandy soil and blood glistening in the moonlight. The trail would lead Spader's men right to their hiding place.

Teeth clenched, she darted out and looked around. A dead bush was only a little way down the path. She sprinted to it and snatched it up, then ran farther from the cave, brushing the footprints away with the branch and covering the blood droplets. The wind was picking up, and it caught some of the sand grains. Perhaps that would help.

She turned and started sweeping back the way she'd come, realizing she'd wasted time doing it the other way, but apparently her mind was too numb to work logically.

Just as she reached the crevice, she saw the top of a man's head appear below her. Quickly she darted inside.

Ramsay was still standing with his shoulders pressed to the wall. He looked like he was asleep, but his eyes snapped open again when he saw her.

"What?"

"I saw one of Spader's thugs."

"Alone?"

"I only saw him. There could be more."

"Did he . . . see you?"

"Don't know," she admitted, wishing she could be certain she'd gotten away.

"We've got to get farther inside." He turned and staggered down the tunnel, and she followed, glad she had a gun, until she considered that shooting in here would make a tremendous noise—and bring the rest of the searchers down on them.

She switched on her flashlight, playing it in front of her, still hardly able to see where she was going. Even in his weakened condition, Ramsay seemed surer of his footing. He led her around a curve in the tunnel, then stopped.

"Turn off your light."

She switched off the beam, plunging them into darkness.

"What if the guy comes in here?" she asked, struggling to hold her voice steady.

"We'd better wait and find out."

"Shouldn't we go farther back?"

"He won't expect us so close."

Ramsay stepped in front of her. A moment ago she'd thought he might pass out. Now he was standing more erect.

She pressed her lips together and waited with her pulse pounding and her ears tuned toward the crevice. When she heard a muffled sound from the front of the cave, she went stiff.

Beside her Ramsay tensed as they stood in the darkness, listening to cautious footsteps and seeing what must be the beam of a flashlight advance toward them. At least they could mark the tracker's progress.

CHAPTER

TWENTY-ONE

RAMSAY GATHERED EVERY ounce of strength he still possessed. The first thing he saw as the thug rounded the curve was the barrel of his gun, ready for action. Jerking it from the man's grasp, Ramsay sprang forward, knocking the tracker off his feet. The flashlight clattered to the ground as he brought his prey down.

Prey. It was a long time since he'd thought of humans in those terms. But old instincts sprang to his aid.

He had surprise on his side. As he'd calculated, the tracker assumed that they'd tried to hide farther back in the cave.

Even wounded, Ramsay had the strength advantage. Summoning hidden reserves, he bashed the man's head against the stone floor, then felt him go limp.

"Ramsay, are you all right?"

"Yeah."

"Is he . . . dead?"

"Yes," he lied. The guy wasn't gone yet. But he would be soon. "*Futuo*," he cursed under his breath as he calculated risk against necessity.

"What?"

"He seems to be on his own, but I've got to get rid of him . . . in case one of the others comes looking for him or us and finds the cave. Can you guard the entrance?"

"Yes," she answered, but he knew she was struggling to hold her voice steady as she peered at him in the flashlight beam.

"You look terrible."

"I'll be okay."

He pulled the pack off the man's back and stuffed the gun inside.

"Ramsay."

He turned to her and pulled her close. "We'll get out of this."

"It's all happening too fast."

"Yeah."

He held her for a moment, sending her silent messages of strength and confidence.

"You're making me feel better," she murmured. "How are you doing it?"

"We're making each other feel better," he answered, trying to block out everything but her. He'd needed her more than he'd been willing to admit, and now she was back in his arms. He longed to keep her there, but his business was too urgent.

Letting go of Madison, he stepped away. With a grimace of distaste at what he had to do, he picked up the guy and his pack and started down the tunnel toward the cavern he'd seen on his previous trip. As soon as he was out of sight, he shifted the man in his grip, exposing his neck. Plunging his feeding teeth into flesh, he drank warm blood, feeling it flood his system, giving him the strength he was going to need to get himself and Madison out of this trap.

As he drank, he felt the man struggle in his grasp.

Acting on instinct, he quieted the thug with a savage bite to the windpipe. Ignoring the sputtering and gasping, he kept moving. For a long time, he'd thought of himself as civilized. It seemed that his savage nature wasn't far from the surface.

But he had an excuse. This guy had come into the cave prepared to kill him, but the better man had won.

Man?

Well, he wasn't exactly that. And he'd just proved it with his actions.

The trip to the cavern felt endless, but finally he saw the tunnel open out ahead of him.

He staggered to the underground precipice and stood swaying at the edge, looking down in disgust at the thing in his arms. A man who would kill because he was paid to do it.

At least that knowledge made him feel better as he flung the body out into space, watching it disappear into the darkness and finally hearing a dull thud as it hit bottom. He should feel relieved.

Instead, he shuddered, trying to banish the darkness churning inside him.

As he hurried back toward Madison, a sudden spasm gripped his middle, and he had to grab the cave wall to keep from falling over. Breathing hard, he staggered forward a few more feet, then stopped again.

Gods! This had happened to him before, years ago. There must be something wrong with the bastard's blood! It could be an illness, but Ramsay didn't think so. It was more like a drug dose. The guy had been high on something, something he'd been taking for a long time. He'd built up a tolerance to the stuff, but it was too much for Ramsay.

He stayed where he was, gasping, leaning against the wall and fighting not to pass out. Sweat had broken out on his body, and he felt a strange itching along his ribs.

Somehow, he pulled himself together and started putting one foot in front of the other again. His brain felt like it was doing flip-flops inside his head, and when he stepped around the corner into the dim morning light, his vision blurred.

Madison had been staring toward the cave entrance. She whirled as she heard his slow, shuffling approach, the gun in her hand. When she saw it was him, she lowered the weapon. As she came forward and peered at him, she gasped.

"Ramsay?"

"Got to . . . lie down," he managed to say.

Turning, he started back the way he'd come, leaning against the wall. Madison caught up with him, slipping her shoulder under his arm to help support him. She shined the light ahead of them, and when they came to a fork in the tunnel, she hesitated.

"Which way?"

He could barely speak, barely think. Trying to remember where he was and where he should be going, he pointed to the left.

When he lurched forward, Madison kept pace with him as he stumbled along, hoping he wasn't going to fall on his face.

They turned a corner, and he stopped again.

Madison raised her flashlight, playing it along the tunnel. "There's a side passage," she said.

"Not yet," he gasped. They had to get farther into the cave, in case someone started searching.

"You can't."

He didn't bother to answer. Teeth gritted, he kept going, until finally he stumbled and pitched forward.

He would have landed on his face if Madison hadn't broken his fall.

"Ramsay. Oh Lord, Ramsay. You must have a concussion—or worse."

In some part of his mind, he realized she thought this was from the explosion. No point in explaining that he'd made a bad mistake in his choice of dinner.

"Do you know somewhere we can hide?"

Did he? He'd been here before, but now he couldn't remember.

When he didn't answer, Madison eased him down to the floor.

He made some kind of sound low in his throat, then closed his eyes. He had started to shiver, and he tried to fold his arms across his chest, but that was beyond him.

KENT Spader scowled as he stepped into the middle of the open area where the archaeology team had been cooking their meals.

"Report!" he shouted.

One by one, his men reappeared, some looking worried, others defiant.

"Everybody in the camp is either dead or gone," Patterson said.

"You're sure about that? Nobody's hiding?"

"Not unless they jumped into the latrine."

Kent barked out a laugh, then sobered. "I want Dartmoor."

"Understood."

"What about Hawker? Has he reported back?"

"Negative."

"He went into the hills?"

"Said he had a hunch."

"You can't get him on his two-way."

"Negative."

Spader glanced up toward the tomb. It was gone, obliterated under a ton of rock. That was what he'd come here to do, but he also wanted to get his hands on the witch who'd been poking around in places that should have stayed buried. As he stood in the gray, predawn light, he considered his options. What if somehow Dartmoor and Gallagher had met up with Hawker? The man was good, but maybe Gallagher was better, damn him.

"I want the area around the camp searched," he barked. "Two-man teams. Nobody on his own. Understood?"

"Yes," the hired thugs echoed.

"Use caution. Ramsay Gallagher is dangerous. He may be armed. I want each team to report back at half-hour intervals."

MADISON looked down at the unconscious man who had slumped to the cave floor. The last thing she wanted to do was leave Ramsay, but she knew that he simply couldn't walk any farther. There were no good choices, but she had to make a decision.

"I'll be back," she whispered, then started off down the tunnel. He'd been here before. He thought they needed to go farther into the cave. Did that mean he'd found a place? Or was he just making a strategic decision?

She kept moving, shining her light ahead of her, sweeping the beam on the floor and to the sides. She came to an opening in the left-hand wall. After a moment's hesitation, she took the side tunnel, moving cautiously since she had no idea what she was going to find.

There was a sort of room at the end, with blankets and some trash. Apparently someone had slept in here, but that didn't mean it was a good place to take Ramsay. Was there a better place farther into the cave? Would he be able walk there? If not, she didn't think she could carry him.

She turned and left the room, hurrying back to the main tunnel, where she moved farther into the mountain. Far away, she thought she heard a roaring noise and wondered if it was coming from the sea. That was where the main passage led, wasn't it?

Was it better to go down that way?

She stopped and pressed her fist against her mouth, struggling to hold back a sob. The only thing she knew for sure was that she had to get Ramsay to a safer place. *But where?*

She stood still, taking several deep breaths. Making a snap decision, she kept going down the tunnel, then took the next side passage she saw.

This time the tunnel was longer, with several turns. She came to a wide place but instead of its being a dead end, there was a tunnel that led farther into the hill. She followed that and found that it circled around, leading to what looked like the main passage. That meant she and Ramsay wouldn't be trapped.

It felt like a sign. This was where she should take him. Running back the way they'd come, she scooped up the supplies from the first sleeping room and took them to the cave she'd selected. The blankets were smelly, but they were better than nothing. After spreading them out to make a bed, she ran back to where she'd left Ramsay. He was lying on the floor, unmoving, but when she bent down beside him, his hand flew up and struck at her shoulder.

"Vandar," he choked out.

"What?"

"Vandar. How?"

His eyes took on a fierce look as he delivered another blow, this one to her chest. He was a powerful man, but his strength had obviously ebbed, thank the Lord.

"Ramsay, don't."

"I thought I killed you."

What was he talking about? An old enemy?

"Ramsay. It's Madison. Please. You're with Madison."

CHAPTER
TWENTY-TWO

RAMSAY'S EYES SNAPPED open. At first they seemed to see something far away in time and space. Then he focused on Madison.

"Who is Vandar?" she asked.

His fingers dug into her arm. "Where did you hear that name?"

"From you. Who is he?"

"He's a monster . . . me."

"You're confused."

"No."

She wasn't going to argue with him about something that apparently had no bearing on the here and now, even if it was obviously important to him.

"We have to get somewhere safe. Can you walk?" she asked, even though she had little hope of his getting to his feet.

"Yes," he answered.

To her shock, he pushed himself to a sitting position. Clawing his hand on the wall, he pulled himself up and stood swaying on his feet. He was up, but how far could he get?

Determined to waste as little time as possible, she helped him shuffle down the tunnel, toward the sea entrance.

Somehow they made it to the side passage where she'd left the supplies, and she steered him to the left. He took only a few more steps before his knees buckled, and he went down like a sack of rocks.

"Ramsay," she called out, crouching over him. "Ramsay."

"If I can't kill Vandar, run for it," he muttered.

"Okay." This Vandar guy must be very important to him, yet she had no idea what he was talking about.

He said something else.

"Descensus in cuniculi cavum."

It sounded like Latin.

"What?"

"Down the rabbit hole," he muttered.

Then he added, *"Semper eadem."*

She recognized that one. It meant "always the same."

He went on to something else she couldn't understand. But his voice had become urgent.

"What?" she asked.

He only repeated the garbled words. Then he switched to what sounded like gutter Spanish. Something she probably didn't need to translate. Apparently the man could speak a dozen languages—and probably curse in all of them.

The conversation wasn't getting either one of them anywhere.

"I'm going to leave you for a minute, but I'll be right back."

This time he didn't answer.

She set the flashlight on the floor beside him, then ran back to where she'd left the blankets. After snatching one up, she hurried back. He was lying unmoving with his eyes closed again, but when she crouched down beside him, he made a small sound.

"It's okay."

His eyes stayed closed, but his lips moved. His voice was so low that she had to lean over to hear him. "Where am I?"

"In the caves that lead down to the ocean."

"The man . . ."

"You killed him."

He winced.

"I've got to get you to a safer part of the cave."

He tried to sit up, but this time he didn't have the strength.

"I'll do it."

She laid the blanket on the stone floor beside him. "Can you roll to the side?"

"Maybe."

He helped her do it, then fell back heavily when she had the blanket under him. Grabbing the portion at his head, she tugged, pulling him across the floor.

"Too heavy for you," he muttered, then put his feet on the floor, pushing himself along as she pulled. They were both breathing hard by the time she got him into the sheltered cavern.

"Trapped?" he asked.

"There's another way out."

"Um." His voice was very faint now, and when she bent back toward him, he was sleeping. At least she hoped it was normal sleep and that he hadn't passed out. She was worried about his injury, worried that one of the falling rocks could have caused serious damage inside his skull—maybe bleeding into the brain. That would account for the hallucination he'd had about the Vandar guy.

When he moved restlessly on the blanket, she bent over him. His hand scrabbled at his ribs as though he was trying to claw at something there.

"Ramsay?"

He didn't answer, but his fingers still tore at his side.

"Let me help you."

She tugged his shirt out of his waistband and pulled it up. When she brought the flashlight close, she gasped as she saw what looked like silver scales that had formed on his skin over his ribs. They were each about two inches wide and two inches long, but not square.

They looked totally alien against his flesh, yet they seemed to have grown from his living cells.

She'd been naked with him after the vision quest, and she was sure she would have noticed something like this. They hadn't been on his ribs before, yet they were here now.

She stared at the anomaly for long seconds, hoping that she had imagined it. But the scales didn't disappear.

Gingerly, she reached out and pressed her finger to one. It was hard to the touch, unyielding. Lord, what could it mean? His hand reached toward the aberration, still clawing at the strange patches. When his fingers touched hers, his eyes snapped open.

"What is it?" she whispered.

He ran his fingers over the scales.

"You didn't have those before."

"Yeah." He cleared his throat. "I've had some weird diseases. I think this is from something I picked up in the tropics."

"What?"

"Not sure what it was called. Some kind of growth that . . ." He paused again. "That comes back when I'm sick."

"Oh."

"It's not contagious."

"Okay." She realized as they spoke that he was sounding more coherent.

"You feeling better?"

"Yeah."

When he tried to sit up, she pressed against his shoulder. "Just rest."

When he relaxed, she said, "You were speaking Latin."

"Was I?"

"Um-hum."

"I studied it . . . in school." He laughed.

"What's funny?"

"I was thinking that it was a long time ago."

"You didn't learn Latin curses in school."

He laughed again. "You'd be surprised."

Changing the subject abruptly, she asked, "Who is Vandar?"

He tensed. "How do you know about Vandar?"

"You said his name, before you lapsed into Latin."

His vision turned inward.

"Who was he?"

He hesitated. "Someone who decided he was my enemy. He tried to kill me. I knew that one or the other of us would have to go."

"And you won."

"Yeah."

"You're not going to tell me about it?"

When he didn't speak, she dragged in a breath and let it out. "I guess it's your business."

He found her hand and squeezed. "Long story. I don't have the energy for it now."

Yes, she should let him recover. "Thank you for saving me . . . from the rocks."

He looked relieved that she was dropping the questions. "I had to protect you."

"And you got hurt."

"I'm getting better."

"I hope so." As she spoke, she flashed back to the explosion. She'd barely had time to think about what it meant. Now realization came crashing in on her. "It's all gone," she whispered. "All that work. Spader destroyed it."

She couldn't hold back a sob as the enormity of it all finally slammed into her.

Ramsay reached for her, gathering her to him, stroking his hand across her back.

"You're a strong woman," he whispered.

"I don't feel strong," she gasped between sobs.

"You got me here."

The way he spoke and the feel of his arms around her tore at her emotions, and her tears came faster and harder. She'd held herself together for so long, and finally she'd reached the end of her strength.

CHAPTER
TWENTY-THREE

RAMSAY ROLLED ONTO his side, his arms enfolding Madison as she wept. "It's all right. It's all right," he murmured.

"No. You don't understand what it means to me."

"I think I do."

"How could you?"

He teetered on the edge of a decision, torn between honesty and self-protection. Or perhaps it was guilt and desire.

He held Madison close, wanting to comfort her, and wanting so much more. Like honesty between them. But recent memories flickered in his mind. He'd bashed a man over the head—then drunk his blood as he prepared to fling him into the cave's deep pit. What would she think if he told her about that?

She'd asked him a question. He couldn't tell her that perhaps his whole past and future had been wound up in that tomb. To her it was an archaeology discovery. To him it might be everything.

Because he wasn't prepared to reveal any of that, he sent her silent messages, designed to calm and reassure. He felt some of the tension ease out of her and hated that he was using his powers on her, yet at the same time he was grateful that he could do it.

So many conflicting emotions warred within him. When he finally spoke, his voice was thick.

"I've survived great loss. Things as bad as the loss of the tomb."

She nodded against his chest. "What?"

"I've lost the love of my life," he murmured.

"Oh."

"It was a long time ago."

"Will you tell me about it?"

"Yes. But not now." He didn't want to dwell on his loss. Not when Madison was in his arms. It didn't matter how she'd gotten there. What mattered was her response to him now. He'd calmed her with his thoughts, but he hadn't tried to change her mind about him. And she was letting him see all her vulnerabilities.

He tipped her head up and brought his lips to hers for a comforting kiss.

She'd kept away from him for days. Probably she hadn't trusted him. Maybe she'd thought that getting more involved with him was a bad idea, and maybe Coleman had warned her against him.

He'd been sad about that—and relieved at the same time.

Now he couldn't hang on to the reasons why he'd kept his own distance. The emotional chasm between them vanished as he kissed her and ran his hands over her back and hips, pressing her body more tightly to his.

"What are we doing?" she murmured.

"Not too much, unfortunately."

He shifted his lips, playing with the tender curve of her ear, then sucking gently on the lobe, drawing a sigh of pleasure from her.

His hand moved, slipping under her shirt, his fingers spreading across the warm skin of her back.

"I missed you," she whispered.

"Yes," he answered, just as a noise far away made him tense.

She felt the sudden tension go through him.

"What?"

"There's somebody in the caves. We have to assume it's Spader's men."

She made a small sound of distress. "What are we going to do?"

"We can't stay here."

He pushed himself up, then stood, wishing he felt steadier on his feet as she gave him a critical look in the light from the flashlight beam.

Scooping up her pack, she slung it over her shoulder.

"Where are we, exactly?" he asked.

Gripping his arm, she whispered, "When you were here yesterday, did you see a room where someone had left blankets and other supplies?"

"Yeah."

"These are the blankets. I moved them to the next room down the passage."

"I didn't go into it."

"Well, I saw that it had another exit." She gestured behind her.

"Good thinking." But even as he spoke, he was considering alternatives. "Did you check it out?"

"I'm sorry. I was busy with you."

"You did fine."

He kicked at the blankets, heaping them into a lump, making it look like nobody had been lying here recently.

"I've got to turn off the light."

Her fingers tightened on his arm as he plunged them into darkness.

"Can you see?" Madison whispered.

"Not much, but I can find my way around."

Making a snap decision, he crossed the room and took

the exit that neither one of them had explored, assuming that it wasn't going to lead to some precipice.

Once in the tunnel, he stopped and listened again. He could still hear footsteps, but it sounded like they were farther away. Reaching for her hand, he guided her along the passage.

It was level for several yards, then it dipped downward.

"What can you see now?" Madison whispered.

"I can make out some light ahead of us." Still clasping her hand, he walked cautiously toward the light. He could also hear the waves now.

Bending, he put his mouth to her ear. "It's the passage leading down toward the sea."

"What happens when we get there?"

"Don't know yet."

As they kept moving, he tuned his ears for sounds of pursuit, but the waves were louder now, blocking out anything coming from behind.

When they reached a place where the tunnel merged with the main stairway leading to the landing spot, there was more light.

Looking around, he spotted a rock outcropping jutting from the wall.

"You hide there," he said. "I'll lure the guy farther down the stairs."

She looked like she was going to object.

"Go on."

"You threw away that guy's gun, didn't you?"

"Yeah. So it wouldn't connect us to him."

"Do you want this one?"

"You keep it."

After a few moments' hesitation, she ducked behind the rock, and he turned to inspect the hiding place. Satisfied that she was hidden, he started quickly down, pausing at a place where the stairway took a turn, thinking this might be the best spot for an ambush.

Below him, the waves roared, but he thought he could make out the sound of someone coming down the steps.

Hoping they wouldn't turn around and find Madison, he pressed his shoulder against the stone wall, waiting. He wasn't in great shape, but getting rid of their pursuers was his only option.

The footsteps came closer. Whoever was on the stairs was in a hurry, probably thinking that he and Madison were trapped at the sea entrance.

Ramsay waited, tensing. As a man came around the corner, he gave the guy a push, sending him rattling down the stairs.

But the thug checked his fall by grabbing at the wall. As he lay on the stairs, he turned and whipped out his arm, a gun in his hand.

Ramsay saw the weapon and ducked before the guy fired. The blast boomed in the tunnel, but the bullet went over his head. He was already hurtling after the shooter, using his superior speed. Reaching the man, he bashed his gun hand against the rocks.

The thug screamed and dropped the weapon, which clattered down the stairs. Recovering, he kicked out, catching Ramsay in the midsection. He struggled against the pain as he leaped forward, throwing himself on the attacker.

Could he disable the man and get some information?

Dodging a fist, he delivered a blow of his own as they kept toppling down the steps.

The man tore himself away, increasing his downward speed. They were close to the bottom now, and the guy couldn't stop his momentum.

As he reached the water-slick landing, he slid across the stone dock, then flew over the edge into the water like he'd been on a water slide at an amusement park. Only this wasn't for fun.

He screamed as the waves caught him and pulled him out to sea, then slammed him back against a rock outcropping.

Ramsay pulled himself up, holding the wall as he approached the landing at the bottom of the stairs. He was in time to see the man being swept out to sea again by an outgoing wave, then disappearing below the surface.

He stood on the bottom step, trying to catch his breath. The tide was lower now, and he saw that Gavin had either been misinformed about using this exit as an escape route— or he'd been lying to keep Ramsay from getting any ideas.

With the water level down, there might be a way out along the cliff. If he and Madison hurried.

He had started back up the steps toward her when another gunshot rang out.

Futuo!

CHAPTER
TWENTY-FOUR

RAMSAY TOOK THE steps two at a time. As he rounded the curve, he saw another one of the bastards angling around, trying to get another shot at Madison.

She fired first, sending the guy toppling backward down the stairs.

Wide-eyed, Madison peeked out from behind the rock. "Did I get him?"

"Yeah."

"There were two of them."

"The other one got swept out to sea."

When she gained the stairs, she reached for him and held on. "I heard the shot," she whispered. "I didn't know if he'd hit you."

"Same here."

They clung together for a long moment.

"Is it ever going to end?" she whispered.

"Yeah. We're going to beat them."

He wanted to keep holding her, but they couldn't stay where they were. Stepping away from Madison, he gave the man on the stairs a kick, propelling him downward. He toppled over and over, finally coming to rest on the wet landing.

Madison winced but said nothing.

Ramsay followed the man down and pitched him into the water. "There could be more of them. We have to get out of here."

She looked at the churning waves where the thug had disappeared. "How? There's no boat."

"Your friend Gavin said it was impossible to get out this way. Let's hope he's wrong."

Taking Madison's hand, he led her to the side of the landing platform, which jutted out into the water several yards. "The tide's out. I think we can follow the beach."

"What if there's no way up the cliff?"

"Then we're in bad trouble. But I think it's the best chance we have. More of Spader's men could start searching the cave when these two guys don't come back."

She nodded, her gaze sweeping the narrow rocky beach where waves lapped.

"Hardly any space to walk."

"And none at all when the tide is in. Come on before it's too late."

He climbed down and turned to reach for her hand, helping her down to the sand.

"Best if we can get around a curve, so no one can see us from here."

"Okay."

He started off, slogging across the rocky beach, stepping around boulders that were in the way. Some looked like they'd recently tumbled down from the cliff face, maybe as a result of the explosion at the tomb, and he hoped no more were going to break loose.

Although Madison kept pace with him, he could hear her breathing hard.

He stopped and looked back at the landing. Nobody else

had appeared, but he couldn't count on a clean getaway until they were out of sight.

The waves were lapping closer to the cliff, washing their footprints away where they'd stepped from rocks onto sand. At least that was good.

When he'd given Madison a chance to catch her breath, he started walking again, looking over his shoulder from time to time.

They were about two hundred yards from the stone dock when he saw a figure on the platform and pulled Madison down behind a boulder.

"What?" she whispered.

"Someone else made it to the bottom."

They stayed where they were, and Ramsay dared a peek around the rock.

Two more men were standing on the jetty and gesturing, but they were looking the other way up the beach.

He waited with his heart pounding, willing them not to jump down on this side.

They stayed where they were, and he saw one of them pull out a walkie-talkie.

"They're making a call," he told Madison. "To Spader, I guess."

The water was lapping higher on the beach, and Ramsay's legs were already getting wet.

He looked at the rising tide, then back toward the jetty. How long could they stay here before they had to make a run for it?

Time stretched, and he watched the breakers creeping closer. Risking another glance toward the dock, he saw that the men were still there, probably ordered to guard the only exit to the caves.

Finally, Ramsay grasped Madison's shoulder. "We can't stay here any longer. Start moving along the beach. Stay low."

She nodded and started crawling farther from the guys guarding the platform. He followed her, waiting every moment for a shout behind them, but apparently the boulder was still blocking the line of sight from the dock. Madison made it around a curve and scooted forward, giving him room to join her. They both sat for a few moments with their backs to the cliff. Then he stood and started walking again.

She followed, but now every wave lapped at their legs, soaking their knees.

KENT Spader spoke into the walkie-talkie. "You haven't found them in the caves?"

"I think they were here. We found fresh drops of blood near the entrance. But there are a lot of tunnels and side passages."

"Keep looking. What about the sea entrance?"

"Mack and Carl are down there. It's pretty rough water. They said nobody could get out that way," the man on the phone reported.

"Let's not make that assumption."

Kent clicked off. Muttering to himself, he wandered into the hut that Madison had used for her office and bedroom and began riffling through the papers he'd found. But she'd been careful not to leave anything important lying around. It was all probably in her computer. Only the laptop was lying on the floor. One of his men had knocked it off the desk and screwed up the hard drive. Maybe they could get something off it and maybe not.

"Hellfire!"

He had accomplished half his mission. Nobody was going back into that tomb. If they tried to blast their way in, they'd only destroy more of it. But he still didn't have Madison Dartmoor, and he was tired of sitting here waiting for news. He was going to go out searching, because if anyone could get Dartmoor out of that cave, it was Ramsay Gallagher.

*   *   *

RAMSAY turned and scanned the sea, watching the tide roll in. A large breaker was sweeping toward them, crashing farther up the beach than any of the others. He planted his feet in the sand and grabbed Madison's arm as the wave broke, then flowed out again, tugging strongly at them and knocking Madison off her feet. It would have pulled her out to sea if he hadn't been holding on to her.

When she finally picked herself up, her clothing was soaking wet.

"Got to get you out of here." Ramsay looked up the beach. Ahead of him he saw a crevice in the cliff. Hoping they could use it to climb up, he forged ahead, practically pulling Madison along.

"Keep going."

"I don't know if I can."

Another wave came roaring in, this one bigger than the one before. But they had reached the crevice. He pushed Madison inside, shielding her from the brunt of the rushing water.

When the breaker had rolled out again, he turned to the cliff, seeing that there were depressions in the rock. Someone had carved a sort of ladder to the top of the cliff.

He pointed. "We can get up this way."

"Maybe *you* can."

"And you. Start climbing. I'll be right behind you in case you slip."

Another wave battered them, soaking them both.

Ramsay craned his neck up, inspecting the cliff wall. He judged it was about thirty feet high.

Without wasting any more time, Madison pressed the toe of her boot into a niche below it.

Ramsay watched. The ladder had been made for someone taller, but she managed to work her way up several feet.

He climbed onto the wall behind her, his heart in his throat as he watched her unsteady progress.

About twelve feet from the ground, she slipped, and his hand shot up to steady her.

"Okay?" he asked when she'd grabbed the wall again.

"Yes." It sounded like she was speaking through gritted teeth.

He looked down, seeing the ocean roll relentlessly toward the shore. The place where they'd been standing was almost invisible now.

Madison began to move more quickly.

"Don't rush it," he called out.

"I want to get out of here."

"Yeah."

As she worked her way up another few feet, the wind picked up, chilling Ramsay's wet shirt and pants and whipping at his body.

When Madison stopped to rest, he came up behind her. "Too bad you're not wearing a skirt," he observed. "I'd have a great view."

She made a snorting sound and started upward again. Her progress grew slower, and he knew her arms weren't used to this kind of exertion. Still, she continued doggedly upward, until one of the handholds gave way beneath her fingers.

He wanted to scream as her arm flailed in the air. Quickly he reached up again, pressing her bottom toward the cliff. Centuries ticked by before she had a firm grasp on the wall again.

"Okay?" he called out.

"Yes."

She said nothing else, and he knew she didn't have energy to spare.

Just get to the top, he silently chanted over and over. *Just get to the top.*

Without looking down, she started moving again, and he held his breath, willing her to make it the last few feet. She did, with only a minor slip, then rolled out of view.

"Gratia deis!" Thank the gods. He quickened his pace. "What do you see up there?" he called out.

"Open . . . country." As she spoke, he could hear her teeth chattering. They both needed to get out of the wind and into some dry clothing.

Hurrying to join her, he grabbed at the next handhold. It crumbled under his fingers.

DOMINIC listened to the phone ringing on the other end of the line. No answer.

Gavin was supposed to report in before the end of the night, but he hadn't so much as left a message saying he couldn't get away from his duties. A coded message. Of course he couldn't let on that he was keeping in touch with Dominic behind Madison's back. But he could call a woman who was supposed to be his girlfriend.

He held the phone in his hand, his fingers squeezing the instrument. It looked like calling Madison was his only alternative.

He dialed, waiting again. One, two, three, four rings. Finally he got a recording saying she was unavailable. He debated leaving a message, then decided against it.

When he hung up, he clenched his teeth in frustration. He hated being stuck back here in California, waiting for news. But that had been his choice.

He paced back and forth across his bedroom, his gaze swinging to the phone each time he passed. Feeling like a father checking up on his daughter out on a date, he called the security station at the entrance to the dig site. Once again nobody answered, and he knew that something was badly wrong.

He'd assumed Spader had given up his mad quest to shut down the site. Maybe he'd been foolish in that assumption.

Once again he made a call, this time to a contact he had in the police department where the site was located.

"Signor Mancuso?" he said when he had the man on the phone.

"Si."

"I'm concerned about Signorina Dartmoor, the archaeologist who is conducting the dig we discussed."

The cop was like policemen all over the world. He simply waited for more information.

"I haven't been able to get in touch with anyone there. I would greatly appreciate it if you could send a man out to the site."

There was a pause on the other end of the line, and the man spoke in accented but good English. "Do you have any other reasons to be worried?"

"A man threatened Dr. Dartmoor when she was at a conference recently. I thought he'd backed off, but he may be up to some mischief at the dig."

"We'll get someone out there within the next few hours."

"Can you go now? I can make a substantial contribution to your department."

"I'll see what I can do."

The cop clicked off. Dominic hung up and stood staring out the window at the ocean. He'd acquired a very interesting piece of information a few months ago that had occupied a great deal of his time and energy. Madison would be interested to know about it, but he'd been keeping it to himself because he always played his cards close to his chest.

It was important enough that he'd sent a team down to Peru to investigate. Now he couldn't help wondering if he should have been paying closer attention to what was going on in Italy.

CHAPTER

TWENTY-FIVE

AS RAMSAY SCRABBLED to find purchase, he felt fingers tangle in his hair, holding him up. When his toe connected with the rock, he pushed himself upward, then flopped onto the ground beside Madison, breathing hard.

"Are you all right?" she asked urgently.

"Yeah. Are you?"

"Yes. Lucky you're not wearing a toupee."

He laughed. "Glad you're in good enough shape to make jokes."

Knowing they were in a vulnerable position, he raised his head and looked across the open countryside, seeing no people, only a herd of cows grazing peacefully along the edge of the cliffs. There was a road about a hundred yards away. No vehicles were visible.

The fields were full of tall grass that came to their waists, but they were still too exposed. They needed to find shelter. And warmth. He was chilled to the bone by the seawater and the wind, and Madison was shivering. He pulled her close, holding on to her, grateful that the two of them had made it to the top.

She clung to him before he eased away.

"Got to get you warm and dry," he said in a husky voice.

"You, too."

"I'm fine," he answered automatically.

Madison swept back her damp hair and looked around. "I wish I'd explored this side of the mountain."

"You were focused on . . . your work."

"For all the good that did me."

"Don't think about that now. You're alive. That's the important thing."

He kept his arm around her as he started toward the road, scanning the area, alert for any signs of danger. They reached the rutted surface, and he stopped for a moment.

"Which way?"

"Away from your camp. Which I assume means going left."

"Um-hum," she answered. "At least I know that much."

They kept moving, and he wished he could do more for Madison than keep his arm around her.

He stroked his hand up and down her arm, trying to work up some heat. The wrong kind of heat, it seemed, because touching her was making him long to make love to her.

She slid him a sidewise look, and he grinned.

"Think warm thoughts."

"You're helping."

Even as they bantered, he kept watching for anyone in the area, and every minute or so, he looked behind him. The fourth time he turned, he saw a beat-up truck driving slowly toward them.

Madison also turned. "Thank God. They can give us a ride."

He tensed as he watched the car approach. Then he caught sight of the driver.

"*Futuo*," he shouted as he threw Madison into the grass. "It's Spader. Get down. Crawl as far away from here as you can."

She gasped, and he saw her moving away from the road, then lost track of her as he focused on the truck.

It came to a halt, and Kent Spader jumped out, holding a handgun. "Where's Dartmoor?" he growled.

"The tide got her. She didn't make it."

"You're lying. I saw her dive into the grass."

"Maybe that's what you wanted to see," Ramsay countered. "We should talk," he added, trying to establish a mental connection with the man. If he could do that, maybe he could influence his actions and buy himself some time.

"About what?"

"I have information you want," he answered. As he spoke, he was trying with every ounce of will to change to dragon form. He could feel a tingling in his body, on his skin, that came before the change. When he got that far, elation surged through him. But it appeared that was all he could accomplish.

Desperately, he focused on the silver scales that had appeared over his ribs after he'd drunk the bad blood, willing the dragon skin to cover the rest of his body. Nothing more happened. He was still blocked, and he wanted to howl in frustration.

"What information?" Spader challenged.

He swallowed, bringing his attention back to the man with the gun. "I know where to find the original of that moving statue thing."

"I already have a line on where to find it. I'm betting it's at Coleman's estate. And I'm going to get it—as soon as I take care of you and Dartmoor. That will be the end of this evil project. Once and for all."

"What do you mean by 'evil'?" Ramsay asked.

"Have you no respect for the nobility of mankind?"

"Of course I do."

Spader laughed. "I don't think so. You want to prove that we're nothing. Less than nothing. That we never could have evolved from apes without help."

Ramsay swallowed, wondering what to say now. Obviously the idea of alien–human contact made Kent Spader's skin crawl, and he was willing to do anything it took to prove it wasn't true—even destroying evidence and murdering innocent people.

"I know better. Mankind is destined for greatness. Everything we need is right here on earth," Spader continued.

"You don't even know what we discovered before you blew up the tomb," Ramsay tried.

"Nothing. You found nothing. And I buried your work site before you could go any further with this travesty. My contacts at the compound kept me informed."

"Gavin?"

Spader laughed. "Yeah. One of them." He raised his voice. "Hey, Madison, you thought your little assistant was working for you. I bet you don't know he was reporting to Coleman, too. He was a damn busy guy."

"And he was lying to you," Ramsay ground out.

"Stop with the malarkey. You've been screwing up this operation since you butted in where you don't belong."

"That's not the way I see it," he answered.

Spader raised his voice, no longer addressing Ramsay. "Madison, I know you're out there in the grass. If you don't want me to shoot your boyfriend, get over here."

"Don't do it," Ramsay shouted. "He's going to shoot me anyway."

Spader squeezed off a shot that landed inches from Ramsay's foot.

"Next time, it's your kneecap."

Ramsay threw himself to the ground, rolling away, hearing more rounds follow him. But he could still count on his reflexes, and the grass hid him, for the moment.

I can take care of myself, he silently broadcast to

Madison. *Don't come out of hiding.* He repeated the message as he crawled through the grass, trying to put distance between himself and the man with the gun. Could he circle around? Get in back of the bastard?

Or had he connected with the man enough to send him a message. It didn't feel like it, but he tried. *Watch out for lions in the grass. They're coming to get you. If you don't want to get eaten, get out of here.*

Crawling to a boulder, he used it for a shield as he raised his head to see what was going on. Spader was swinging the gun from side to side, pointing the weapon first one way and then the other. Maybe the trick was working.

Lions in the grass. Watch out for lions in the grass. They're coming to get you. If you don't want to get eaten, get out of here, Ramsay repeated, focusing the message on Spader, hoping it was enough to confuse the man. And hoping that Madison was as far away as she could crawl.

Spader squeezed off a couple of shots. "I'll get you," he shouted.

In the next second, Ramsay saw something that made his heart leap into his throat. Behind Spader, something moved in the grass. Not a lion. Madison hadn't gotten the hell out of there. She had worked her way behind Spader. As Ramsay watched, she broke cover, her gun in her hand.

CHAPTER
TWENTY-SIX

RAMSAY HEARD THE gun click. It didn't fire, but Spader swung around, facing Madison.

"Drop it, witch."

Ramsay was already on his feet and running, so fast that he could hardly see anything around him. His total focus was on the man with the gun.

Realizing his mistake, Spader was already turning. But he was too late.

Ramsay knocked the guy to the ground, landing on top of him.

He made a wheezing sound, struggling for breath, but he was still trying to get his weapon into firing position.

Ramsay grabbed the gun hand, twisting it inward as Spader squeezed the trigger.

The bullet hit Spader in the chest. He gasped and went limp.

From the corner of his eye, Ramsay saw Madison dashing forward.

"That was dangerous," he growled. "Standing up with your gun."

"He was busy trying to murder you. I assumed I could get him."

"I think the seawater disabled the gun."

"Yeah. I didn't think of that. Is he dead?"

Ramsay bent over Spader. He'd dealt with a lot of dead and dying men. "On the way out," he said in a grim voice. "The bullet punctured his lung and hit his spinal cord."

"Good. He told you he killed the men in camp. I don't think he was just bragging."

"Yeah," Ramsay agreed.

"He was going to kill you," Madison continued. "Then he was going to question me and finish me off."

"Agreed," Ramsay answered in a gritty voice. Raising his head, he looked around. As far as he could tell, only the cows had witnessed the scene.

Stooping down again, he began searching the man's pockets. He found a walkie-talkie, which he pulled out. Also a wad of Italian money, which he counted. It was a considerable amount and solved one of their problems, since neither one of them had been prepared for traveling when they'd run from the camp.

He put the cash in his pocket.

"The police will find him," Madison said in a choked voice.

"And they'll find his fingerprints on the gun in his hand."

"Will they think he shot himself?"

"It depends on how much they want to investigate the death of a foreigner who was obviously up to no good in their country."

Madison answered with a little nod.

"One more thing I've got to do," he said, pressing the send button on Spader's walkie-talkie.

"This is one of the guards from the archaeology camp,"

he said in a voice that faked a thick Italian accent. "Since I'm using his walkie-talkie, you can assume that your boss is no longer around. He met with an unfortunate accident. If I were you, I'd get the hell out of here before I come looking for you, too."

Without waiting for a reply, he clicked off and met Madison's gaze. Reaction was setting in, and she looked shell-shocked.

"Are we safe now?" she whispered.

"I don't think anybody's coming after us," he said as he pulled her close and held on tight. He could have lost her, and he was still coming to grips with what that would have meant to him. He wanted to keep her safe. He wanted her in his life, but was he prepared for all the consequences of a real relationship? He still couldn't answer that question.

All he could do for the moment was hug her tightly. "Let's get out of here," he whispered.

"Where are we going?"

"Away."

She glanced at the truck. "Can we drive that?"

"Not a good idea. We don't want anyone to figure out that we were involved with Spader."

"Oh, right," she said in a low voice.

He gave her a close inspection. "You've got grass and dirt all over you."

"So do you."

He brushed off her back, while she did the same for him. Then they each did their own fronts.

"I can't believe he's gone," she said. Her voice was weak, and he knew she had spent about all her mental and physical capital.

"You'll get used to it."

"What do we tell the police?" she asked.

He thought about that. "You don't have to tell the truth about what happened when someone tried to kill you. Not if coming clean is going to cause complications. The best thing to say is that we found the camp under attack and ran."

"That's . . . illegal."

"What Spader and his men did was a lot more illegal. And I've got a gut feeling that telling everything we know is just going to get us in trouble. Our best bet is to say we made it out of the camp without getting caught."

She nodded as she worked her way through the advice. "So we never saw Spader?"

"No," he clipped out, then considered more details. "We saw armed men coming down the road. After the explosion, we assumed the camp was under attack, and we ran to the caves, then came out at the stone pier and walked along the base of the cliffs until we found a place to climb up."

She nodded. "I hope I can keep that straight."

"You will. All of it happened."

She managed a laugh. "And a few other details."

"None of them are anyone's business but ours." Taking her hand, he led her down the road.

To his relief, it wasn't long before they came to a village with houses constructed of the same stone as the camp, but larger and in much better repair, although they were clearly several hundred years old. One of the largest buildings had a sign out front advertising that it was a bed-and-breakfast. Also good, because neither of them had their passports and he didn't want to go through any long explanations.

After leading Madison through a pretty flower garden to the front door, he left her sitting in a chair in the front hallway and went to look for the proprietor. He found a plump, dark-haired woman cleaning the kitchen.

"Do you have a room?" he asked in Italian.

She looked him up and down like he was a tramp who'd been sleeping in the fields. "What happened to you?" she demanded.

"We had a spill while hiking. We need a room. Your best room."

When she hesitated, he got out the wad of money that he'd taken from Spader. "I know this is short notice. I'm willing to pay well."

"I can accommodate you," she said.

"Thank you, Signora . . . ?"

"Signora Beldona," she answered.

"Thank you so much."

He'd figure out what they were going to do next when they'd both gotten some rest.

"All set," he told Madison when he returned. She was sitting with her head thrown back against the wall, but she pushed herself up straighter when he reappeared.

They followed the woman up a flight of steps to the second floor, and then into a comfortable room with a small private bath. It was simply furnished but clean. A hand-made rag rug was centered on the wooden floor, and the bedspread was faded cotton.

"This is fine?" the woman said.

"Yes. Fine. Thank you," Ramsay answered.

Once inside, he closed the door and reached outside the window to close the wooden shutters. Then he turned on a small lamp beside the bed.

"Thank God," Madison murmured. "I feel safe for the first time in hours."

THE voice on the other end of the phone line was somber. "Bad news."

Dominic Coleman tensed. He'd been waiting for a report from the police inspector in Italy.

"Give it to me straight," he said.

"We have searched the archaeologists' camp. There are twelve dead bodies in the houses, at the guard posts, and on the grounds. No one else is there."

Dominic forced himself to ask, "Is . . . is one of the dead a woman?"

"No. At least not where we've searched. But we've only gone over the main camp."

He let out the breath he'd been holding. Maybe Madison had escaped. He prayed she'd escaped.

"We're still looking for victims." There was a pause while Dominic imagined the inspector consulting a notebook. "You're referring to Signorina Dartmoor?"

"Yes."

The police captain continued, "There's an old network of smugglers' caves in the area. We're searching them now."

"Yes. I'm aware of them. Thanks."

The captain cleared his throat. "There appears to have been an explosion at the dig site."

"An explosion? What are you talking about exactly?" Dominic wheezed.

"We've reviewed your permits, and we have the proposal Signorina Dartmoor turned in to the Antiquities Commission. It designates the area she was excavating. There's nothing at that location but a pile of rubble."

"You mean the tomb?" Dominic asked, barely able to get the words out.

"I'm afraid so."

Dominic sat down heavily in an armchair and struggled to take in the magnitude of the disaster. Apparently everybody at the dig site was dead, and the tomb itself was destroyed. Spader must have been planning the attack carefully. He must have mounted a major invasion of the site.

"Did you catch any of the perpetrators?"

"They've disappeared." The cop paused. "I suspect you have some idea who did this."

Was there any point in hiding the truth? Dominic considered for a moment, then said, "A man named Kent Spader has had goons stalking the site almost since Dr. Dartmoor began excavating. I can send you information on him if you give me your e-mail address."

Signor Mancuso provided the address, then said, "We're widening the search area."

"Yes. Thanks."

"Do you have the names of all the people working at the site?"

"Yes." He corrected himself. "Not the guards. They were hired locally."

"Unfortunate that you don't have that information."

"I'm sorry."

"What names can you give me?"

"Dr. Madison Dartmoor. Her assistant, Gavin Kaiser. Dr. Calvin Collins. Dr. Harold Martin. They were working with Dr. Dartmoor. And Ramsay Gallagher."

"What position does Gallagher hold with the expedition?"

"No official position."

"How did he happen to be there?"

"He met Dr. Dartmoor at a professional conference."

"And that was enough reason to have him join the group?"

"I know that sounds flimsy now, but he rescued Dr. Dartmoor from a kidnapping attempt," Dominic explained.

"At a professional conference?" the inspector asked sharply.

"Someone wanted her to reveal aspects of her work that she wasn't prepared to discuss," Dominic said lamely.

"Who?"

"The same man, Kent Spader."

"What aren't you telling me?"

"Nothing that would be of any interest to anyone outside the archaeology field."

"Let me be the judge of that."

Feeling trapped, Dominic said, "There were questions about the origin of the tomb."

The inspector waited several moments before speaking. "Which are?"

"We think it wasn't Roman or Greek. It may have represented a totally different civilization."

"It's well known that there were civilizations here before Rome. You mentioned the Greeks, for example. They had colonies in the area."

"This one might not have been recorded."

"So it may be of unusual significance?"

"Yes."

"All right. And you trust Ramsay Gallagher?"

Did he? Dominic hesitated.

"Could he be involved in what happened?" the inspector pressed.

"I hope not," he answered. "Will you keep me posted on your progress?"

"I'll get back to you when I can."

The inspector clicked off, and Dominic was left wondering exactly what the hell had happened at the dig site and whether Madison had escaped.

CHAPTER
TWENTY-SEVEN

RAMSAY TURNED BACK to Madison. "Let's get you out of those ruined clothes."

She stood passively while he unbuttoned her shirt and pushed it off her shoulders, then pulled each arm in turn from a sleeve. Next he unbuckled her cargo pants and slicked them down her legs. When he got to her boots, he stopped, realizing he should have taken them off first.

"Better sit down," he said in a thick voice.

She sat in a chair, and he knelt before her, unlacing the boots so he could pull them off and then her pants.

Standing again, he tried not to notice that she was only wearing her bra and panties as he sat on the edge of the bed to untie his own boots, then pulled them off.

His clothing was smeared with dirt, so he unbuckled his belt, undid his zipper, and stood so he could step out of his pants.

Cautiously, he eased his shirt partway up, checking his ribs with his fingers. The damn scales were gone. *Gratia deis.*

When he'd pulled his shirt over his head, he saw that Madison was standing a few feet in front of him.

"You need to rest," he said in a thick voice.

"I need you," she answered, reaching for him and wrapping her arms around his waist.

He's been worn out, emotionally and physically. The feel of her body against his brought instant arousal.

"Don't," he choked out.

"Don't try to push me away because you think it's the right thing to do."

"It is. Right now."

She cupped her hand around the back of his head and brought his mouth down to hers.

The moment their lips touched, he stopped thinking. All he could do was draw in the sweet taste of her, the scent of seawater that was a stark reminder of what they'd been through together.

The feel of her mouth on his was like a jolt of molten sensuality that sizzled along his nerve endings.

Unable to stop himself, he drank from her like a man who had thought he would never drink again.

She made a needy sound, her mouth opening to give him better access, and he was greedy to take what she offered. Yet he also knew that this time had to be different. He'd made love to her twice, and each time some outside influence had been working on them.

Not now. He wanted only the two of them, giving and taking from each other because it was what they both craved.

"You're sure?" he murmured.

"How can you doubt it?"

He answered with a soft laugh as his hand slid down to her hips, reveling in the feel of her silken skin beneath the thin fabric of her panties.

They were in the way, and he slipped his hands inside, slicking them down her legs. When they pooled around her feet, she stepped out of them, and he ran his hands over the rounded curve of her ass, then lower, to find her sex. She was wet and aroused for him, and he made a low sound in his throat as he stroked her there.

"I don't think I can stand up much longer," she whispered.

Frankly, he was having the same problem, but he reached to unhook her bra and send it to join the panties before he leaned down to pull the covers aside and lower her to the bed.

Before he followed her down, he dragged his shorts off, his cock springing out as he freed it.

This could go very fast now, if he let things get out of control. But he was determined not to rush. Naked, he gathered her close, stroking his fingers over her back, down her flanks, pulling her against his body.

When she made a sound of approval and rubbed against him, he felt as if the two of them were going to ignite and set the bedsheets on fire.

Easing away, he took her breasts in his hands, his thumbs stroking over the hardened tips, bringing a whimper to her lips.

"Ramsay?"

"Let me enjoy this."

"You're going to make me come."

He laughed. "Oh yeah, I am."

Bending, he sucked one taut nipple into his mouth, while he slid his hand down her body and into the folds of her sex, dipping inside her, then dragging his finger up to her clit, over and over.

She cried out, moving her hips raggedly against his hand, her fingers digging into his shoulders as she threw her head back and cried out.

He continued to stroke her, giving her every ounce of pleasure he could before she fell back against the pillow, breathing hard.

She stared up at him. "You . . ."

"Plenty of time for me. For both of us," he murmured as he began to stroke her and kiss her all over again.

He wanted to be on top of her. Inside her. But not until she was ready for him again.

Greedily, he clasped her to him, wedging his aching cock into the cleft at the top of her legs.

Yet his own satisfaction was only a small part of what he craved. There was so much more, but he couldn't speak any of it. He could only give her pleasure.

Lowering his head, he caressed her breasts with his face, then turned his head so that he could take one pebble-hard nipple into his mouth, sucking on her, teasing her with his tongue and teeth while he used his thumb and finger on the other nipple.

When she arched into the caress, he shifted so he could trail one hand down her body, dipping into her folds again. She moved against his hand, making a low sound as she showed him that she was aroused as she had been before.

"Now, please, now," she begged, and he was helpless to deny either one of them the pleasure of their joining.

Positioning himself between her legs, he entered her in one swift stroke.

She circled his back with her arms as he began to move within her, trying to keep the rhythm slow.

He wanted to lower his feeding teeth to her neck, to add to his pleasure by taking some of her blood, but he would have to cloud her mind to do that, and he wasn't willing to take that step.

His focus changed as he felt her inner muscles tighten around him, the contractions like small electric shocks communicating their urgency to his cock. And while orgasm still gripped her body, his own release grabbed him. Throwing his head back, he shouted out his pleasure.

Shaken to the depths of his soul, he collapsed against her, his head drifting to her shoulder, and she reached to soothe her fingers through his hair, turned her head so that she could stroke her lips along the line where his hair met his cheek.

He shifted to his side, and they lay clasping each other for long moments. When he reached for her hand, she knit her fingers with his.

"Thank you," she whispered.

"Thank you," he answered.

"What did it mean to you?" she asked.

"More than I can tell you."

He heard her swallow. "Will you tell me your secrets?"

"You think I have secrets?"

"I know you do."

He was shaken by what he was feeling. Instead of speaking, he gathered her close, sending her thoughts of sleep.

"What are you doing?" she murmured.

"Nothing."

"I've felt that before."

His chest constricted so painfully that it was difficult to draw a full breath. She had made love with a man named Ramsay Gallagher. *A man.*

But would she run screaming from a dragon-shifter? One who wanted to drink some of her blood? It was hard to imagine any other reaction.

CHAPTER
TWENTY-EIGHT

RAMSAY DOZED FOR a few hours, then eased out of bed. When he looked back at Madison, he saw she hadn't stirred, and he knew she must be exhausted. Hopefully, she'd sleep for the next few hours.

Their clothing was strewn around the floor, and he wished there had been some way to get it cleaned while they slept. He pulled on his underwear, pants, and shirt, then picked up his boots and socks and carried them out of the room with him where he put them on.

Downstairs, he found Signora Beldona, who gave him a speculative look.

"You want a meal?" the innkeeper asked.

"Not now. If the signora wakes up, tell her not to worry. Tell her I went out to get some things, and I'll be right back."

"Si."

"Can you tell me where to find a clothing shop?"

"There's a small one in the square," she answered, then gave him directions to the center of town, which was only a street away.

He hurried out, following the directions the woman had given him. He would have liked to go back the way they'd come and drink some blood from one of the cows he'd seen in the fields. But that was going to have to wait.

In the shop, he bought himself a pair of jeans and a button-down shirt, knowing he'd feel better when he could change into something clean. And Madison would appreciate something pretty, he thought as he looked through the women's clothing and selected a bright cotton dress, a shawl, and some sandals. Over the years he'd learned a lot about women's sizes, and he was pretty sure he'd gotten them right.

As he headed back to the bed-and-breakfast, he saw a police car parked outside.

"*Futuo*," he muttered under his breath as he quickened his steps.

He gave the small vehicle a long look as he drew closer. Had the cops somehow discovered they were from the ill-fated archaeological site? Or maybe this visit had nothing to do with them. Maybe it was about some local dispute involving Signora Beldona.

Composing his features, he stepped inside and found a short, dark man talking to Signora Beldona. He was wearing a uniform that indicated he was fairly high up in the department, but Ramsay couldn't be sure of his exact position.

As soon as Ramsay entered the room, the owner of the bed-and-breakfast flushed, probably because she'd called the cops as soon as he'd gone out.

The policeman's attention switched to him.

"I want to ask you some questions," he said in fairly good English.

"Certainly," Ramsay answered, figuring he might as well continue in English. "To whom am I speaking?"

"I am Police Inspector Mancuso."

"Pleased to meet you. I'm Ramsay Gallagher," he answered as though they were having a social exchange, even though he had no illusions about the man's purpose. This was strictly business.

He watched the inspector carefully, sure that his name had registered.

"What is your business in this region?" the cop asked.

"What is yours?" Ramsay countered.

"I'll ask the questions."

"I was at Dr. Madison Dartmoor's dig."

"You're not there now."

Ramsay kept his voice steady. "Dr. Dartmoor and I were outside last night when we saw her assistant going into the tomb with another man. The tomb exploded. We were caught by falling rock. Then we saw armed men entering the camp. We assumed the camp was under attack and fled to the smugglers' caves."

The inspector kept his eyes on Ramsay. "You say you and Dr. Dartmoor fled? Where is she?"

"Upstairs. Sleeping."

"They had one room," Signora Beldona added helpfully.

"I'd like to speak to her as well," Mancuso said.

"I'll get her."

"I'd rather the signora did that."

Ramsay nodded, hoping his face didn't betray his annoyance. Obviously the inspector didn't want the two of them to speak to each other privately. Had he already discovered Spader's body in the field?

"I brought Dr. Dartmoor some clean clothing," he said, then turned to the innkeeper. "Please bring it up to her." Opening the bag, he took out the pants and shirt he'd bought for himself.

When the woman started up the stairs, he turned back to the cop. "And I'd like to change my clothes as well. You can stand outside the bathroom door if you're afraid I'm going to run away."

They both walked to the back of the house, to a small

bathroom. Ramsay ducked inside and quickly changed into the clean outfit.

When he came out, Madison was coming down the stairs, looking worried. "What's happened?"

Ramsay gestured toward the inspector. "I'm assuming Inspector Mancuso has been to the camp and found the tomb buried under a ton of rock, and now he wants to ask us what happened."

Madison looked at the inspector. "Is that correct?"

The man glared at Ramsay before turning back to Madison. "I'd like to speak to you alone."

A look of panic bloomed on her face. "I'd rather stay with Ramsay," she said.

"I want to hear your stories separately," the man said in a tone that brooked no argument.

"Does Dominic Coleman know about the . . . explosion at the tomb?" she asked.

"I've been in communication with him," Mancuso clipped out.

"Oh Lord. He must be worried to death about me. I have to call him."

"You can do that later."

"You don't get one phone call?" Ramsay asked.

The cop gave him a dark look. "One more remark from you, and you're under arrest."

Madison gasped. Ramsay pressed his lips together.

Satisfied, the cop turned to Signora Beldona. "Is there a room I can use for the questioning?"

"The parlor."

Ramsay gave Madison a direct look. "It's okay. We don't have anything to hide. Just tell him what happened."

"Okay," she murmured.

The cop looked at Ramsay. "I'd like you to wait upstairs."

"Sure," he agreed. *So there's no chance of my hearing your conversation with Madison.*

The inspector waited while he walked up the stairs, then led Madison into the parlor and shut the door.

Signora Beldona was staring up at him.

"Thanks a lot," he mouthed in Italian.

When she shrugged and turned away, he walked into the bedroom and stood looking around. Madison's clothing was gone from the floor, but she hadn't had time to make the bed. It was still mussed, and he crossed to it, pulling up the sheet and spread, breathing in the scent of their lovemaking.

"Madison. Don't panic. It's going to be okay," he whispered, hoping it was true.

He knew the cop was just doing his job. He'd come upon a very messy mass murder scene, and he wanted to make sure that the survivors weren't involved in the killing. But that left them in a precarious position. If the details of their stories didn't match, he would keep going after them. Then he'd find out that Ramsay had been struggling with Spader when the gun had gone off.

They'd have to prove it was self-defense when it was their word against a dead man's.

His heart was pounding as he lay down on the bed. The tension wasn't doing him any good. Closing his eyes, he went through a relaxation routine that he'd learned long ago. Then he prepared to send his mind outside his body.

He could do this. He had done it many times in the past. But that was when he'd had his full powers.

Don't put up obstacles, he warned himself. *Just let it happen. You've got a strong connection with her. You can reach her.*

When he felt more in control, he let his consciousness flow outward, seeking Madison. Yet he couldn't simply try to get inside her mind. He couldn't let her know what he was doing, because Mancuso would see her reaction.

He tried to reach her. But all he felt was a terrible void.

CHAPTER
TWENTY-NINE

STRUGGLING TO MAKE a connection with Madison, Ramsay sent his thoughts back to the last time they'd been in this bed together.

They'd been kissing and touching. Making love.

It had been so full of passion. Not just physical passion. A joining that opened them to each other on so many levels.

Madison, he murmured. *Madison, come back to me. Join with me. Let me see what you're doing now.*

He could feel himself drifting closer to her. Closer. Closer. But he couldn't make the contact.

It was like when you were trying to think of a name, and it wouldn't come to you, but you could feel it just hanging out of reach in your mind.

He knew he couldn't force it. Instead he thought of how much he . . . loved her.

He loved her!

The revelation was like a bolt of lightning striking him. And like a lightning strike, it hurt.

What good did his love do him? Or her?

While he was trying to cope with the new knowledge, his mind made another leap, and he was in the room with her. Not literally. Mentally. He was standing in the corner of the parlor, watching her and the cop. Only neither one of them could see him.

Or could she?

She shifted in her seat and looked in his direction.

He tensed, waiting for her to cry out or jump up. But she only shook her head.

"Signorina?"

Her attention snapped back to the cop. "Yes?"

"You just have to tell me what happened. In your own words."

She sat up straighter and focused on the inspector. "Ramsay and I saw Gavin going into the tomb—with another man neither one of us recognized. I was going to ask him what he was doing, but Ramsay held me back."

"This was at night?"

"Yes."

"Why were you up?"

"I was restless. I got out of bed."

"Okay. Let's go back to the moment before the explosion. You said Ramsay held you back. Why?"

She shifted in her seat again. "He sensed something."

"Do you mean he knew something?"

"No. He . . . senses things."

"What do you mean?"

"He has instincts about people. I think he never trusted Gavin, and he didn't want me to rush into . . . a situation neither of us was expecting."

The cop didn't comment, so she went on.

"When the tomb exploded, Ramsay threw me to the ground. He covered my body with his. Rocks fell on him. One of them hit him in the head. It was bleeding. The wound must still be there. You can find it."

She started to stand, but Mancuso waved her back into her seat.

"We can do that later. What happened next?"

"We saw armed men coming into the camp. Ramsay said we had to hide in the caves. He was injured. He had to lean on me when we climbed the hill."

"And then?"

She hesitated, and Ramsay knew she was remembering what had happened. One of the thugs had come after them. Now she was thinking that Ramsay had killed the man in self-defense.

The men didn't find us. We hid in the cave. I was injured. You took care of me.

She straightened and looked toward the corner of the room.

Maybe she could see him in some ghostly way. He smiled encouragingly at her.

When she began to speak again, it was with more assurance. "Ramsay was injured. I was worried that he had a concussion. I found a place for us to hide in the cave, and I took care of him. I was frightened that he might have bleeding in his brain, but he got better. Finally, he told me he could walk, but we didn't want to go back to the camp, so we explored and found an exit down by the sea."

"Nobody found you in the cave?" Mancuso asked.

"Nobody found us."

"Why didn't you go back to the dig site?"

"We'd heard gunfire, and we didn't know the situation there. We went down to the water entrance to the caves. The tide was out, and Ramsay said we could run along the base of the cliffs. Only the tide started coming in, and the waves were breaking on us. We found a place where we could climb up. He almost fell. I had to grab him by his hair."

She stopped and took a breath.

"Then what happened?"

"We were in a field. We saw the road and followed it to the village. We got a room here. We were both exhausted. We . . . slept."

"That's all?"

Her face hardened. "Our relationship is none of your business."

"It is if it relates to this case."

"We just slept," she said, punching out the words.

"Okay."

"I'd like to go call Mr. Coleman now. Then take a shower," she said.

"Not yet. I want to check some details. You didn't run into anyone in the field?"

"No."

"You didn't hear a gunshot?"

"No."

"Let's go over it again."

Madison sighed and sat back.

Mancuso started anew, making sure she told the same story. Finally, he seemed satisfied.

"Tell Signora Beldona to send Mr. Gallagher in here."

"All right."

As she walked stiffly out of the room, Ramsay switched his mind back to his own body.

He heard the women talking downstairs and climbed out of bed. When he reached the ground floor, Madison stared at him.

The cop had also stepped out of the parlor.

"How did it go?" Ramsay asked Madison.

"All right." She kept her gaze fixed on him, and he knew she wanted to say something private. But that was out of the question.

"You'd better go call Coleman," he said. "He may not even know we're alive."

"Yes." She turned to Signora Beldona. "Is there a phone I can use here?"

"Si. In the kitchen. Let me show you."

Yeah, Ramsay thought. *The phone you used to call the cops.*

Mancuso turned to Ramsay. "I'd like to examine your head. You have a wound?"

"Sure." He leaned down so that the inspector could reach the crusted place where a rock had hit him. When Mancuso touched it, Ramsay winced. "Still tender," he said, although it was healing well, the way he usually healed. Lucky for him that he hadn't taken a shower and wiped away the dried blood.

"Come into the parlor," the cop was saying. "I want to get your version of events."

"I'm sure my version is the same as Madison's," he said as he followed the man inside the room.

Mancuso shut the door and gestured Ramsay to the same chair Madison had occupied.

"Make yourself comfortable."

He bit back a sardonic comment as he sat. No point in antagonizing this guy any more than he'd already done.

"Tell me in your own words what happened."

"Starting when?"

"From before the explosion."

"My memory right around there is a little fuzzy. I guess from the head injury."

"Do the best you can."

He started telling the story, matching the details to what Madison had already said.

Mancuso listened, making a few notes.

"And you didn't encounter any of the men who invaded the camp?" he asked.

"No."

"And you didn't know the attack was coming?" he asked suddenly.

"How would I know?"

The inspector shrugged.

"I didn't know about the attack before it happened," Ramsay said in a firm voice.

"But you threw Dr. Dartmoor to the ground just before the explosion."

"I had a bad feeling about Gavin and the other man going into the tomb."

"Why?"

"It was suspicious. I didn't recognize the other man. I figured that if he was in the camp, the guards at the road were already dead or disabled."

"That doesn't explain your reaction before the explosion."

He shrugged. "I can't explain it. I just sensed something was going to happen."

"Sensed?"

"That happens to me sometimes. Like when you know the phone is going to ring before it does."

The cop nodded. "Why were you wandering around the camp?"

"I couldn't sleep. We hadn't been here very long. I was jet-lagged."

Mancuso circled back. "You had no inkling anything was going to happen?"

"No."

"And you didn't encounter a man named Kent Spader?"

"No."

"But you know him?"

"No."

"He was at the conference with you in Las Vegas."

Ramsay shrugged again. "There were several thousand people there. Dominic Coleman told me about him, but I didn't meet him."

"Told you what?"

"That he wanted to stop Madison's project."

"Why?"

"As far as I can tell, because he's a nutcase."

"You didn't make a call on his cell phone?"

Ramsay kept his voice even. "How could I? I said I didn't see him."

"I mean—here in Italy."

"No. I didn't see him here, either."

The cop tried again, asking his questions in various ways, but he wasn't able to get Ramsay to make a mistake.

"How many men invaded the camp?" Ramsay asked.

"We're not certain."

"Did anybody besides Madison and me get away?"

"We're not sure yet."

"Was Kent Spader personally directing the invasion?"

"He may have been." Mancuso stood up. "You can go, but I'd like you to remain in the area."

"Do you happen to know if our passports are still at the camp? Both Dr. Dartmoor and I left them in our huts."

"I have them," the inspector informed him.

"Then I guess we *will* be sticking around. What about my credit cards and the money I had with me?"

"That will be returned to you."

"Thank you," he said. He had a lot of experience with vanishing into thin air. If he wanted to leave Italy, he could do it easily, but he didn't think Madison had the same luxury.

They stepped into the hallway and found both Madison and Signora Beldona waiting for them.

"Did you reach Signor Coleman?" the inspector asked.

"Yes. He was relieved to find out Ramsay and I are all right." She kept her gaze on Mancuso. "He says he spoke to you. He says he was expecting a report from you."

"I don't take orders from him." The cop's expression turned fierce. "I'm in the middle of a mass murder investigation."

"Yes, of course," Madison murmured. "Sorry. But you must realize that Ramsay and I have been running for our lives. We didn't know if the men who invaded the camp were going to catch up with us."

"Understood," the cop answered, then turned toward the door. Ramsay and Madison watched him leave.

Madison glanced at the signora. "I'm worn-out. And Ramsay is still recovering from his injury. We'll be in our room," she said, then started up the stairs.

Ramsay followed, wondering what the tone of her voice meant.

As soon as he followed her into the room, she closed the door and whirled to face him.

"All right, I want some straight answers."

"About what?"

She began speaking rapidly, her gaze boring into him.

"Down there, when I was talking to Mancuso, I felt you watching me. Listening to me. I even thought I could see you standing in the corner of the room. But you weren't there. And . . . and other times. I've felt like you were getting inside my mind. Not just then. In the vision quest. And in Las Vegas, even. I'm tired of your playing games with me. I want you to explain what's going on."

She was spewing out a lot of doubts she must have bottled up. Finally she ran out of steam and stood facing him, her expression tense.

When he took a step toward her, she stepped back.

"Don't touch me. If you touch me, you're going to do something to my head, aren't you?"

CHAPTER
THIRTY

RAMSAY STOPPED AND slipped his hands into his pockets, wondering what he was going to say.

He sighed.

"You're getting ready to spin me some story," she accused.

"No. I told you I've always had some psychic abilities."

"Like what, exactly?"

"The cop probably asked you why I stopped you from following Gavin into the tomb. It was because I sensed something bad was going to happen. In the moment before the explosion, I had the strong conviction that if you went in there, you'd be killed. Then the bomb went off."

She answered with a tight nod. "What about the vision quest? What about when Mancuso was interviewing me, and I felt you there?"

"I didn't know what was going to happen at the vision quest. I was as surprised as you were. But I've felt us getting closer."

She wasn't willing to take that at face value. "In Las

Vegas, we didn't even know each other, but I think you were working on me then."

"I wanted to keep you safe; is that so bad?"

"You tried to influence me."

He could have denied it. Instead he nodded. "And when the cop took you into the parlor, I tried to connect with you. I didn't know if I could reach you, but it seems I did."

"Unless you tell me what's going on with you, I'm going to walk out of here."

The defiant look in her eyes made his chest tighten.

"How did you do it?" she demanded.

"I thought about the two of us. Of us making love, of how wonderful it was having you in my arms, with no barriers between us," he said in a thick voice.

"A nice story."

The next words came from deep in his soul. "Then I thought about how much I love you."

He felt his breath catch. He hadn't meant to say that. Not at all. But the words had tumbled out of his mouth.

Her expression turned from wariness to joy.

"You love me?"

He had said it. He couldn't take it back, although he didn't share her joy. He might love her, but that wasn't going to solve any of his problems.

Still, when she rushed across the room, he held out his arms and gathered her close.

Closing his eyes, he held on to her, because she felt like the only point of stability in a wildly tilting universe.

She tipped her head up, her mouth meeting his for a long, passionate kiss.

"Ramsay. Oh, Ramsay. I'm so happy. I love you. I kept fighting it because I was afraid to trust you. Now I know we're going to work it out."

Were they? Her joy and her optimism tore at him, but all he could do was hold her, kiss her, stroke his hands over her back and shoulders, then down to her hips. He could love her. He could make love to her. But he couldn't protect her from the future.

"There's more you need to tell me, isn't there?"

"Yes."

"I want to hear it. But not now. Now I just want you naked, in bed."

"Oh yeah."

"Or maybe we should make a stop in the shower first," she murmured. "That cop made me feel dirty."

"He was doing his job."

"He thought you were involved in the killings."

"He had to explore that possibility."

"Are you defending him?"

"Just trying to be fair to his point of view. He knew I reacted before the explosion. That's made him think I could have been working with Spader—even though I wasn't."

"I'm sorry I brought him up," Madison whispered. "I don't want anyone in this bedroom but us."

Ramsay made a sound of agreement, but he was thinking about what they'd had to do to stop the men who were following them yesterday. And what he'd done in Colorado at the bridge. Killing wasn't difficult for him. He'd done it many times over the years. How was Madison going to react when he told her about some of the chapters in his unsavory past? And how would she like to find out his real age?

He didn't want to think about that. He didn't want to think about any pain to come. Instead, he brought his mouth back to hers, turning his head one way and then the other, using the heat between them to cauterize his mind.

They forgot about the shower and were heading back to the bed when a knock at the door made them jump.

"What is it?" he called out.

"*Scusi, signor*," the innkeeper called out. "But Signorina Dartmoor has an urgent phone call."

They both tensed.

After glancing at Madison, he dragged in a breath, then crossed to the door and pulled it open.

"You must go down to talk on the phone," the innkeeper said.

"Sorry," Madison whispered.

"Not your fault."

She hurried out of the room and down the stairs. Ramsay followed her to the kitchen, where a phone was hanging on the wall.

Snatching up the receiver lying on the nearby counter, she said, "Hello?"

After listening for a few moments, she said "Yes, we're fine."

Then she looked at Ramsay. "It's Dominic. He wants to talk to you."

Ramsay crossed the room and took the receiver from Madison. "Hello."

"Are you and Madison really all right? She's not just saying that?"

"We're fine."

"What happened at the dig site?"

He thought about what he should say, considering that Inspector Mancuso could be tapping in to the conversation. It should be okay to give Coleman the same information that he'd already given the cop.

"One of Spader's men came in and had some kind of interaction with Gavin Kaiser. They went into the tomb, and there was an explosion that destroyed it."

"You're sure?"

"Yes."

Coleman made an angry sound.

"After the explosion, I believe his men attacked and killed everybody they could find. But Madison and I got away." He gave a condensed version of their flight, omitting any mention of contact with the bad guys.

When he was finished, Coleman spoke. "I want you out of there."

"That's impossible. Inspector Mancuso has our passports."

"I can deal with that."

"How?"

"You don't need to worry about the details yet, but I want the two of you to meet me in Peru."

That was the last thing Ramsay had expected to hear.

"I thought you don't travel."

"I'm making an exception."

"Why . . . there?"

"It's a great vacation spot," the billionaire allowed. "I'll get you plane reservations and book you into a luxury hotel in Lima. In the Miraflores section of the city. You'll like it."

Ramsay struggled to take all that in. He wanted more information, but he understood that he wasn't going to find out anything over the phone.

"Please convey the plans to Madison."

"All right."

When the connection clicked off, he turned to Madison. "He wanted me to give you some information."

"Why didn't he tell me directly?" she asked with an edge in her voice.

"I assume he didn't want you to start asking a bunch of questions."

Her jaw tightened. "But he could tell *you.*"

"He knew I could wait."

"Oh great." She flapped her arm in exasperation, then turned and started up the stairs toward their room. He followed her, watching the tense set of her shoulders.

When they'd both stepped into the room and he'd closed the door, she whirled to face him. "I've known him for years. I've worked with him on this project. And he trusts you more than he trusts me."

"I don't think it's a matter of trust."

"What would you call it?"

He felt trapped. "You're going to react to anything I say."

"You bet I am."

Before the phone call from Coleman, they'd been heading for the bed—to make love. Now Ramsay felt like a chasm had opened up between them.

"He wants us to meet him in Peru."

She dragged in a startled breath. "Why Peru?"

"He wouldn't tell me. All he gave me was the destination. Except for that, I'm as much in the dark as you are."

She answered with a small nod, then said, "But how do we get out of here without passports?"

"He said he'd take care of that. Can he?"

She gave a harsh laugh. "I imagine he's planning to buy our way out of here the way he buys anything else he wants. It will be interesting to see if he can do it, given Mancuso's bulldog attitude."

CHAPTER
THIRTY-ONE

RAMSAY HAD LEARNED a long time ago that money gave you power. Coleman apparently had absorbed the same lesson. Only hours after Mancuso had left, a private car delivered a large envelope to the bed-and-breakfast. In it were Madison's and Ramsay's passports and also first-class plane tickets from Rome to Lima. The driver of the car had instructions to take them to the airport.

Wearing the clothes he'd purchased in town, they climbed into the car. Ramsay kept looking around, expecting a police vehicle to come speeding after them with sirens blazing, but they arrived at the airport without incident.

Well, without anything that had to do with the police. He could feel the gulf between himself and Madison widening. She had been overwhelmed when he'd said he loved her. Apparently she'd had some time to think, and she'd decided love wasn't enough. He silently agreed, although he had his own reasons.

But he couldn't speak to her about anything personal until they were alone.

All he could do was reach for her hand and squeeze it after they'd gotten settled on the plane. She looked at him, then away.

"I promise we're going to talk—as soon we get to our hotel in Lima," he said.

MADISON hoped she'd managed to keep her expression neutral. "I'll believe that when I hear it," she said.

Somewhere in her mind, she acknowledged that she sounded childish. But too much had happened for her to even attempt to behave normally.

Or—what was normal?

Back in Italy, Ramsay had said he loved her, and that had been enough to send her into his arms. She'd wanted to make love with him—until the phone call from Dominic. Which had been like a cold wave drenching her.

What was wrong with her? Was she some kind of wimp who let strong men dominate her? First Dominic and then Ramsay?

Maybe it was because she'd been so lost and alone after her parents had gotten killed. During that terrible time, Dominic had stepped in and taken over the father role. She'd been so grateful and so emotionally tied to him. She'd even let him influence her choice of careers. What would she have become if left to her own devices? She didn't even know.

Still, she'd been an excellent student. And excellent at supervising the dig in Italy. But what were her motives? To succeed in her field? Or please her surrogate father?

She gripped the arm of her seat, stealing a sidewise glance at Ramsay, who was staring straight ahead, looking miserable. She wanted to reach out and lay her hand over his. To comfort him? Or reassure herself?

She didn't know which. But she did know she couldn't sit silently beside him for hours.

When she cleared her throat, he turned toward her.

"I'm sorry," she whispered. "I'm . . . on edge."

"Of course. So am I."

"Why do you think Dominic is sending us to Peru?"

He looked around the first-class cabin. Most of the other passengers were wearing earphones and staring at the individual television screens in front of them.

"He said it was a good place to vacation."

"Do you believe that?"

He laughed. "I know it is."

"You've been there?"

"Yes."

"What do you think is the real reason?"

"Well, speaking as a tourist . . ."

She shook her head. "You're never just a tourist."

He shrugged.

"You're interested in everything and everybody. And you can't help sucking up information like a sponge."

"Not *everybody*," he said in a soft voice. "Just certain people."

She knew he was trying to bridge the gap between them. But she still needed to keep the conversation on a neutral level.

"My area of concentration was Europe. But I've had survey courses about Latin American prehistory. I know about the Incas, of course. And other civilizations farther north, like the Aztecs or the Mayas. Tell me why we might be going to Peru."

"There were cultures there long before the Incas. The earliest recorded civilization is the Lithic, dating back to 9,000 B.C. The Incas are in the fifteen hundreds. And there are many peoples in between."

"You've got that information at your fingertips?"

"Yeah."

She looked over her shoulder, then lowered her voice. "Do you think Dominic's sending us to a research site?"

Ramsay shrugged. "I guess we'll find out."

"We're starting in Lima. If you had to guess, where would you say we're going?" she pressed.

He'd thought about that. "Of course, the most famous archaeological site in Peru is Machu Picchu. It was abandoned by the Incas in the fifteen hundreds, covered by the jungle, and discovered by Hiram Bingham in 1911. But it's been extensively excavated and studied. I'll be surprised if he'd focus on it."

"Then what?"

"What do you know about the Nazca lines?"

"I've heard of them, of course. The enormous images carved into the desert. They're too big to see if you're on the ground. The only way you can spot them is from above."

"There are a couple of dozen images. The one you see reproduced most often is a hummingbird. But there's also the figure of a man. Giant hands. A spider. A monkey. Other animals."

She nodded. "I'm guessing you know how they were put there."

"Yeah. The first few inches of rock are dark colored. Below that is light rock. Archaeologists think the Nazca people etched them about two thousand years ago by scraping away the top layer."

AS he talked about the lines and the Nazca culture, Ramsay could tell Madison was following his words carefully, and that gave him something to hang on to. He kept talking, telling her what he knew about ancient civilizations in Peru.

She brought him up short when she said, "It sounds like you were there. I mean, back in ancient times."

He managed a laugh. "I guess I get all wound up in a subject when it interests me."

"You and Dominic have that in common."

He couldn't stop himself from saying, "Maybe that's

what attracted you to me." He watched her face carefully as he said it.

"It was a lot more than that."

"Yeah, the bodyguard factor."

Her voice thinned. "Are you trying to back out of what you said?" She swallowed. "I mean, when you said you loved me."

"I'm not backing out," he answered, thinking that perhaps she would be the one to run screaming from the relationship.

"Okay. I guess we can't talk about it here."

To Ramsay's relief, Madison closed her eyes and went to sleep. He wished he could do the same, but there was no escape for him. And he was wondering where he was going to find a blood supply in the city.

As soon as they cleared customs, Madison began looking around the terminal for Coleman. He wasn't there.

Then she spotted a man holding a sign with their names. He'd been hired to meet them and drive to the Miraflores Grand. But he had no information beyond their names and destination.

"I guess Dominic's tired, and he's waiting for us at the hotel," Madison said.

Ramsay shrugged. "I don't know what he has in mind. I thought he didn't travel much."

"He doesn't. He must consider this trip important."

As soon as the car pulled up, Madison rushed into the hotel. Even before she registered, she asked to be connected to Señor Coleman's room. The clerk checked his records, then looked up at her with an apologetic expression.

"I'm sorry, Señorita. There's no one by that name in the computer."

She looked back at Ramsay, her face pinched. "I don't understand."

The clerk was speaking again. "I do have a message for you."

He handed her an envelope. After she'd read it, her expression was still disappointed—and puzzled. "He was in Lima, but he left right away. He wants us to spend the night here and get some rest. Then he's got us booked on a plane to Arequipa in the morning. What's in Arequipa?"

"Right in town?" He thought for a moment. "At the museum, there's a very well-preserved mummy of a young girl who was apparently killed in an Inca rite."

"But you don't think it's the Incas we're interested in."

"Right." He glanced at the desk clerk. "We'd like to check in."

"Of course. I have a lovely suite for the two of you."

"Excellent," he answered, thinking that Coleman was covering his bases. They could choose to sleep in the same bed—or separately.

Madison pressed her lips together, apparently getting the message that they'd be better off continuing the conversation upstairs.

When the bellman had showed them to the tenth-floor suite and left, Madison turned to him.

"What else is in Arequipa?"

He dredged up an answer, since he wanted to postpone any personal discussion.

"Back in colonial times and into the twentieth century, the first daughter in each Spanish noble family in Peru always married. But the second daughter was forced to become a nun. There's a famous monastery—we'd call it a convent—in Arequipa where they lived totally cut off from the world. Even when they had a visit from their family, they were screened behind a double set of thick grilles."

"They didn't have any choice about going into the convent?"

"Not really. When the bishop questioned them, if they said they weren't acting of their own free will, they'd be cast out in disgrace."

"That's horrible."

"Yeah. A good example of how women have been treated down through the ages," he answered vehemently, then was sorry he'd made an editorial comment. What if she said it sounded like he'd been there in the fifteenth century?

She walked to the window and looked out over the city.

"I'm sort of like that."

"Huh?"

"I wonder what choices I would have made if I hadn't let Dominic Coleman guide my life."

"But you're a success in your field."

"Maybe I was, until my project got blown to hell."

"Don't."

He joined her at the window, slipping his arm around her as he looked over rooftops with laundry drying on lines. Down at street level, a dog trotted along the sidewalk. Probably a stray.

Madison curled into his embrace, then shook him out of his reflective mood when she said, "Let's stop stalling. What were you going to tell me about yourself?"

"I see you haven't forgotten about that."

"Tell me your big secret. And yes, I'm sure you have one."

CHAPTER
THIRTY-TWO

RAMSAY SWALLOWED AROUND the lump in his throat, but he knew he had to do some more explaining if he didn't want Madison to walk out the door. "You remember the vision quest."

"Of course."

"We went back to a time when the . . . shape-shifters were here. And it looked like they'd . . . mated with the people they encountered on earth."

"Yes," she murmured.

"I told you I wasn't sure it was real. I still don't know if it was, but I think I'm descended from them. That's why I was so interested in your research. I wanted to know where I came from." Which was true as far as it went.

Madison turned to stare at him, taking that in. "Is that where you get your . . . psychic powers?"

"I think so."

"You think everyone with mental powers has the same heritage?"

He shrugged. "I don't know about other people. I just know about myself."

"Why do you think it's true of you?"

"I wasn't lying when I told you I was fascinated by the idea of extraterrestrials influencing mankind. When I heard about your research, I knew I had to find out what you'd discovered. Then I saw that statue you'd brought to Las Vegas, and it seemed familiar. Either I have some connection to the dragons—or I'm obsessed." He laughed. "You know, like a mental patient who thinks he's Franklin Delano Roosevelt or Alexander the Great."

"Please! Let's stick with what you really think you know. If you're descended from the shape-shifters, what about your parents? Who were they?"

"That's part of the mystery. I was adopted by a couple who found me wandering around on my own."

"Are they still alive?"

"No. They died years ago—leaving me to fend for myself again."

"But you did very well for yourself."

"They left me a lot of money," he said, fudging the facts again. Really, after he'd accidentally killed his harsh master, he'd found the man's stash of gold coins. Which had been enough for him to change the way he lived. "I figured out early how to make my way in the world."

When she started to ask another question, he turned her toward him and folded her close.

"I don't usually talk about myself."

"I get that."

"I've told you more than I've told anyone else in a long time. Can we drop it for now?"

"Yes," she murmured, and he thought she was satisfied—for the time being. But he was sure that she was going to come back to him for more explanations, and he wondered what he was going to say.

Instead of speaking he wrapped her more tightly in his arms, wanting her so fiercely that it took his breath away.

She stayed where she was, tipping her face up to his. He lowered his head, seeking her mouth. His lips moved over hers with a hunger that had grown since the last time he'd held her.

He needed her, more than he'd been willing to admit. And he was afraid that he was going to lose her.

Kissing her with a desperate urgency, he slid his hands over her shoulders and back and then down to her hips, pressing her more tightly to his erection.

He felt as if he were drowning, with no one to save him except the woman in his arms.

Perhaps she was feeling the same thing, because she tightened her arms around his waist as she deepened the kiss.

He was lost in the intoxicating taste of her, the feel of her mouth on his. He forgot about the mystery of why they were in Peru. There was only the reality of the warm, pliant woman in his arms. Swamping his senses, threatening to drive every coherent thought from his mind.

When her hands slid to his hips, and she rocked her body against the rigid flesh behind his fly, he thought he would go up in flames. He wanted her now. This moment. Yet he wouldn't allow himself to rush to completion.

Tenderly, he gathered her up in his arms and carried her to the bed, threw back the spread, then laid her down on the crisp sheet.

With hands he couldn't hold steady, he undid the buttons of her blouse and spread the fabric before reaching behind her to unhook her bra and push it out of the way.

She gave him a slow smile as she shrugged out of the blouse and bra, then said, "Undress for me."

"What?"

"I want to enjoy watching you take off your clothes."

He grinned back at her, glad that she felt comfortable enough with him to make the request. Or maybe she needed to exercise some control.

Before standing, he kicked off his shoes and socks. Then he walked a few feet from the bed where he slowly peeled his T-shirt up his chest before pulling it over his head. Their eyes locked as he reached for the fly of his jeans. His gaze never leaving her, he lowered the zipper, then skimmed the pants down his hips, and stepped out of them. His cock strained against the knit fabric of his briefs, and he watched her focus on that.

"Take off the shorts."

"If I do, it's going to be hard to go slowly."

"I don't want you to go slowly. I want you inside me now."

The words were like an arrow piercing his resolve. He dragged the shorts off and saw that she had kicked away the rest of her clothing just as quickly.

When she held out her arms, he came down on top of her, gasping at the feel of her naked flesh against his.

She clasped him to her, rocking against him, then reversed their positions so that she was the one on top. In one smooth motion she took him inside her, then went perfectly still, resting on top of him, looking down with a wicked expression on her face.

When she lifted her breasts toward him and began to play with the nipples, he made a muffled sound.

He heard the ragged edge of her breathing—and his—as she sat on top of him, playing with her breasts, driving him toward madness.

He knew he said something incoherent. A plea. In what language? When she began to move above him, he sighed out his gratitude.

She might have intended to make her movements slow

and deliberate, but she was soon rising and falling with frantic urgency, driving both of them toward completion.

He struggled to hold back, waiting until he felt her inner muscles clenching around him before he allowed himself to let go, then cried out as wave after wave of satisfaction washed over him.

Reaching up, he pulled her down, clasping her to him, kissing her damp hair, her cheek, her brow.

"Oh Lord, Ramsay," she whispered. "Oh Lord. You've taken me captive."

"No more than you've taken me," he answered, holding her close, praying to all the gods in the universe that he could keep her with him.

Coleman had said they were in Lima to rest. Ramsay understood the wisdom of that, but he couldn't stop himself from bringing his mouth back to Madison's for a long kiss. If he was going to lose her, he wanted memories to warm him through the long, lonely nights.

He made love to her again and was still greedy for more, but he knew they both had a long day ahead of them.

"We should sleep," he murmured.

"Yes."

He held her in his arms, feeling guilty about sending her drugging thoughts. But that was his best option.

When he was sure she was sleeping soundly, he eased out of bed and stood looking at her for a long moment.

Then he slipped quietly out of the room and finally out of the hotel.

Most of the Miraflores district was dark, but he knew where he could find what he was looking for. Gambling was legal in Peru, and there were a number of casinos within easy walking distance of the hotel.

As he started down the dark sidewalk, he heard footsteps behind him.

He stopped, and the follower stopped. Yes, there was definitely someone in back of him.

His mind ranged over the possibilities. It could be a mugger who thought he could score off a rich American. Or it could be more personal. Coleman wasn't in Lima, but what if he'd sent someone to check up on Ramsay? Or Ramsay and Madison? He couldn't be sure which.

He speeded up, still walking but knowing that the man in back of him was now running to keep up.

Rounding a corner, he stepped into a darkened doorway, blending with the shadows and watching as a short, dark man trotted down the sidewalk, then stopped, looking around.

When Shorty took several steps back and didn't see his quarry, he went ahead again, more slowly at first and then faster.

Ramsay watched him disappear. It was tempting to reverse the hunt and take the man down. He could find out if it was just a random mugger or someone sent by Coleman. But if it was the latter, he didn't want the billionaire to know the tail had been discovered. And he didn't want the guy to wake up in the morning with unexplained teeth marks on his neck.

After waiting long enough to make sure he was alone, Ramsay set off for his original destination, a casino near a small mall that sold native crafts.

The establishment was decorated in gaudy red and gold, but the paint and fabrics were a bit worn around the edges. Most of the floor space was taken up with rooms, including one where a large crowd was still playing slots and various games like roulette, blackjack, and poker.

Ramsay bought a stack of chips, then wandered to the roulette tables, placing bets at random, not caring whether he won or lost.

Instead, he was studying the other patrons, judging their suitability as blood donors.

He played for fifteen minutes, lost all his chips, and strolled outside again, his senses probing the darkness. As far as he could tell, the man who had followed him hadn't figured out where to pick up his trail.

He stood in the shadows as several patrons left the establishment. When one he'd noticed earlier started toward a nearby parking lot, he followed the man to his car. There was an attendant, of course, but the guy had fallen asleep at his post.

Coming up behind the casino patron, Ramsay said softly in Spanish, "You forgot something."

The man turned, and Ramsay stepped quickly forward, pulling him into an embrace and clouding his mind as he drew a quick draft of blood.

It pleased him that he was getting his old skill back. He didn't need to use sex as part of the encounter. But the physical contact still let him blur the man's mind.

When he was finished, he helped the man into his car and left him leaning over the steering wheel.

Making a quick decision, he stepped to the parking attendant's booth and took more blood. Mindful of the man's probable poverty, he left him a large tip for his donation.

The feeding session had taken less than three minutes. Feeling refreshed, Ramsay strolled back toward the hotel, enjoying the quiet of the city at night.

As he approached the hotel entrance, his steps slowed. The man who had initially followed him was standing in the shadow of some shrubbery.

Unable to ignore him this time, Ramsay turned and started toward him. "Looking for me, Shorty?" he asked.

The guy stiffened.

Ramsay repeated the question in Spanish.

Instead of answering, the man bolted. Ramsay took off after him and caught up easily.

Pulling the man into an alley, he twisted one arm behind the guy's back.

"Please. Don't hurt me," Shorty begged.

"Why were you following me?"

When the man hesitated, Ramsay twisted the arm, stopping short of breaking it.

CHAPTER
THIRTY-THREE

SHORTY MADE A moaning sound. "Please, señor. Let me go," he said in Spanish.

"That depends on what you have to say. Why are you following me?" Ramsay repeated in the same language.

"I wasn't following you."

"Don't lie to me." Ramsay punctuated the order with an arm twist.

The man screamed, then said in a rush of words, "I was paid to do it."

"By whom?"

"I don't know."

"You've got to know who's paying you?"

"A man I know . . . from the street."

Ramsay ran through the scenario and decided it could work that way. "Just me? Or me and the señorita?"

"Both of you."

"But if we went in separate directions?"

"You."

He held the man close, probing his panicked thoughts, trying to determine the truth of his words—and the truth behind them. He still didn't have all his faculties, and it took him some time to simply skim the surface of Shorty's mind, but he could glean enough to know that the man had been approached in Kennedy Park by someone he'd worked for on previous occasions. Someone who had taken his orders from a third party, and he hadn't passed on that information.

He felt the man's terror as he held him. He could drain the guy's blood and leave him next to a trash can. Or break his arm. Ramsay felt the violent impulse stirring inside himself. It was tempting to teach this guy a lesson.

But that would only be for his own gratification. It wouldn't provide any additional information. With a sigh, he let the man go, and he stumbled away, struggling to stay upright. When he gained his footing, he took off running.

Still wondering who was keeping tabs on him, Ramsay headed back to the hotel. In their suite, he took a shower before slipping back into bed with Madison.

She murmured a question. "Where were you?"

"Restless. Out for a walk."

"You do that a lot."

"Old habit," he answered, feeling his chest tighten.

"Okay."

He debated telling Madison that they were being watched, then decided not to worry her.

"Go back to sleep. We have a long day ahead of us."

"What happened out there?"

"Nothing," he said, sending her soothing messages.

She reached for him and pulled him close, and he closed his eyes as he rested his cheek against her warm breasts.

Holding her was a touchstone to the softer side of himself. Outside he'd been ready to take revenge on a man who was only following orders; here he knew what was important.

He threaded his fingers through Madison's hair and across her back. It was easy to get her to relax, but he still hated manipulating her.

THEY had time for the breakfast buffet that was part of the package with the room. As they made selections from the tables of baked goods, fruit, bacon, eggs, and sausage, Ramsay watched the other guests. Nobody seemed to be paying them any special attention. But when they stepped outside to leave for the airport, he spotted a man across the street keeping them in view. Not Shorty from the night before. Someone else.

Madison followed his gaze.

"You know that guy?"

"Never saw him before."

"He's watching us, isn't he?"

"I think so."

"Why?"

Ramsay shrugged. "Maybe Coleman's making sure we arrive safely in Arequipa."

She drew in a quick breath. "Why shouldn't we?"

"After what happened in Italy, maybe it's a good idea to be cautious."

They arrived at the airport without incident, paid the internal flight tax, and boarded.

As far as Ramsay could tell, no one followed them onto the plane. Once again they were met at the airport by a man who drove them past snowcapped peaks and into the city.

"Why are there so many white stone buildings?" Madison asked.

"They're made from a local volcanic rock," he told her.

"Are the volcanoes active?"

"No. But this is an earthquake zone. There was a bad one in 2001."

Like Madison, he scanned the passing scene, but he was more interested in making sure nobody was following them than in taking in the sights of Peru's second largest city.

He saw no one suspicious, which suggested that Coleman was the one responsible for the surveillance of the previous night. Now that they were going to meet him, there was no need to keep tabs on them.

Madison gripped his hand.

"What?"

"Are we going to tell Dominic what really happened?" she asked in a low voice, and he realized she must have been worrying about it since Italy.

"Do you want to?"

"No."

"Why not?"

"I guess . . . the fewer people who know, the better."

"Yeah," he answered, thinking he didn't want to give Coleman anything to hold over them and glad that Madison was reevaluating her relationship with the guy.

Before they registered, Madison spotted her mentor sitting in a comfortably furnished lounge area that looked like it might have been transported from a European manor house.

When Coleman saw them, he pushed himself out of a chair beside the massive stone fireplace. Madison ran to him and they hugged.

Ramsay watched the reunion with interest. He wasn't jealous, he told himself, but he knew her relationship with the old man was strong. When they were alone, would Coleman give her reasons not to trust her new lover?

"I was so relieved to find out you were all right," Coleman said. "I want to hear the real story, but"—he glanced around the lounge—"in private, I think."

Madison nodded.

"I've booked us the best suite in the house, but first I

want you to drink some of the coca leaf tea that will help you with the altitude."

"Do I need it?" Madison asked.

"It's a good idea," Coleman replied, reaching for his cane, then walking over to the urn at the side of the lounge.

Ramsay looked the older man up and down as he poured cups of tea for all of them. "I thought you rarely traveled."

"That's right."

"But you've come here."

"Because I thought it was important."

"You didn't use a cane at home."

"Better safe than sorry."

When they'd finished the robust tea, they all took the elevator to the third floor, to a suite with three bedrooms, three bathrooms, a living room, and even a formal dining room. Although Ramsay had no intention of sleeping anywhere but beside Madison, he wasn't going to start off making a fuss about it.

Coleman had already ordered lunch, which was waiting for them in the living room.

After getting comfortable in the seating area, Ramsay sipped some bottled water, determined to let this meeting play out at its own pace.

"I'd like to hear what really happened at the site," Coleman said.

Madison glanced at Ramsay.

"Just tell him what happened—the way you told Inspector Mancuso," he said in a reassuring voice, wondering if she could really fudge the facts when her mentor was staring at her.

She nodded and began to tell the version they'd agreed on. Coleman seemed satisfied with the account. When Madison was finished, he turned to Ramsay. "Do you have anything to add?"

"I think she's given you the picture."

"Both of you had quite an ordeal."

"It came out all right," Ramsay answered.

Now that they'd gotten their narrative out of the way, Ramsay relaxed and ate a ham and cheese sandwich. Although he wanted to hear what Coleman had to tell them, he was content to let the man unveil his plans at his own pace.

But Madison was too anxious to sit quietly. She set her tuna sandwich in front of her on a plate and said, "What's in Arequipa?"

Coleman gave her a satisfied smile that made Ramsay struggle not to react. This was more proof that there was something wrong with the relationship between them, and it had nothing to do with his personal stake in the triangle. Or maybe it did.

The billionaire deliberately took a bite of a chicken salad sandwich and washed it down with sips of tea before he said, "Arequipa is the gateway to the Colca Valley. Colca Canyon is the deepest canyon in the world, almost ten thousand feet."

"You're kidding," she answered. "Why haven't I heard of it?"

"Well, it looks far less spectacular than the Grand Canyon because it's much narrower."

"What else?" she prompted.

"The region is very arid, with vast stretches of land that only a vicuna could love. There are also some springs and cultivated pre-Columbian terraces where the locals are still farming. Tourists come to a spot along the rim of the canyon where condors soar on the rising thermals."

The travelogue was getting to Ramsay, and he couldn't stop himself from demanding, "What does this have to do with us?"

Coleman smiled, and Ramsay realized too late that the man had been deliberately pushing him to beg for information.

He reached for a briefcase on the floor beside his chair and took out a folder, which he passed across to Ramsay. When he opened the cover, his breath caught. Inside was a photograph of a statue. It was much like the man/dragon artifact he'd seen at Coleman's mansion—and like the copy Madison had brought to Las Vegas.

It was standing upright, and a man's hand held a ruler next to it, so he could see it was about ten inches high—about the same size as the other one. As he passed the photo to Madison, he saw that the one below it showed the figure transformed into a dragon.

"These are authentic?" he asked.

"Yes."

"You only have the pictures?"

"The artifact's in a safe place."

"But it originally comes from somewhere near Colca Canyon?"

"Yes."

"Where, exactly?"

"It was found by a llama herder, after he escaped from a landslide."

"You're lucky he didn't turn it over to the government," Ramsay observed.

"He was smart enough to know that he wouldn't make any money that way."

"How did you end up with it?"

"I have agents all over the world who know the type of artifacts I want to buy."

Madison leaned forward, her expression tight. "How long have you been keeping this from me?"

"I've had it for several months," Coleman answered easily.

"And you didn't tell me!"

"What were you going to do, drop your project in Italy and come down here?"

"No," she said in a low voice. "But I would have liked to know about this find."

She shuffled through the whole pile of photos, then looked up at Coleman. "Did you have someone specific in mind to work the dig?"

"Let's not get into that."

Ramsay could feel Madison's disappointment. She'd thought she had a special relationship with this man, and he'd just let on that it wasn't true. Or at least not to the degree she'd assumed.

Before she could say something she'd be sorry about later, Ramsay said, "But now you've brought us to Peru."

He expected the man to address Madison. Instead, the billionaire's gaze swung to him. "I have the artifact, but I haven't located this new tomb site. I was hoping you could help me find it."

"Why do you think *I* can do that?" Ramsay asked in a level voice.

"I had reports from Italy. I knew that you'd suggested where to find the main tomb. Madison's team had started digging in that location when the explosion changed everything."

Beside him, Madison shifted in her seat. Ramsay hated to make it worse for her, but he wanted everything spelled out.

"And Gavin was working directly for you as well as Spader. Right?"

"Yes."

When Madison made a small sound, Ramsay reached for her hand, knitting his fingers with hers, and he knew the gesture wasn't lost on Coleman. If he'd suspected the two of them were close, now he could see it for himself. Would the new relationship get between him and Madison? Ramsay selfishly hoped so. He was hoping she'd figure out for herself that Coleman wasn't the man she'd thought he was. It would be wrenching for her to come to that conclusion, but she'd already been questioning her life choices.

Pushing the process along a little more, he asked in a calm voice, "Did you arrange for someone to keep us under surveillance in Lima?"

CHAPTER
THIRTY-FOUR

COLEMAN KEPT HIS gaze fixed on Ramsay. "You went out last night. You lost the man tailing you. Then you came back to the hotel and spotted him again. You chased him and almost killed him."

Madison looked from Ramsay to Coleman and back again. "That happened last night?" she whispered.

"I wouldn't describe it that way."

"How would you describe it?" Coleman asked.

"I spotted him. I lost him. Then when I came back to the hotel, he was waiting for me again, and I decided to ask who had sent him."

"What did you find out?" Coleman asked, tension in his voice.

"He didn't know, so I let him go."

"Where did you go after you lost him the first time?" Madison asked.

"A gambling casino. I got a hundred dollars worth of chips, played until I lost the stake, and left."

"You said . . ."

"I was restless. Are we going to get into an argument about it?" Ramsay asked, annoyed that Coleman had managed to turn the tables on the question.

"No," Madison said in a tight voice. He suspected that they'd be discussing it later.

"Let's get back on track," Ramsay said. "We're here to find a tomb somewhere in the Colca Canyon area."

"I have a contact in a little town called Achoma. He can take us to the general vicinity."

"Okay," Ramsay answered. "But we're not exactly equipped for getting into anything heavy."

"I've had clothing for you and supplies delivered here," Coleman answered easily. "Each of you will find what you need in your rooms. And the equipment will be in the vehicle."

Ramsay had decided it wasn't worth making an issue of the sleeping arrangements. But apparently Madison was feeling rebellious.

"We're staying in the same room," she told Coleman. On her way across the seating area, she glanced at Ramsay. He got up and followed her.

Without looking at the contents she began moving luggage from one bedroom into the other. He grabbed two duffel bags and helped her, then closed the door.

"I'm sorry," he murmured.

"Not your fault."

Reaching out, he pulled her to him, and he felt her trembling in his arms.

"I thought . . ." Her voice broke, and she stopped speaking.

He stroked her back, her hair, still feeling a confusing mixture of emotions. He didn't like being manipulated by Coleman. He didn't like Coleman manipulating the woman he loved. But he did like the way she was turning to him. Still, he suspected that could be dangerous for both of them. Coleman was a man who needed to keep control of any situation. How was he going to react to Madison's drawing away from him and turning to another man? Or was he deliberately pushing her away?

"Don't let this get to you," he murmured.

"How can I not?"

"Remember you're your own woman."

"Am I?"

"Yes."

"He's been directing my life for years, and I was so grateful that I never questioned him. He even went behind my back with Gavin."

Ramsay swallowed. "You want to walk away from him?"

He felt her fingers tighten on his shoulders. "You mean this minute? It's tempting, but I want to see this new tomb." She hesitated for a moment, then rushed on. "I'm starting to think I'm just along because he needs *you*."

"He needs your help, too. You're the trained archaeologist."

"And you've got encyclopedic knowledge—and intuition."

He stroked his hand up and down her arm. "We'll find the tomb. Together. And decide if it's worth our time. If not, we'll walk away from Coleman and start a project of our own."

She lifted her head, her eyes questioning his. "Can we?"

"Of course. I've got the money to do it."

"You're as wealthy as he is, aren't you? But you don't flash it around."

"I don't know how much he has. I have enough to be . . . comfortable."

She laughed. "Comfortable. Right. You're as rich as . . . as . . . a medium-sized country, aren't you?"

He didn't deny it, only held her and stroked her, still

unsure of the future. He'd like to just say no to Coleman. But if that new statue was authentic, it seemed that his people had been here, too. And he couldn't give up the chance to find his origins.

"About your going out last night," Madison said.

"Yeah, I was waiting for you to mention that."

"Maybe you can get used to sharing things with me?"

"I've been by myself for a long time. It's hard to break old habits."

"Try."

"Okay," he answered, even when he knew that was still impossible.

They spent the night in Arequipa, but there was little chance for Ramsay and Madison to continue the conversation. Most of their time was taken up with Coleman, checking the equipment and getting more information on the tomb site.

"You've provided guns?" Ramsay asked as they discussed the equipment.

"Yes."

Madison looked at him.

"You think that's necessary?"

"After what happened in Italy, you don't?"

"You have a point."

"I'd like to check them out," he said.

Coleman showed them the Sig Sauers he'd acquired.

Ramsay checked the weapons and ammunition. "You know how to shoot these?" he asked Madison.

"Yes."

He would have taken her to a firing range for some practice, but that wasn't on Coleman's agenda.

Instead, he had Google Earth photos of the area, which he wanted Ramsay to look at and comment on the chances of finding the tomb. The country was dry and arid, except for the margins of the Colca River.

When he and Madison finally made it into bed, she put her mouth close to his ear. "It's like he's determined to keep you busy."

"Uh-huh."

"Why?"

"Don't know. Maybe he's worried about this expedition."

"You think he knows something he's not saying?"

She hesitated. "Maybe."

"That's just wonderful."

"Or he's trying to be friendly," she added quickly.

Ramsay had the feeling Coleman wasn't big on friendship, but he kept the opinion to himself. He saw the utility of getting along with Madison's mentor, at least for the present.

And the truth was, the man had provided the best leads Ramsay had gotten to his origins.

The next morning, they ate breakfast at another well-laden buffet and drank some more of the coca leaf tea.

"Make sure you put on sunscreen and wear the hats I got for you," Coleman told them. "The sun here is fierce."

After smoothing on sunscreen, they left in a Land Rover stuffed with supplies.

Ramsay drove, heading northwest. Madison sat beside him in the passenger seat, and Coleman had a seat in the next row, but there was little conversation.

At first the road surface was good, but it deteriorated as they wound upward, into a dry, dusty landscape. When they reached the crest of the mountain, Coleman informed them that they were at an elevation of sixteen thousand feet.

"Everybody okay?" he asked.

"Fine," Ramsay answered. "Altitude doesn't bother me much."

"I'm feeling a little light-headed," Madison admitted.

"Well, we won't be this high for long," her mentor answered.

Ramsay hadn't been to this part of Peru before, but the road signs were clear. They arrived at Achoma a little after noon. It was a small town with one-story houses made of mud bricks. Some roofs were thatched or made from what looked like bamboo poles. Others were covered with sheet metal held down with bricks or rocks.

The largest building was a Catholic church with an elaborately carved facade, which commanded one side of a dusty square. The streets were hard-packed dirt.

Across from the church was a row of shops and a small café tended by women in colorful native dress: wide-brimmed hats, long skirts, and cotton blouses topped with embroidered vests.

"Stop there," Coleman directed.

They pulled up at the end of the block in front of a shop selling everything from bottles of cold drinks to clothing.

"I'll be right back," Coleman said as he got out. "Wait for me."

"I don't think so," Ramsay answered as he followed the billionaire into the shop. Madison was right behind him.

Coleman gave them an annoyed look, but he didn't order them back to the vehicle, which was lucky, because it was better not to let on to the locals that these visitors were having an argument among themselves.

"I want to speak to Tomaso Laredo," Coleman said in adequate Spanish to the woman sitting on a low chair just inside the door.

"He's not here."

"Tell him Señor Coleman wants to speak to him."

Ramsay went back to the Land Rover, grabbed a bottle of water, and brought it to Madison. "How are you?"

"I've felt better."

"Make sure you stay hydrated." When she'd drunk

some of the water, she handed it back to him, and he took a swig.

Outside, a barefoot, half-grown boy was herding six long-legged woolly animals up the street.

"Llamas?" Madison asked.

"Alpacas. You can tell by the face. The alpaca nose is shorter, more like a sheep."

Five minutes after they'd arrived, a short man with dark leathery skin, wearing jeans, a blue shirt, and a wide-brimmed hat, hurried toward the store.

"Señor Coleman?" he asked Ramsay.

"No. He's inside." The question gave him some information. This guy hadn't actually met Madison's mentor.

Coleman came out, and the four of them gathered in front of the shop.

"I can take you to the area," the man said in Spanish. "I can show you where I found the statue. But that's all."

"Good enough," Coleman said, then turned to Ramsay. "He'd better sit in front with you."

Ramsay hesitated. He didn't like this whole setup much. Coleman had said he had a contact here. He hadn't said it was the man who had found the statue.

"It's a long ride into the desert. Maybe we'd better use the facilities," he said.

"Good idea," Coleman agreed.

When they asked for the *baño*, the shop owner led them to a couple of outhouses around back.

Madison disappeared into one. Ramsay and Coleman headed for the other.

"You trust this guy?" Ramsay asked when they were alone together.

"Yes."

"You haven't met him before."

"So what?"

"I think we should ask him some more questions."

"I'm in charge of this expedition. And I'm ready to go. You should be, too," Coleman said with an edge in his voice.

"Why?" Ramsay asked.

"Because you're descended from the dragon-shifters."

CHAPTER
THIRTY-FIVE

RAMSAY HOPED HIS expression didn't change as he stared at Coleman. "You son of a bitch. If you know that, then you had a bug in our room at the Lima hotel."

The man shrugged. "Right."

"That's an invasion of privacy."

"I have a lot riding on this. I'm not leaving anything to chance."

Ramsay balled his hands into fists. He wanted to punch the guy in the jaw. Barring that, he wanted to turn around and drive back to Arequipa, since Coleman had just proved he was unethical; but where would that leave Madison? They were in a small town in the middle of a Peruvian desert. Would Madison leave with Ramsay or go on with Coleman? He wasn't sure he wanted to find out, but he knew he wanted to find the tomb out in the desert.

Madison came out of the ladies' facility and gave them a long look. "Something wrong?" she asked.

"No," Ramsay bit out. He would tell her about Coleman's eavesdropping, but not while they couldn't do a damn thing about it. At the moment, he was thankful that he hadn't said anything more specific to Madison about his origins or about her relationship with Coleman, but the bastard had listened to them making love.

When they returned to the vehicle, Tomaso was talking to the kid with the herd of alpacas. They stopped speaking abruptly when Ramsay and Coleman appeared.

What was that all about? Ramsay studied Tomaso without looking directly at him. Was the guy hiding something? Planning something?

"So you're the one who found the artifact," Ramsay said in Spanish.

"Si."

"When did you find it?"

"Four months ago."

Coleman jumped into the conversation. "It's getting late. We don't want to be out there after dark."

"Yeah." Still uneasy, Ramsay went to the back of the vehicle, opened the hatch, and found the bag with the weapons Coleman had purchased. After handing one of the Sigs to Madison and one to her mentor, he took the remaining pistol for himself and stuck it in the side pocket of the vehicle, along with extra clips.

"Do I get one?" Tomaso asked.

"No." Ramsay climbed behind the wheel. Tomaso got in beside him. Coleman and Madison were in back.

"That way," the man said, pointing toward the far end of town.

They drove past more mud-block houses, then back onto the two-lane highway, until the man in the passenger seat pointed toward a track into the desert. "That way."

Ramsay turned off onto what could be barely called a road and headed past cactus, century plants, and other vegetation that needed little water.

The land became hillier, with outcroppings of rock. Every so often, Tomaso would give directions, and Ramsay would follow. But as the Land Rover jounced along, he was starting to wonder if they were taking a direct route.

"Do you know where we're going?" he asked.

"Si, señor."

"How far is the next turn?"

"I can't tell you exactly. I'll know it when I see it."

"Just let him do his job," Coleman snapped.

"That way," the man said again, pointing toward a giant pile of rocks.

Ramsay glanced back at Madison, who was sitting rigidly in her seat. Then he looked up at the crest that jutted high above them.

As he studied the promontory, a glint of metal flashed behind a rock. Reacting without even thinking, he slammed his foot on the brake and threw the vehicle into reverse, seconds before the crack of a rifle sounded and a bullet glanced off the fender of the SUV.

The Land Rover screeched to a halt behind a huge boulder. As Ramsay cut the engine, more bullets hit the rocks and the hood of the vehicle.

"Get down," he shouted to the others in the car.

They scrunched down in their seats as bullets slammed through the hood and into the engine. He was pretty sure the vehicle wasn't going anywhere. How far were they from town?

"We've got to get out of here," he said.

He'd seen some cover to the right. "Duck low. On my signal, head for the rocks over there." He gestured. "Take your weapons, but don't fire. I'll keep you covered."

"What about you?" Madison gasped as she ripped off her seat belt.

He reached across the seat, pressing his hand over her shoulder. "I'll be okay. Get ready to run."

A gun battle wasn't his preferred method of fighting, but it was his only choice at the moment. And really, his preferred method wasn't even an option. He couldn't change into a dragon form. And if he did, how would Madison and Coleman react?

He slipped out of the driver's door, using it for a shield, and raised the Sig, firing at whoever was up on the rocks as the three passengers ran to safety.

The attackers had rifles. Ramsay had only the handgun, which didn't have nearly the accuracy at this range. But it was the best he could do.

Moving to the back of the vehicle, he saw Coleman disappear. Tomaso and Madison had already made it to shelter.

Still firing, he ran after them, putting on a burst of speed that no human could have matched.

When he slipped behind the rocks with the other three, Madison clasped him to her.

"Thank God you made it."

She tipped her face toward his, and his heart stopped. "You're hit."

She brought her fingers to her nose, and they came away covered with blood, which she looked at in shock.

"I'm not hit."

"Then what?"

"The altitude," Coleman answered. "It's giving her a nosebleed."

She found a tissue in her pocket and wiped off the blood while Ramsay turned toward their guide.

"What the hell is going on?"

His eyes were wide with fear.

Ramsay shook him. "Explain this ambush to me. Did you set us up?"

The man was shaking as he answered, "No, señor."

"Then why are those guys shooting at us?"

When he clamped his lips together, Ramsay slapped him across the face. "I want some answers."

"They know I got some money. They know I was leading you out onto the desert."

"What? You blabbed all over town?"

He looked stricken.

Ramsay switched his attention to Coleman. "I guess you trusted the wrong guy."

"What are we going to do?" the billionaire asked.

"You have your cell phone?"

Coleman got out his phone and tried to get a connection, but it didn't appear to be working out here in the middle of the Peruvian boondocks.

"Now what?" Madison asked.

"*A fronte praecipitium a tergo lupi,*" Ramsay muttered.

"What?"

"It's Latin," Coleman translated. "He means they've got us between a rock and a hard place. Or literally, a precipice in front and wolves behind."

"Yeah," Ramsay answered.

A volley of shots rang out, echoing off the rocks and sending rock chips into the air, too close for comfort. But there was still a solid barrier between them and the shooters.

"It's at least two guys," Ramsay said.

"Do you think they're coming down?" Madison asked.

He glanced toward the promontory. "That might be their plan, but I think we can convince them it's too dangerous. You have your weapons?"

Madison and Coleman both nodded.

"Sorry we didn't get some target practice yesterday," Ramsay muttered, wishing he'd done a lot of things differently. In truth, he'd known this was a risky expedition, but he'd come here anyway. Now he silently acknowledged that he should have been more cautious.

From long experience, he didn't waste time worrying about what he should have done.

Instead he said, "I'm going to circle around and get behind them, and you're going to fire off a few shots in their direction every so often to make them think I'm still here."

As he spoke, he looked up at the afternoon sun beating down on them, wishing they'd been able to grab water bottles as well as weapons.

With a glance at Coleman, he took off the wide-brimmed hat he was wearing and put it on Madison's head. When it fell over her eyes, he gently tipped it back.

"They'll think it's me, which will give me time to get in back of them."

"I don't much like that plan," Madison murmured.

"Neither do I. But what's the alternative—sitting here and waiting for them to come down?"

Madison firmed her jaw. "Okay. If you put it that way."

"Don't worry if you don't hear from me for a while."

When he pulled her into a tight embrace, she clung to him as though they might not see each other again. Wishing he had a better alternative, he turned and crouched low, moving to the other end of the rock formation. Then with the rocks between him and the shooters, he moved slowly into the desert.

When he was about a hundred yards from the ambush scene, he stopped, dragging in several lungfuls of air. Then he took off, moving with superhuman speed, hoping he was just a blur in the sun. Cactus thorns tore at his pants legs as he ran, but he didn't slow down.

MADISON crouched behind the rocks, feeling as if the world had turned upside down. One minute they'd been on their way to the tomb, and she'd been daydreaming about the prospect of picking up the work that had gotten blown to bits in Italy. In the next moment, men had started shooting at them.

She looked at Dominic, who was sitting on the ground, his back against a rock and his face pasty.

"You had no idea this was going to happen?" she asked, working not to sound accusing.

He glanced at her, his face taut. "Of course not."

"Try your phone again."

"What's the point?"

"Try it!"

He got out his phone and attempted another call, but the result was the same as it had been before.

Turning, she looked for the other man who had been with them and didn't immediately see him.

"Tomaso?"

He didn't answer, and she couldn't step out from behind the rocks to look for him, but when she scanned the ground, she saw a trail of footprints leading away through the dust.

CHAPTER
THIRTY-SIX

WHEN MADISON GASPED, Coleman gave her a questioning look.

"What?"

"Your friend is gone."

"*Gone?* What do you mean, 'gone'?"

"Tomaso took the opportunity to get out of here."

"I guess he's afraid he'll get shot."

She gestured toward the rocks where the attackers had them pinned down. "Or he's working with those guys."

Coleman's expression turned sick.

"What game are you playing?" she asked.

"No game. I just want to find that tomb."

"And you're willing to take any risk to get there."

"I didn't think it was a risk."

There was nothing she could say. Not now. Staying under cover, except for the top of the hat Ramsay had lent her, she fired off a couple of shots in the direction of the hill—then ducked back around the rock as the men returned fire. At least she knew the guys were still up there, still thinking that Ramsay was pinned down and shooting at them. That was something.

TEN minutes later, Ramsay reached the other side of the hill and stopped to catch his breath. He might have superhuman speed, but he wasn't used to this altitude.

From the shelter of a boulder, he studied the back of the outcropping where the shooters had made themselves comfortable. Too bad he couldn't fly up there, because if those guys figured out that he was climbing up in back of them, he'd get a face full of lead.

Could he fly up? *The hell with Madison and Coleman.* They couldn't see him now. They wouldn't know how a dragon had come to swoop down on the attackers.

He stood with his eyes closed, willing it to happen. But minutes ticked by. Perhaps he felt something. Maybe a tingling sensation over his ribs. But the end result was the same as it had been every other time he'd tried since the battle with Vandar.

With a curse, he gave up and began to climb the hill, careful with each hand- and foothold so he wouldn't start a rockslide.

Each time he heard shots echoing off the rocks, he gritted his teeth, but at least he knew Madison was still down there, firing. And the men at the top of the outcropping were maintaining their focus on the group they had pinned down.

Yet he couldn't stop worrying about Madison. She'd agreed to his plan without question. She was one of the bravest women he'd ever met. Would she be brave enough to stay with him when she found out what he was? And what was that, exactly? He wasn't sure anymore.

He was almost to the top of the hill when another exchange of gunfire split the air. Was Madison the only one shooting? Or was Coleman doing his part, too?

Maybe this was Ramsay's best chance. Pulling himself up the last few feet, he peered over a ridge of rock. About three yards ahead, he could see the backs of two hombres dressed in long-sleeved shirts, boots, dusty pants, and wide-brimmed hats. They were both facing the boulders where the passengers from the Land Rover had taken refuge and were both resting their rifle barrels on large rocks that gave them cover.

In one smooth motion, Ramsay vaulted up and dashed forward, knocking the two men off their feet before they could turn around. They went down, the air whooshing out of their lungs. Yanking them up again, he kicked their weapons away.

The dumber one reached toward his belt and pulled out a small revolver.

As the man squeezed off a shot, Ramsay swerved to the side, his own weapon leaping into his hand as he shot the man in the heart.

Seeing the tables were turned and desperate to get away, the other guy scrambled to the edge of the cliff, where a shot from below caught him, and he fell forward beside his partner.

The sudden silence was deafening.

"The other one's dead. Don't shoot," Ramsay called. "Understand?"

"Yes," Coleman answered.

Wondering if the guy was going to take a shot at him anyway, Ramsay crawled to the edge, staying low.

He'd wanted to question these guys, but that was impossible now.

When he looked over the edge, he saw Coleman staring up at him, a gun in his hand.

"You shot him?" he called down.

"Yes. What about the other one?"

"He pulled a gun on me, and he's dead. I could have handled both of them."

"I didn't know that."

"Are you all right?" Ramsay asked.

Madison came out from around the rocks. "Yes."

"Gratia deis."

"You speak Latin when it comes to the crunch?" Coleman asked.

"Yeah. Old habit."

"Can you come down this side?" Coleman asked.

Ramsay inspected the area, spotting a path that descended toward the valley, and started down.

Five minutes later, when he reached the ground, Madison threw herself into his arms, and they clung together.

"I was worried about you," she whispered.

"Same here."

"You and Coleman are okay. What about Tomaso?"

Coleman's features hardened. "He disappeared."

"That's just great. I wanted to get some more information out of him. Just like I wanted to question that guy you shot."

"I couldn't tell that you weren't in trouble."

Although it was a reasonable answer, it didn't satisfy Ramsay. Still, they had more immediate concerns.

"Remember, they put a couple of bullets into the engine. I don't think we're going anywhere tonight. Keep me covered," he said to Coleman and Madison as he walked back to the vehicle and raised the hood. Confirming his assumption, the engine would not turn over.

Madison drew up beside him. "How are we getting out of here?"

"Walking."

"Now?"

He looked up at the sun, which was dipping low in the west. "It will be dark soon. That's a dangerous time to move around the desert. We should wait until tomorrow."

"What about the tomb?" Coleman asked.

"What's more important to you?" Ramsay shot back. "Finding the tomb or getting out of here alive?"

"If you put it that way—you know the answer."

He turned back to Madison. "I'm going to push the car off the road."

"By yourself?"

"Yeah."

He looked around at the immediate vicinity, then angled the Land Rover toward the rocks where they'd taken shelter. Several times he had to stop and turn the wheel to change course, but he finally got the vehicle around the rocks and out of sight of the road.

When he finished, Madison and Coleman were both staring at him.

"You're not even sweating," Coleman marveled.

"Good genes." He gave the billionaire a direct look, but the man said nothing else.

"We're going to spend the night here?" Madison asked, looking around at the barren landscape.

"You and Coleman. In the vehicle."

"What about you?" she asked in a quavery voice.

"I'm going to look for Tomaso."

"You said it was dangerous to tramp around the desert at night."

"It's not as dangerous for me."

"Ramsay . . ."

When her voice trailed off, he reached for her hand and squeezed. "I'm not going to take dangerous chances."

"Just semidangerous chances?"

He laughed. "Something like that."

Walking to the back of the vehicle, he checked the supplies. "We should all drink some water. You can eat some of the power bars we packed." He pulled out the jackets they'd brought. "It gets cold here at night. Get into the Rover and crack the windows. Madison, you stand guard first. Wake up Coleman when you get tired. You take the backseat. He can take the front."

She looked like she wanted to object, but she did as he

asked. Coleman's expression turned sour, but he silently took orders.

Ramsay also pulled on a jacket and a backpack. In it he put water, a flashlight, and a power bar.

The tense expression on Madison's face had him leading her around the edge of the rocks and several yards from the Rover where they could have a little privacy.

As he took her in his arms, he said in a low voice, "I'm sorry I got you into this."

"This isn't your fault."

"I should have asked more questions—and laid down some ground rules, but Coleman was pretty insistent."

"He's good at taking charge and making everyone else fall into line."

Madison must have caught Ramsay's inner debate.

"What?"

"I know you've trusted him for years. I wouldn't trust him now."

"Because he got us into this mess?"

"For a couple of reasons. We don't really know why those men attacked us. And we don't know Coleman's relationship to Tomaso, but we do know that he bugged our hotel room in Lima."

She made a sound of distress. "How do we know that?"

"He told me when we made that washroom stop."

"Oh Lord. He was listening to us . . . making love."

"And talking confidentially. Like when I told you about my background."

Her breath hitched. "Or when I told you about my relationship with him. Unfortunately, I've always trusted him."

"I didn't tell you to make you feel bad. I told you so that you'd be careful around him."

"What's he going to do?"

"I wish I knew."

"Should I stay up all night?"

"Try to stay up until I get back."

He pulled her to him, holding her tight. He'd just given her some damaging information about her best friend. He hadn't given her the same kind of information about himself.

After hugging her tightly, he eased away. "Don't tell him I told you about bugging our room."

"I won't."

"I want to watch you get into the vehicle. Maybe you should . . . uh . . . disappear behind some rocks before you lock yourself in."

"Yes. Right."

They both returned to the vehicle, where she pulled out a packet of tissues.

Ramsay gave Coleman the same instructions, made sure they had ammunition for the Sigs, and waited until they were locked in before looking for footprints leading away from the vehicle. In a few minutes, he'd picked up the trail.

He could see Tomaso had been running. After the man had gotten a hundred or so yards from the hiding place, he'd slowed down, circling back to town.

The trail was several hours old, but Ramsay had no trouble following it, and no trouble seeing where something had startled the man. *An animal? A condor? A human?*

At any rate, Tomaso had started running again, not toward town anymore, but in a different direction.

MADISON shifted in her seat, turning to look out one window and then the other. The guys who had been shooting at them were dead, but they might have friends who'd come looking for them.

She wished Ramsay were here.

"How long before he comes back?" Coleman asked, echoing her thoughts.

"As long as it takes, I guess."

Her mentor turned to look at her. "You think he *will* come back for us."

"Yes."

"You trust him?"

"Of course. Don't you?" she asked, struggling to keep her voice low and even.

Dominic dragged in a breath and let it out. "I haven't trusted him from the beginning. Never completely."

"But you wanted him to help you."

"Before I knew what I was getting into."

"You don't think he had anything to do with that ambush, do you?"

"I hope not."

There was more she could have said. More Dominic could have said, but they were both choosing to keep their thoughts to themselves. She hated that. Once they'd been so close, discussing everything together. Or had that just been an illusion? She knew how he could act when he'd decided someone was his enemy.

She shivered.

"Cold?"

"A little."

"Too bad we can't turn on the heat."

She snuggled down in one of the blankets that they'd gotten out of the back. "Why don't you try and get some sleep."

"You'll wake me later?"

"Of course," she answered automatically, still nervous about Dominic's attitude toward Ramsay.

RAMSAY followed the trail through the sandy soil. From the long scuff marks after each footprint, he could see that Tomaso was running faster, but his energy was flagging. He was acting like something had come after him. But there weren't any tracks beside or behind his.

Was he running from a condor? They were huge birds, some with a ten-foot wingspan, but he hadn't heard of them going after a full-grown man.

Ramsay studied the ground. It was rocky to the right of Tomaso's trail. Could someone have followed him—keeping to the rocks? Or come back and wiped out his trail.

Ramsay couldn't be sure.

He moved cautiously, then stopped short when he came to a small canyon that was hard to see because the land stretched out perfectly flat on the other side.

When he saw sand kicked up at the edge, he knelt to look over. About a hundred feet below him, he spotted something white. It resolved itself into a man's shirt.

"Tomaso?" Ramsay called.

There was no answer and no movement below.

"Tomaso?"

The response was the same. Wishing he had one of the ropes that were packed in the supplies back at the Land Rover, Ramsay tested the raw edge of the drop-off and decided it was stable enough. And there were hand- and footholds he could use.

He slung a leg over the edge, grabbing on to a protruding root and testing to see if it would hold his weight before using it to lower himself half a yard, where he felt for another foothold. He was able to brace his boot against a rock and lower himself again.

When a rock gave way under his foot, he cursed and pressed himself against the canyon wall, digging in his fingernails and searching for a foothold.

Finding it, he waited for a moment to make sure he wasn't going to fall before proceeding downward again.

It was slow work, because he was very conscious that he was out in the middle of nowhere by himself, and if he fell, he was in big trouble.

It felt like hours before he finally reached the bottom.

Tomaso was lying on his stomach a few feet away, with his arms twisted outward and his head at an unnatural angle. When Ramsay knelt and put his hand on the man's neck, he found his skin was cold and his neck was broken. He'd been dead for several hours.

Quickly, Ramsay searched his pockets but found nothing of interest.

"Who are you really?" he muttered.

The dead man didn't answer, and Ramsay felt like he'd been on a wild-goose chase. He'd left Madison and Coleman alone, and they could be in danger.

That thought made his stomach knot. He had to get back as soon as he could.

He looked up, scanning the canyon walls. He'd have an easier climb if he walked about ten feet to his right.

As he hurried toward the new position, a spot high up on the wall glinted in the light of the setting sun, and he stopped short.

CHAPTER
THIRTY-SEVEN

STARING AT THE canyon wall far above him, Ramsay saw a place where something that wasn't rock glinted. There wasn't much of it. Maybe nobody else would have spotted it. But his eyesight was superhuman.

Since he couldn't fly up there to have a look, he began to climb, then stopped when he reached the spot.

It wasn't easy to hang on with one hand and scrape dirt away from the canyon wall with the other, but when he'd cleared an eight-inch patch, he could slide his fingers over what felt like a sheet of metal embedded in the rock.

He reached to brush away more dirt, but stopped when some of the rock below his foot crumbled.

Inspecting his work, he saw that he'd cleared a swatch at least a foot and a half wide, but he was sure the metal plate was bigger.

The native people who had lived in the area had dug holes in the canyon walls to store food and also bury important people. The holes were called *colcas*, which had given Colca Canyon its name.

This could be one of those, except that they weren't sealed with metal doors. When he tapped on the flat surface, it sounded hollow. There was a space behind it, but he couldn't tell how large.

Excitement bubbled inside him. Was this it? Had Tomaso led him to it?

He would have liked to bang at the barrier with a rock, but he was dangling about fifty feet from the floor of the canyon, and gymnastics were not an option. Also, he didn't want to end up damaging this thing because he couldn't judge what he was doing.

He needed better light and the rope they'd packed. Which meant he'd have to go back and tackle the doorway in the morning.

With a sigh, he climbed to the top of the canyon and rested, debating his next move. This could be the tomb Coleman was looking for. Or it could be something else.

He could go back and say he'd found nothing. Maybe that was the best option. He'd have to think about it.

And then what? Come back here by himself. Or with Madison?

Coleman would be keeping track of this place.

It was getting dark. Which created another problem. Both Madison and Coleman were armed. If he came at them through the dark, he might get shot. But if he let them know he was coming, he might lead an attacker to them.

On the way back, he smelled blood and decided that he'd be better off with some nourishment. Silently he crossed to a herd of llamas being tended by a young man. One of the animals had wandered a little way from the others. Standing behind a boulder, he silently called it toward him. After a few moments' hesitation, the animal trotted forward, and he pulled it close, murmuring gentling words with his voice and his mind as he tipped its head up and took some of its blood.

The herder hadn't stirred, and Ramsay figured he was

sleeping. Still, he made a wide circle around him as he headed back to where he'd left the Rover.

Finally, in the darkness, he saw the silhouette of the vehicle's roof and hood.

He waited for a few moments in the darkness, then ducked down and approached silently until he could see inside the windows. Coleman was in front, sitting with his back against the passenger door and his feet stretched out across the seats. Madison was in the next row of seats, facing in the opposite direction. Coleman looked like he could be sleeping. Madison was sitting straight and rigid, her back braced against the door.

When he was almost to the vehicle, he reached out toward her with his mind.

Madison. Don't say anything out loud. Nod if you can you hear me.

She stirred and looked around, seeing nothing, then moved her head up and down. He felt a little buzzing inside his skull and wondered if she was trying to say something to him. If so, the message wasn't getting through.

I'm to the right of the Land Rover. Don't shoot me. Tell Coleman you think you see me.

She answered with a little nod, then said, "Dominic, I think I see Ramsay. Don't shoot him."

The billionaire stirred. "Where?"

"On the right."

Coleman lurched up, his gun in his hand.

"Don't shoot. It's him."

"How do you know?"

"I recognize his silhouette."

Thanks.

Ramsay closed the distance between them and rapped softly on the window. Pulling his face close to the glass, he said aloud, "Don't open the door yet. I want to get in fast to minimize the light. Into the backseat."

Madison clicked the door locks. In seconds, he was inside. When she turned toward him, he pulled her close.

"Are you okay?" she asked.

"Yes. Are you?"

"Yes."

Ignoring Coleman, they clung together, until the billionaire cleared his throat. "Did you find the guy?"

"Yes. I followed his trail through the desert. It looked like something spooked him. He tumbled off the edge of a canyon rim."

"He's dead?"

"Yeah."

Coleman sighed. "Another dead end."

Ramsay hesitated, then said, "Not exactly. I found something interesting in the canyon wall."

"What?" Coleman and Madison both asked.

"A metal plate that's not a natural feature of the area. But it's about fifty feet from the top of the canyon rim. I couldn't get a good look at it without a rope. We'll go there tomorrow."

He could feel excitement vibrating inside the SUV as the others took in the significance of his find.

"Do you think it's the tomb?" Coleman asked.

"I have no way of knowing."

He wanted to take Madison outside where they could talk privately, but that wasn't an option.

So he settled down beside her, holding her close, knowing she wanted to be alone with him.

We can't, he silently told her as he turned his head, sliding his lips against her cheek and her ear, telling her to sleep.

When she finally did, he relaxed. But he stayed awake, waiting for morning.

In the gray light before dawn, Coleman stirred. "You're going back to the tomb?"

"If that's what it is."

"You can find it again?"

"I can track Tomaso—the same as I did yesterday."

The billionaire looked around, then climbed out of the truck. Madison and Ramsay followed.

Coleman flexed his arms and legs and winced. "I don't think I'm up for the trip. I pushed myself pretty hard coming here, and last night was hard on me. I think I'd better let the two of you go out, and I'll wait here for a report."

Madison looked at him with concern. "You're sure?"

"I wouldn't get very far walking. I was going to tell you that last night. When you finish out there, you're going to have to send a car for me."

"You've got your gun," she said. "And water and the power bars."

"Of course."

"I don't like leaving you."

"I'll be fine."

Ramsay gave the old man a considering look. "Make sure you drink plenty of water."

"I will."

He and Madison gathered supplies, including the rope, tools, water, and some power bars. They also put on more sunscreen and grabbed hats.

Ramsay carried most of the equipment, giving Madison the food and water.

"How long do you think we'll be?" Madison asked as they started off along the trail Tomaso had left.

"Hard to say. I would have liked to camp out there. But we can't leave Coleman indefinitely."

"Agreed."

"You really think you found the tomb?" Madison asked as they tramped past a clump of cactus.

"All I know is that I found *something*."

It was still cool, and they made good progress.

"How far are we going?" Madison asked.

"Maybe a half hour."

When they got to the scuff marks, Ramsay stopped and pointed. "This is where he started running—not toward town."

"What do you think happened?"

"Maybe the ghosts of ancient dragons spooked him."

She shivered. "You believe that?"

"There are all sorts of superstitions in this part of the world. From the Incas and before them."

"It's not a dragon."

"Give me a minute." He left her sitting on a rock while he searched the ground to the left. Last night he'd been in too much of a hurry to make a thorough search. Today he spotted a set of tracks coming toward Tomaso's trail.

"Apparently someone else was here yesterday," he told Madison when he came back to her.

"Who?"

"I wish I knew."

She looked around. "I don't see anyone now."

Neither did Ramsay, but he kept alert as they headed for the canyon.

As they approached the drop-off, he slowed down, making sure Madison was aware of the edge and also making sure nobody was hiding down there waiting for them.

She peered over, saw Tomaso's body, and winced.

"He broke his neck when he went over."

"I'm sorry."

"I'd like to know why he was in such a hurry."

He retraced his steps of the night before, stopping above the place where he'd found the metal door and testing the stability of the edge.

"Down there." He pointed. "But you can't see anything from this angle."

"How do we get down?"

"I'll go first. You'll stay here until I can get the door open—if I can. And make sure it's safe."

First he pounded three pitons into the ground two feet

from the edge and attached ropes. Then he strapped on a tool belt and fixed a loose canvas strap around his waist and rappelled down.

When he reached the level of the metal plate, he slid the loose strap down, turning it into a seat so that he could comfortably dangle above the canyon floor.

Looking up, he saw Madison watching him. He wanted to tell her to get back from the edge, but he didn't think it would do much good. So he gritted his teeth and set to work.

First he used a wide scraper to remove dirt from the metal plate, using his legs to move himself from one location to another.

When he was finished, he'd cleaned an area; he called up, "I think I can see the edges. The plate is about forty inches square."

"Okay. Now what?"

"I figure out what's holding it in place."

He saw no hinges. No handle. No lock. Nothing that gave a clue about how to get inside. But when he pressed his hands against the surface, he felt a kind of tingling on his skin, like the tingling when he was trying to change. The sensation grew into a shiver that vibrated through his body.

He had no real knowledge of what he was doing. Yet as he ran his fingers over the surface, he felt something happening. Something he couldn't explain.

The metal seemed to heat, but not to the point of pain. As he moved his hands, the panel began to move with them.

He slid his fingers to the side, and the whole plate shifted, disappearing an inch into the rock on the right side.

As a small opening appeared, he felt a whoosh of stale air rush out.

"What was that?" Madison called down.

"You heard something?"

"Yes."

He closed his eyes, sliding his fingers farther to the

right, taking the panel along with them, his excitement growing as the opening widened. He still didn't understand how he was moving the damn thing, but he was sure it had been designed for someone like him. Someone with mental powers unavailable to humans.

Or was that just a fantasy he'd made up to explain a mechanism he didn't understand?

"What's happening?" Madison called out.

"The plate's opening." Pulling his flashlight from the tool belt, he shined it inside. The beam disappeared into the darkness.

"I'm going in," he called up.

"Don't!"

"It's okay," he answered, even when he had no idea if there was a trap inside.

Using his legs to change his position, he went into the hole feet first. To his relief, they made contact with a floor.

When he stood up, he found that he was at the top of a flight of stairs.

"Talk to me. Are you all right?" Madison called, her voice rising in anxiety.

"Yes, I'm fine," he answered, his voice echoing off the walls.

"What do you see?"

"Not much."

"I'm coming down."

His protective instincts leaped to the fore. "No!"

Of course she ignored him. Moments later, she was lowering herself down the third rope. Standing at the edge of the opening, he reached out and steadied her, pulling her toward the entrance. She pushed herself through, and he guided her to a standing position, then pulled her close.

"Where are we?" she whispered, and he felt her shiver.

"Cold?"

"Yes. And . . . spooked. Somebody went to a lot of trouble to build this place."

"It's not a *colca*."

"What's that?"

"Holes the native people dug in the sides of cliff walls. They sometimes used them for burials." He played the light around a huge, cavernous space. "But this is much larger than anything they created."

"Is it a natural cave?" she asked, pulling out her own light and shining it around the chamber.

"I don't know yet." Taking her hand, he clasped his fingers with hers. "But it could be dangerous."

"How?"

"We don't know who used this place last—or for what. You know damn well there could be booby traps or drop-offs that you can't see in the dark."

"Then I guess we'd better stick together—and be careful."

"I can't persuade you to go back to the top and let me do the exploring?"

"You must be kidding." She turned to Ramsay. "How did you get inside?"

"I slid the panel to the side."

"It could have been there for hundreds of years. Thousands. But I didn't hear it scraping or anything."

He shrugged. "I guess it was well engineered."

He held the flashlight in his right hand, playing it on the stairs, and Madison did the same.

"Want to go down?" he asked.

"You're kidding, of course. You know I want to."

Cautiously they walked down fifteen steps carved into the rock.

"They're all the same size," Madison murmured, and he understood the significance of the observation.

He nodded. Ancient steps were usually of uneven thicknesses and widths.

"Which shows advanced building skills," she added.

They came down to a wide floor, which also seemed to be carved out of the native rock. The ceiling was high above them now, but the room appeared to be about twelve feet wide.

There were no side passages as there had been in the smugglers' caves back in Italy, a lifetime ago. They kept walking forward to another flight of steps.

"No carvings. No statues. Just bare walls—and the steps," Madison murmured.

"Yeah."

At the top of the second flight, Ramsay clasped Madison's hand, and they descended together.

At the bottom was a much larger cavern. And when Madison shined her light on the walls, she gasped. There were pictures all over them. Pictures like the ones at the tomb site in Italy. Only these were in much better condition.

Disregarding Ramsay's warning, she ran toward the left wall, shining her light on the scenes.

Ramsay followed more slowly, his heart pounding as he marveled at what he saw. Like dreams and visions he'd had over the years. He had always wondered if he'd made them up. Here was proof that they had been real. Maybe he had been with these people, or ones like them, before his conscious memories.

These paintings were so much more vivid than the ones he had seen in the tomb in Italy.

They were rendered by an artist of considerable skill, one who knew perspective and proportion. And who was adept at the use of color. They showed people at tables eating meals of fruit, vegetables, and meat, people in houses built of what looked like the local mud bricks but houses with a totally different style. They were two stories, with tile roofs and large windows filled with glass. Around them were gardens, planted with what he recognized as local vegetation and also flowers and bushes that must have been imported from other places.

The snow-covered mountains were in the background, without the terraces they had seen as they'd traveled here.

Among the people were dragons, and it looked like the two species were mingling freely. Or perhaps they were all shifters, some in dragon and some in human form. There was no way to know from a quick inspection. If he had the time, perhaps he could pick up clues.

In the other tomb, there had been the suggestion of a rupture between dragon factions. He wasn't seeing anything like that here. Did it mean there hadn't been any infighting? Or that the artist had chosen to depict only the pleasant aspects of life?

Madison had moved farther into the room. When she came to one section of the mural, she gasped. He hurried over to find out what she was reacting to and saw a dragon holding a woman in an embrace. Her head was thrown back while he bent his mouth to her neck.

"What's he doing?" she asked.

"Drinking her blood, I imagine," he answered, keeping his voice mild. The dragon wasn't standing. He was lying down, and as Ramsay studied him more closely, he saw a gash on his side where scales had been torn off.

Madison made a low sound, obviously distressed by the explanation. "You mean he's a vampire?" she breathed.

He struggled to make what she was seeing acceptable to a twenty-first-century woman. "He's not a vampire in the sense that you're thinking. Not an evil creature of the night, like Dracula or some monster from a horror movie. He's not going to kill her. He's only going to take some blood." And maybe something else as well, he thought as he looked more closely at the couple, studying the expression on their faces. They looked like they were connecting on a deep, spiritual level that sent a jolt through him. He'd taken blood from sexual partners over the years. He'd always clouded his partners' minds, keeping the blood-drinking to himself. But maybe it had meaning he'd never realized and never expected.

"Where do you get all that?" Madison asked, and he brought his attention back to her.

"Because of the way they're depicted. It's tender, not violent. The woman's not struggling. She's not pushing him away. She's hugging him to herself. And the expression on her face is sweet. I think they're lovers," he added, working to justify the picture, then pointed to the gash on the dragon's side. "He's been hurt. Maybe she's healing him."

"Like *that*."

He shrugged.

Madison looked more closely. "You're just guessing!"

"It makes sense," he clipped out, wishing they hadn't gotten into this conversation.

She turned to look at him. "Are you remembering something from your dreams?"

"Not precisely. I mean not the dragon and the woman. But the kind of scene we're seeing here."

"Coming here means something to you that it can't mean to me."

"It means a lot to you, too. It proves you were on the right track in Italy."

He walked farther into the huge room, playing his light over the walls, searching for another scene that they could talk about.

"Look at this. They're gardening. I can see some of the same plants they raise today. Corn. Peppers."

She came closer. "And some I don't recognize." She pointed to low-growing plants.

He laughed. "Potatoes. I think there are something like three thousand kinds of potatoes in Peru."

"How do you know what vegetable it is? They grow underground."

"I've visited farms. I recognize the foliage and the shape of the plants." He cleared his throat. "Maybe it will be easier to find the tomb in here than at the site in Italy," he said, to take the focus of the conversation off the two of them.

Madison followed him, their footsteps echoing around the large chamber.

"The room's empty. No furniture. No statues," Madison pointed out.

"Yeah. Which brings up the point that we still don't know where the statue came from."

At the end of the room was another metal doorway, something like the one that had blocked the entrance to the underground complex, only this one was much larger. It seemed to be at least nine feet tall and six feet wide. Enough space to accommodate a dragon with his wings folded, Ramsay thought, his heart pounding inside his chest. Still he struggled to keep his excitement in check.

The exterior door had been set into the rock with no special ornamentation. Here it was edged with elaborately carved stone blocks.

"This must lead to the inner room," he murmured as he ran his fingers over the carving of a dragon. There were symbols woven into the pattern, symbols he was sure meant something, but he had no idea what. "Or it's a booby trap designed to finish off anyone who makes it in here."

"Why a trap?"

He shrugged. "That's as good a guess as any."

Madison pressed her fingers against the door, then swept her hand back and forth. "Can you open it?"

"There's no obvious mechanism. I mean, no doorknob. No handle, no hinges."

"You got this far. How did you open the outer door?"

He wasn't going to tell her that he'd used some mental ability that he couldn't explain.

"I slid it to the side. But I'm not going to rush to try it again. We don't know what's in there."

"Are you going to tell Dominic what we found?" she asked, the question hanging in the chilly air of the tomb.

"You think we shouldn't?" he asked, surprised that she'd even posed the question.

"I'd like your opinion."

They were so absorbed in the conversation that they were both startled when light flooded behind them and a voice said, "Put down your guns and your flashlights. Hands in the air. Turn around slowly."

CHAPTER
THIRTY-EIGHT

MADISON LOOKED AT Ramsay, her gaze full of fear and horror. He wanted to say something reassuring, but under the circumstances, he wasn't sure what that would be.

"Put down your lights and your guns," the harsh voice said again. "Turn around. Hands in the air, if you don't want to get shot in the back."

They turned to find themselves facing a man with a gun. It was Dominic Coleman, standing at the top of the stairs leading down into the chamber with the murals.

"This is a very interesting place," he murmured. "I'll have to make a thorough inspection . . . in a while."

"Dominic?" Madison asked. "What . . . what are you doing here?"

"There's something . . . special about Ramsay. I had faith that he would find the tomb and get into it. So I gave him some time, then followed you here."

Ramsay stood very still, watching Madison's mentor, feeling like a fool. He'd taken the billionaire at his word—and he'd gotten screwed. *Again.*

"What . . . what . . . are you doing?" she sputtered as she tried to come to grips with the situation. "You said you weren't up to coming with us. That was a lie?"

He lifted one shoulder. "A necessary tactic, I'm afraid. I know you've shifted your loyalty to Gallagher. I couldn't trust him, and then I decided that I couldn't trust you, either."

She tried to reach toward him.

"Hands up," he snapped.

"Why are you doing this? We've worked together for years. We shared so much."

"And the situation's changed dramatically in the past few days, don't you think?" he pointed out.

Madison didn't answer.

Ramsay kept his gaze on the billionaire. "What are you planning?"

"To get rid of you. Then get back to the Land Rover and call for help."

Madison stared at him. "But you said your cell phone didn't work."

He shrugged. "I didn't want you to know I could communicate with the outside world. I wanted you to think we were all in this together."

"Weren't we?"

"We used to be," he answered. "Then you changed. That night in Lima you questioned your whole relationship with me."

Madison didn't bother to deny it. Instead, she asked, "And the excuse you always gave was that you were too sick to travel? That was a fake?"

"A convenience."

Madison made a low sound. "I've been a fool to go along with you all these years."

"You've been very helpful to me. You listened to me. Followed my suggestions. You're an excellent student. Excellent at fieldwork. Nobody better. Well, except maybe Ramsay Gallagher. It seems he's a natural."

Ramsay kept his gaze on the man with the gun, but his mind was scrambling for a way out of this mess. Coleman was at the top of the steps with an automatic weapon. If Ramsay rushed him, the man was far enough away to get off five or six shots at point-blank range. Then Madison was next. But maybe he'd have to risk it if that was his only option.

Still another idea was forming in his mind. An idea that had come to him when he'd been looking at the mural. Silently, he reached out toward Madison.

I need your help. Give me your energy.

He saw her turn her head toward him, just for a second. Her features were rigid, and he understood her frustration. Even as he'd made the request, he hadn't been sure what he was asking. He only knew that there was something she could give him, if he could figure out how. Like the dragon and the woman in the picture.

And then what?

The consequences might be personally devastating, but they would both have to face that later. Right now, he had to deal with Coleman.

Give me your energy, he said again to Madison, still hoping that the two of them could figure it out. He was thinking it might have been what the dragon's lover was doing in the mural—in addition to giving him her blood. Or maybe it was what Ramsay *wanted* to be true.

He felt *something*. Some kind of tremor in the air, vibrating between himself and Madison. But not enough. Not nearly enough. And he knew he needed more time.

Ask him questions. Keep him occupied, he silently requested. *But don't stop sending me . . . energy*. Was that the right word? He didn't even know.

Madison glanced at him, then back at the man who had been the most important person in her life for years. In a voice she couldn't quite hold steady, she asked, "What was the ambush all about?"

"I wanted an emergency situation—where Tomaso would run away and Ramsay would track him to the canyon where the tomb should be. I hired the men who ambushed us."

"The figure wasn't in the tomb," Madison said. "It was sealed."

"It was in a *colca*. In *this* canyon. I was sure the tomb must be nearby."

"You couldn't even be sure there *was* a tomb."

He shrugged. "It was a good bet when that statue turned up. While you were busy, I told Tomaso to run back to town and get help. I had the third man at the ambush make sure Tomaso veered off toward the canyon. The guy pushed him over, so Ramsay would find him there and start poking around."

Outrage laced her voice. "Is there nothing you won't do?"

His tone turned smug. "You mean like stage an attack on the site in Italy—so you'd back off on the conference presentation?"

"That was *you*?" she gasped.

"I thought that was a stroke of genius. I needed you to hold off on the presentation. It was too soon to start speculations flying."

"You can't manipulate public opinion."

Coleman laughed. "Of course I can. I understand that the public has to be brought along. Without interference from Ramsay Gallagher. He doesn't share my vision."

"But you were willing to use him."

"Of course. I'm going to change the course of history. Men fight among themselves, but when they have a common goal, they'll work together and prove that we're destined for greatness. With the other species of the universe. Isn't that worth any sacrifice?"

He heard Madison's voice rise. "Did you kill my parents?"

Coleman paused. "I'm not going to answer that."

"You did! Oh Lord, and I cried my heart out to you. Do you have no shame?"

"I have a higher purpose."

"You fiend."

The exchange fueled Ramsay's outrage as he fought to do something that he hadn't done since his battle with Vandar.

His mind jolted back to what he'd seen in the mural between the dragon and the woman.

Give me your love, he said to Madison. *That's the most precious thing you can give me. Love.*

He saw her swallow, saw her face take on an expression that he'd seen before—when they'd been as close as a man and a woman could get.

Even as she poured her emotional focus onto him, she was speaking to Coleman.

"You used me."

"And I can't trust you anymore."

Ramsay heard the conversation somewhere under the buzzing in his ears. In his brain. He could feel something happening, something that he hadn't experienced since the terrible fight with Vandar. Feel his being moving on pathways through his body that he hadn't been able to travel in a long time.

He reached toward Madison with his mind, asking for everything she could give him, even as he felt his awareness of her slipping away. All at once, he could only focus on himself, on the sensations threatening to overwhelm him.

His body turned hot. Then cold as energy flowed through every cell. In his mind, he knew that he was getting closer. But not close enough.

Still, he willed himself to keep going, understanding the goal and what it would mean if he could finally do it. Pain shot through him, and he knew it was because he had not done this thing in months.

But he wouldn't let pain or anything else stop him.

He didn't know he had let loose a great cry of triumph. He didn't know he had burst the seams of his shirt and kicked off his shoes and pants as his body grew larger and rough scales formed along his flesh. He didn't know he had leaped off the floor and flown at Coleman, screeching his anger, while the man made a garbled sound, then turned and ran, trying to escape the angry monster pursuing him like a hound out of hell.

Behind them Madison screamed, and he knew she was watching this scene in horror.

Coleman ran headlong across the first chamber, desperation driving him straight toward the doorway where he'd entered the tomb.

"No," he gasped as he fled from the nightmare monster that snapped its jaws together and flapped its scaly wings behind him.

Without stopping, he hurtled through the opening, his scream echoing through the chamber as he plunged to the canyon floor. *Like Tomaso*, Ramsay thought.

He couldn't get through the opening, not in his present form. And that wasn't what he intended, anyway. He had accomplished his purpose. He had rid them of Coleman. Now he must go back. But not like this.

He stayed near the doorway, reversing the process that had transformed him into the dragon that was his other self.

This time it was easier. Seconds later, he was back in his human form. A naked man standing on the tomb of his ancestors. Or was it a tomb?

Turning, he walked back to the steps, his gaze never leaving Madison as she stood looking up at him.

CHAPTER
THIRTY-NINE

RAMSAY SAW THE tension in Madison's features, saw her clenched fists, but her face was determined, and she stood her ground.

"Coleman went through the doorway and over the edge," he said in a flat voice. "Down into the canyon head-first. He won't be coming after us again."

"I guess I'm no judge of character." Her gaze fixed on Ramsay. "Am I?"

"He worked hard to make you trust him."

"So did you."

The words and the way she spoke them were like a punch in the gut. Still, Ramsay came slowly down the steps, his heart pounding as he watched the play of emotions skittering across Madison's features. He half expected her to take a step back, or try to run around him to get away, but she stayed where she was with her feet firmly planted on the chamber's floor.

"You . . . should have told me you could do that."

"I couldn't."

She made a rough sound. "You just did."

"I mean, I haven't been able to do it since I was injured in a fight and almost died."

"That's where you got the scars?"

"Yes."

"A fight with that guy you kept talking about when you were out of it . . . Vandar?"

"Right." He gave a hollow laugh. "You could call him my evil twin." He reached for the pants lying on the floor. They were torn in several places, but they were wearable. His socks had unraveled. But he shoved his feet into his shoes.

The shirt, however, was shredded.

"You told me you were descended from them," Madison whispered, and he knew she was still trying to come to grips with what she'd seen. "You *are* them."

"It wasn't a lie."

Her tone turned angry. "A lie of omission. You *are* them," she repeated.

"Yeah. First I couldn't tell you because I needed to hide my identity. Nothing unusual about that. Then it was because I fell in love with you." He swallowed. "I was afraid you'd run screaming from me."

"In love!"

"You don't believe it?"

She clenched and unclenched her fists. "Maybe I do."

"That's something."

"I'm trying to figure out how I feel. Are there more . . . people like you?"

"Not as far as I know."

"You said Vandar was your evil twin."

"That's a long story."

"You're going to tell it." It wasn't a question. It was a statement.

"I will. But we should get out of here."

Her features hardened. "Not until you tell me the truth. About a lot of things."

"You think it's smart to hang around here? We don't have our gear. We need to get back to the Land Rover before somebody starts messing with it."

"What if someone attacks us on the way back? Like the guy who chased Tomaso over the canyon edge."

He laughed mirthlessly. "They'll get a very nasty surprise."

He led her back to the doorway. "I'll go up first, so I can pull you."

"You're not going to leave me here?"

"Of course not!"

He made it to the top, going hand over hand up the rope and was pleased to find he wasn't breathing hard. "Get into the sling," he called down.

When Madison had transferred herself to the canvas strap, he hauled her up.

As they stood together at the top, she looked down at Coleman's body.

"What are you going to do about him?"

"We should decide that together."

"You have a suggestion?" she asked in a tight voice.

"Are we agreed that we don't want anyone finding the tomb?"

"Yes."

"Then we have to move the bodies."

"Drag them somewhere?"

He kept his gaze fixed on her. "Fly them somewhere."

She sucked in a breath. "As in . . . the dragon flies them?"

"Yeah."

"And what do we say about Coleman—when they ask us where he is?"

He shrugged. "We don't know. We were ambushed. We fled for our lives into the desert. We haven't seen him since. He could have been kidnapped for all we know. Maybe somebody thinks his relatives will pay to get him back."

"I'm turning into quite a liar. First that performance with Mancuso. Now this."

"I hope you're turning into a pragmatist. Like I said back in Italy, when someone tries to kill you, that gives you the freedom to screw with the facts."

"Spader and his men were one thing. This is about Dominic."

"Stop thinking about him like your kindly old benefactor. He was a master manipulator. He took me in, and few people have done that. Or maybe it was because I was so eager to let him do it when I thought he was helping me discover my heritage."

When she nodded, he went on, "He killed your parents, and he was ready to kill both of us. You think he's worth our making ourselves suspects? In Italy we didn't have a choice. Here, I believe we do."

After thinking that over, she said, "You've got more experience with covering up crimes than I do."

"Uh-huh."

"Then I'll take your advice."

"I want your agreement," he answered.

"Why?"

"Because I don't want to force you into anything."

She gave him a hard look. "Okay."

He emptied his pack, transferring his wallet and his passport to Madison's knapsack before stepping several yards away and turning his back, then taking off his clothes again.

Without any hesitation or uncertainty, he changed, marveling that it wasn't a problem anymore. He could simply do it.

When he looked back at Madison, she was staring at him with an objectivity that he found reassuring.

He nodded to her, then scooped up the knapsack and took off, circling the area, scanning to make sure no one else was nearby. Satisfied, he swooped down into the canyon where he used his talons to shove Coleman's gun into the knapsack. He picked up the carry bag and Coleman in his right front talons. Next he scooped up Tomaso, easily carrying both of them as he climbed into the sky, making for the deep part of Colca Canyon.

When he reached the canyon, he swooped low, dropping the bodies. Then he flew back to Madison, changed again, and pulled on his pants.

"They're gone," he said.

MADISON stared at Ramsay, struggling to rearrange her perception of him. It was still sinking in that he was more than human. He'd said he loved her, but did that mean the same thing to him that it did to her?

"We'd better start for town," he said.

"We'd better get our stories straight. Like we did with Mancuso."

"We can talk on the way back. But first I want to seal the entrance to the tomb again."

Focusing on the practical, she asked, "Could someone else open it?"

"I don't think so," he answered. "Or, not without blasting it off."

"I guess *you* could open it because . . ." She wasn't able to finish the sentence.

"Yeah. I think it had something to do with the way my mind works."

"And you could open the inner door the same way?"

He gave the question some consideration. "Maybe. But that could be a mistake."

"Why?"

"A feeling I have."

She shivered. "Like the curse on King Tut's tomb?"

"Maybe worse."

He stood with his hands at his sides. He'd been careful not to touch her since before Coleman had arrived in the tomb. Now he reached for her, pulling her close.

For a moment she stood rigid. Then she closed her eyes and relaxed against his broad chest, allowing herself to absorb some of his strength. In his arms, it felt like this was the man she had come to know, but he was so much more than that. Too much more?

"*Gratia deis*," he murmured.

Honesty had her answering, "I'm still deciding what I should do." *Stay with him? Run?* Well, not until they were out of the desert, anyway.

"Yeah."

"I think you still haven't told me everything," she whispered.

"I will—when I know we're safe."

Would he really? And would she recognize the truth when she heard it?

He held her for a moment longer, then eased away and went back to the cliff side where he climbed into the sling and lowered himself again.

She watched him dangling over the canyon floor as he closed the door, thinking that if he started to fall, he could fly to safety. When the door was closed, he hoisted himself back up. "Let's get out of here."

"Then what?"

"Another decision point."

As they started back through the afternoon heat, he said, "We'd better talk about Coleman. Is there anyone who's going to miss him?"

She winced. "He kept to himself. Now that I think about it, I don't remember meeting any other guests at his estate. But I'm sure there are people who will wonder what happened to him. Like his servants."

"And if they ask we tell them about the attack."

She answered with a tight nod.

"Is there anything in the car that could be linked to you?"

She thought for a moment. "The clothing's new. But my fingerprints are all over the interior."

"Yeah."

They continued to retrace their steps. When the vehicle appeared around a bend, Madison shuddered as she looked at the bullet holes in the hood.

"Stay here," Ramsay advised. "I'll be back."

She wanted to object, hating to take orders from another dominant male, but she was sure he knew a lot more about covering up criminal activity than she did. He'd already demonstrated that in Italy. How many crimes had he hidden during his lifetime?

His lifetime? My God, how old was he?

She watched him open the back of the Land Rover, get a button-down shirt, cargo pants, and socks out of the luggage Coleman had bought. After changing his clothes, he pulled out a T-shirt and used it to wipe the interior of the vehicle.

"We should take our luggage," he said as he grabbed the two duffel bags Coleman had bought for them.

Twenty minutes later they were on their way to town again, with Ramsay carrying both bags.

"Give me one of those," she murmured.

"That's okay. I can do it."

She watched how easily he managed the load, but then, she'd always known he was strong. And fast. Like when he'd been dodging bullets.

She couldn't handle thinking too much about his abilities, so she asked, "What happens when we get to town?"

"We get the hell back to civilization."

He led her across country, skirting the road they'd taken into the desert, taking a shorter route. Even when she tried to keep her mind in neutral, she couldn't help thinking about the man walking next to her. When he caught her sliding him a sidewise glance, he asked, "What?"

"In the picture, the dragon was drinking the woman's blood," she said, hearing the strained tone of her own voice.

"Uh-huh."

"You pretended you were guessing, but you really did know about that."

He nodded.

Before she could stop herself, she asked the question that had been circling in her mind. "Do you drink blood?"

At least he had the grace to look uncomfortable. "Yeah. I can eat food, too, and get some nourishment from it. But blood is better for me." He laughed. "Think of me as a Masai warrior."

"That's why you go out at night!"

"The Masai have their herds of cows. I've got a herd of deer at my home in Colorado. In Lima the other night, I followed someone out of the casino."

"But you didn't kill him," she said, hoping it was true.

"Like I told you about the dragon with the woman, I'm not Dracula."

"But you *could* kill, if you wanted to," she insisted.

He answered with a tight nod. "I'll tell you everything you want to know. But not until we're safe. Okay?"

"You think we can just . . . disappear?"

"Yeah."

She asked another one of the questions she'd been tossing around in her mind. "Dominic said there was a third man who chased Tomaso to the canyon. I guess the whole ambush was a setup. And those guys wouldn't have killed us. But Dominic killed one of them, so he couldn't talk to you."

"Yeah."

"Dominic wasn't the man I thought he was."

He cupped his hand over her shoulder. "Don't beat yourself up. None of it is your fault."

"I'm still feeling like a . . . dupe."

"He was very careful. Very thorough. And cunning. Remember, he fooled me, too."

"For a couple of weeks, not ten years."

"Because first he made you vulnerable, and then he made you trust him."

She nodded, then asked, "What if someone attacks us in town?"

He kept walking, but his tone changed. "I'm betting they won't. They probably already know the outcome of the shoot-out at the Land Rover. When they see that we're the ones coming back, they'll think twice about starting anything. But if they do, they're going to have to deal with me."

She gave him a considering look. "Yes, that would be a mistake. I guess an ancient legend could come back to life."

"Uh-huh."

Although Ramsay covered the distance easily, Madison's legs ached by the time they walked into town in the late afternoon. Ramsay led her to the commercial strip along the square and settled her in the outdoor café while he went to arrange for transportation.

As she sat at the scarred wooden table, people kept glancing at her. She knew they wanted to ask questions, but nobody approached her besides the café owner, who brought her a bottle of Inca Cola and some fried meat and potatoes. As soon as the meal came, she realized how hungry she was.

With his excellent Spanish, Ramsay arranged for a man in town to drive them back to Arequipa. Apparently the guy who'd chased Tomaso into the canyon was lying low. Or maybe he'd even run away.

She and Ramsay went straight to the airport, where he booked them on the next flight to Lima, which was leaving in a couple of hours.

As she sat in the airport lounge, she kept expecting cops to come swooping down on them, but nobody paid them any attention.

Still, it was a relief to get onto the plane and get out of the area.

ON the flight to Lima, Ramsay was grateful for the lack of privacy. He'd regained his ability to change. He should be feeling wonderful. Instead his stomach was in knots as he thought about the coming conversation with Madison.

The plane landed on time. As soon as they collected their duffel bags, they headed for ground transportation.

When he'd settled them into a cab and given directions to a different hotel, Madison gave him a considering look.

"You're efficient. But then you were efficient back in Las Vegas."

"Is that a criticism?"

"Not of you."

"What's that supposed to mean?"

"I let a strong man make decisions for me for too many years."

"Don't compare me to Coleman."

"I'm not. I'm thinking about myself."

The clarification didn't exactly help.

But the conversation stopped when they pulled up at the Hacienda Grande Hotel, where he'd gotten them a small suite.

When they were finally alone, Madison sat down heavily on the sofa in the living room.

"What makes you think the cops won't come after us?" she asked.

"Nobody in Achoma knows who we are. And there's nothing out in the desert to link the car to us."

"Okay."

"The only name they had was Coleman's. It would take some doing to figure out who the man and woman with him were."

"That's good for us." She cleared her throat. "I thought a lot about the tomb on the way back here."

"What about it?"

"It's a significant find. If I write it up, it will make my career."

"I'm hoping you won't," he answered, fighting the tight feeling in his chest.

"Are you going to kill me to stop me?"

He clenched his hands on the chair arms. "Of course not!"

"Then give me some reasons why I shouldn't break through that inner door."

"Okay," he said, struggling to keep his voice even. "I guess we have to start with me."

He watched her knit her fingers together in her lap.

"I told you I don't remember my parents and that I was found wandering as a small boy—in Italy, near where you were excavating the first tomb. That's why I was so excited about your find."

She gave a small nod.

"I didn't know that I could change my shape. Not until I was a teenager. The old couple who found me treated me like a son. But then there were years of drought and famine. They ended up selling me to a man who was working me to death."

"Selling you?"

"Yeah. There are still places in the world where kids are sold as slaves. Most of the kids live miserable lives. I changed things by killing my master. I don't mean I attacked him. One day, the hatred I had for him bubbled over, and he fell down dead."

She cringed. "You can do that?"

"No. I think it had to do with years of abuse." He kept

his gaze fixed on hers. "Here's the hard part. That was about two thousand years ago."

He watched her gasp for breath. "You're saying you're over two thousand years old?"

"Yes. And like you said back at the tomb, I'm not just descended from those dragon-shifters. I *am* one of them."

"If they're all dead, why are you still here?"

"I must have gotten lost. Or there was a war between factions and somehow I got caught in the middle of it. Or maybe they cast me out because I was defective or something. I've been on my own, trying to figure out who I am for a long time."

She was quiet for several moments before whispering, "You're a being of immense power who has lived virtually forever. You must have been laughing at me the whole time we were making love."

"Do you really think that?" he asked.

"I don't know what to think."

"In the beginning I was using you—to find out something about my own past." He swallowed. "Along the way, I fell in love with you. I couldn't help myself. I didn't want to lose you, and I was pretty sure how you'd react to hearing the truth about me. Like you're reacting now."

She took her bottom lip between her teeth.

"Think about what it's like to live for two thousand years. You have two choices. You can cut yourself off from people, or you can reach out to them. But you'll lose them. Every time. And if you try to stay in one place, people will notice that you're not aging normally."

She wrenched her gaze away from him and looked down. "I'm not sure I can deal with that."

"I know. Few women can."

"But some?"

"I've been lucky to find a few."

He got up and paced to the window, then turned to face

her. "There's more you need to understand. I met a family named the Marshalls about six months ago. They have . . . paranormal powers. When they told me that the earth was going to be invaded, I believed what they were saying. The invader was a powerful dragon-shifter, Vandar."

"Him?"

"Yes. He came from another time continuum."

"What is that?"

"Another timeline. Let me give you the condensed version of the differences. Apparently, there's a universe running parallel to this one. It was a lot like our world until 1893, the year of the Chicago World's Fair. In that universe, a man came to the fair and claimed he could give people paranormal powers. It was true. He did it—but it destroyed civilization because the people with powers and the ones who didn't have them fought with each other. Life in that world is a lot more primitive than it is here. And in the chaos after the World's Fair, a dragon-shifter was caught and tortured by the new psychics who figured out what he was. He escaped from them, but it turned him against humanity. He vowed to enslave and punish as many people as he could. He became totally arrogant and corrupt. He was planning to invade this world and conquer it, too."

She stared at him, and he knew she must be struggling to take it in.

He kept his voice calm when he added, "And until the timelines split in 1893, he and I were the same being. So the evil monster I had to fight and kill to save this world was myself. Or another version of myself."

When she sucked in a sharp breath, he continued, "I could have ended up like him. But life treated me differently."

Before she could speak, he went on. "Something else you need to consider. From what I saw in that tomb, I think it might not be a place where dead dragon-shifters are buried. I think they could be alive in there. Sleeping or in suspended animation. So if you break into that inner room, you may be unleashing monsters on the world. In the tomb in Italy, you couldn't see the pictures clearly because they were faded. But I could see them better. Some of them depicted a fight. Like in our vision quest. Maybe what happened is that the losers ended up dead in the tomb in Italy, and the winners are down here, waiting to come back to conquer the world when the time is right."

He took a breath and kept talking. "I don't know any of that for sure, but I don't want to take a chance on unleashing the hounds of hell on humanity." He sighed. "Maybe Spader had the right idea all along. No good can come of aliens and humans mixing. He was just being too aggressive when he tried to deny it had ever happened."

He had run out of theories and explanations.

"I know I gave you a lot to consider," he said. "And I understand why you wouldn't want to stay with me. Tomorrow, we'll fly back to the States, and you can go back to your career. I'm sure there will be other projects you'll be tempted to pick up. I can finance anything you want to go after. Just let me know. But I'd strongly advise against making the Colca Canyon site public."

He turned and left the sitting room, quietly closing the door behind him. The explanations had wrung him out. His whole body ached, the way it had after the battle with Vandar. Crossing to the bathroom, he pulled off his clothes and stepped into the shower, where he stood for a long time, washing off the desert grime.

After drying off, he changed into clean underwear, slacks, and shirt.

Physically, he felt better. But he couldn't pretend he was handling this. And as soon as he lay down, his mind was filled with gut-wrenching thoughts of the woman in the other room.

He'd given her a lot to chew on. *Too much, maybe.* But he'd wanted her to make the right decision about the tomb. He was sure he knew her character. She wouldn't put her career before the good of humanity. At least he didn't think so.

He strained his ears, trying to hear her through the door. When she turned on the shower, he figured she was washing off the desert.

Maybe washing him off, too. He longed to reach out to her. To make a mental connection, but he sensed that was exactly the wrong thing to do. If she felt him probing her mind, she'd be angry. And she'd have a right to be.

Despair washed over him, drenching his soul the way the shower had drenched his body.

After years of loneliness, and years of caution, he'd fallen in love with her. And told her the truth about himself. He'd revealed more than he had to any other human being, because there was more to tell after he'd learned about Vandar and fought him to the death.

He pressed his hands flat against the mattress, struggling to steady himself. He ached to hold on to Madison, but that wasn't going to happen.

He'd lost her. But he'd lost so much more at the same time. For years he'd had a goal—searching for his origins. Now he might have found them, but he wasn't free to act. The one thing he knew was that he wasn't going to rush headlong into the inner part of the tomb.

Another thought slithered into his mind, and he went very still. He'd talked to Madison about the other universe that the Marshalls had discovered. What if he went there? The tomb in Italy would presumably be intact in that other timeline. If he went through one of the portals between the worlds, maybe he could fly across the ocean and start investigating. Which might prove to be as dangerous to humanity as the tomb here. Like he'd said to Madison, Spader might have had the right idea.

He clenched his fists, knowing that fleeing into the other timeline wasn't the solution to his problems. Vandar had turned into a monster there. Maybe he'd put himself in a similar position.

No, it made more sense to stay in his own world. Now that he knew about the tomb down here, maybe he could figure out what was behind that door by studying the paintings on the wall and the carvings around the door frame. He and Madison had only been in the tomb a short time. There had to be more clues he hadn't seen.

Or maybe he was entirely wrong about that inner room. Maybe it only sheltered the dead.

Automatically, he thought of discussing the possibilities with Madison. Then he reminded himself that she was lost to him forever.

Pain twisted in his gut, and he crossed his arms over his middle as he fought not to let the terrible sense of loss swallow him whole. But his life had fallen into ruin, and there was nothing he could do to fix that.

He'd felt dead after his battle with Vandar, when he'd lost his powers. Madison had made the difference for him. He'd been clawing his way back to his true self, but her love had healed him. She'd changed everything.

He hadn't explained that to her. What was the point? If she were smart, she'd walk away and never look back.

Yet the idea of his never seeing her again made him want to throw back his head and howl in anguish.

Unable to stay on the bed, he pushed himself up, wavering on unsteady legs. Still fighting the pain in his middle, he made it to the window and stood with his arms braced against the sill, staring out at the lights of the city. *It looks better at night*, he thought. The poverty was covered up, and the lights sparkled.

When he heard the bedroom door open, he tensed, but said nothing, listening as Madison crossed the room and came to stand behind him.

"You should get some sleep," he finally managed to say, his voice thick.

"You know damn well I can't sleep."

He nodded. At least she was reacting—not shutting off her emotions.

"You speak Latin in a crisis because you learned it when you were young. When it was the language people spoke."

"Right."

"What did you use to fix my wound?" she suddenly asked.

"My blood. I cut my hand and dripped it on the bullet hole. It has curative powers. But the side effect can be arousal. It did that to both of us because I was already starting to"—he raised one shoulder—"bond with you, I guess you'd call it."

Ignoring the last part, she said, "Aroused us. Like the vision quest. Did you plan that to seduce me?"

"No. I wasn't lying to you. I thought we might get some insights—together. I thought I could control the process. I was wrong."

He felt her shiver. "What?"

"The dragon was drinking the woman's blood. Do you do that—with your partners?"

He wanted to clench his teeth. "You were in the other room thinking about that?"

"Yes. That and a lot more." She swallowed. "Do you do it?"

"Yeah. Sometimes."

"It makes sex better for you?"

He turned to face her. "It can."

The words hung in the air between them.

"Do that with me," she said.

"No."

"Why not? Are you afraid you'll kill me?"

"No. I'm afraid that will make it worse when you walk away from me."

"If you want me to stay with you, you have to . . . share yourself with me. No more lies of omission."

Was that what she really wanted? Or was she trying to prove that she wasn't afraid of him?

They stood facing each other, her gaze challenging and at the same time hopeful, and he knew he had to make this last try, no matter what it cost him. Reaching out, he folded her close, clinging to her. When he felt her tremble in his arms, he couldn't stop himself from thinking this might be his one last time with her.

But he was helpless to deny himself that final pleasure. Eyes closed, he stroked his lips against hers, determined to remember every moment of their lovemaking. It was remarkable how such a light touch could start up a buzzing in his brain. But he had always known this woman's power over him was beyond anything else in his experience.

He savored every nuance of the kiss, starting with that light touch, then gradually deepening the contact. Her tongue met his, and he was intoxicated all over again by the taste of her and the feel of her in his arms.

Still, some part of him was afraid to simply let this encounter take its natural course.

Maybe she understood what he was feeling, because she whispered against his mouth, "I need to know you. I need everything you can give me."

And if he wasn't willing to give it, he was sure that he would lose her.

Eyes closed, he slid his lips over her cheek, to her ear, sucking her lobe into his mouth, feeling her react.

Knitting his fingers with hers, he led her to the bed. As they stood kissing and caressing each other, she began to open the buttons down the front of his shirt, then pushed it off his shoulders, and played with the curly hair on his chest, finding his nipples, drawing small circles around them, making him so hard that his cock strained against the front of his slacks.

And when her hand slid lower and cupped his erection, he made a sound that was part protest and part plea.

When she stepped back, he felt the loss. But she was only giving herself enough space to drag her knit top over her head and unhook her bra. By the time she'd finished, he'd unzipped his pants and kicked them away, along with his shorts. Then he made swift work of her pants.

When she was naked, he pulled her into his arms, holding tight, still unsure if he could do what she'd asked.

She was the one who reached to pull down the covers. When she'd slipped into bed, he followed, gathering her to him.

She stroked her hand over his body, leaving trails of fire everywhere she touched. But when she spoke, he caught his breath.

"What will I feel when you drink my blood? Will it hurt?"

"I can make it so you won't even be aware of it. That's what I always do."

"No. I want to feel what you do. I want you to let me into your mind when you do it."

Could he agree to something so private? Did he have a choice?

"Yes," he answered in a strangled voice.

"Have you ever done that before?"

"Never."

"Oh, Ramsay. Don't be afraid of this."

But he was afraid, afraid that she would walk away from him forever.

Unable to speak, he bent to her breasts, lifting and stroking them, burying his face between them as he tugged at her nipples, then turned to take one distended tip into his mouth as he stroked a hand downward toward her sex. When he reached his goal, his fingers eased her velvet folds apart for his attention.

She was hot and wet for him, as he dipped two fingers into her vagina, then withdrew to the sensitive rim, stroking her there before sliding his finger upward toward her clit, feeling her heated response.

He felt her tension gathering. She had been lying with her eyes closed. They blinked open and focused on his face.

"Show me what it's like for you," she whispered.

He tried to thrust away the cold fear of revealing himself. Silently he reached for her mind as he had done before. Only this time, he strove to make it work the other way. She wanted to know what this was like for him. Could she deal with it?

Don't be afraid of me.

For the first time, he heard her silent voice.

Madison?

I'm right here with you. Let me understand . . . everything.

Understand? Maybe he was the one who had never understood what this could mean. To him.

He parted her legs and plunged inside her, going very still as he looked down into her upturned face. Then he tipped her head back so that he had access to the elegant column of her neck. Before he could stop himself, he sank his feeding teeth into her tender flesh, hearing her gasp as he began to draw from her.

Thrusting aside his fear, he gave himself over to the pleasure, silently urging her to feel it with him.

Oh, Ramsay, that's good. So good. Beyond imagining. You're drinking me into yourself.

He marveled at the give and take between them as he drew her sweet blood into his mouth, letting her essence wash over him, sharing it with her, but only letting it last for a short time. He had never imagined he could be this close to anyone. Lifting his head, he began to move his hips, feeling her frantic response as she drove for completion.

He waited for her to reach the peak. When he felt orgasm grab her, he let himself go, a thundering climax rolling over him as he joined her.

When he shifted to his side, he waited for her to get up and leave the bed. Instead she reached out to stroke his cheek, his lips.

"Thank you for sharing that with me."

"It was . . . all right?"

"Oh yes. More than all right." She swallowed. "I . . . needed you to take a risk . . . to be with me. You thought that might make me walk away from you."

"Yes."

"It made me understand how much you'd lay on the line to keep me. But it was more than that. What I felt. I wouldn't have believed it if I hadn't experienced it."

"Madison." He hugged her to him, embarrassed by the moisture blurring his vision. "I . . . never imagined anything like that either," he said in a choked voice.

"Truly?"

"Oh yes. I've never felt that merging of . . ."

"Your soul," she breathed.

"Yes."

"It was just the beginning for us, I think."

"Oh, Madison. You are incredible."

"You've lived a long time. Had experiences no one else could imagine."

"Yes. But from now on, whatever I do will be with you."

"There's nothing you have to hide from me. Not now."

He hoped that was true, but he only nodded.

"You'll let me come with you when you open the tomb? If you open it."

"It could be dangerous."

"I know. And I want to share that with you, too. I want to share everything we can. For as long as we can. And, I hope I can help. I mean with whatever or whoever's in there."

He nodded, amazed at the conversation, and amazed at the way his life had turned around.

"I love you," she whispered, her voice glowing in the darkness. "And you've helped me find a side of myself I never knew existed."

"You would have."

"I don't think so. Not without you."

"You've put me in touch with my humanity. If that's what you can call it."

"Of course."

"I love you," he said, still marveling at the depth of his feelings as he gathered her close. He was already wondering if there might be secrets in the tomb, secrets that would make a difference for the two of them. What if the dragon-shifters had learned to give their mates long lives? Could he use their techniques? Or perhaps his blood would do it. Perhaps that was the key to keeping her with him for a long, long time. His heart leaped at the thought.

But whatever happened, he knew the darkness had lifted from his life. Darkness he'd never even understood. Madison had changed him for the better, in ways he was only beginning to understand. His love for her had made a difference, along with the strength of the woman herself. And he was determined not to waste a precious moment of the time he had with her.

Keep reading for a special preview of

SHATTERED DESTINY
BY REBECCA YORK

Coming soon from Berkley Sensation!

CHAPTER
ONE

SHE WAS TWENTY miles from safety when disaster struck.

The desert had cooled off, and Sophia Thalia was driving along Blissful Canyon Road, heading back to the spa where she and the other women of her ancient family ran a luxury retreat for the rich and privileged.

Sophia had always lived there, always accepted the responsibilities that had fallen on her from an early age, but tonight's contentious meeting of the Sedona Business Association had worn her out.

As she emerged from a stand of junipers, she leaned forward, watching her headlights cut through the desert darkness.

This was a desolate stretch of road, and at night she was always a little on edge until she reached the turnoff to the resort. This evening it was worse because she couldn't shake the feeling that danger lurked around the next outcropping of red rocks.

When she spotted the small white sign for the Seven Sisters, she sighed with relief. Then, as she slowed for the turn, her premonition slammed into reality. Something came hurtling out of the darkness toward her SUV, and she swerved past the shoulder, almost plowing into a piñon pine before she regained control of the vehicle.

The car rocked back and forth, then settled into a pocket of loose, dusty soil. Her gaze shot to the windshield. Whatever had zoomed toward her had vanished.

Had it been a bat that changed course at the last minute? Or had she managed to dodge whatever it was?

When she tried to drive back onto the road, the wheels spun, digging the vehicle farther into the unstable surface.

"Damn," she muttered as she cut the engine. A tow truck could pull her out. But she'd have to wait here for hours.

She made a low sound of disgust. She'd had a trying week at work, coping with two big problems. The new massage therapy and meditation rooms she'd been pushing for were going to cost a lot more than the original bid. She'd been trying to get some of her sisters to agree that the extra expense was worth it, but so far her point of view was losing.

Then the supplier of the Indian dream catchers and hand-woven rugs they sold in the gift shop had gone bankrupt, just when they were running low on stock. Which meant she was going to have to come up with another alternative—quickly.

Fumbling in her purse, she found her cell phone, but when she tried to get a signal, nothing happened. The phone was dead, although it shouldn't have been. She'd made a point of charging it that afternoon when she'd gotten the bad news that she was going to the meeting in town.

It had been her younger sister's turn to take that duty, but Mrs. Finlander, one of their frequent guests, had made a special request to have Tessa give her a before-bed massage. Really, anyone could have done it just as professionally. But

Tessa had developed a rapport with the woman, and she'd asked Sophia to go to the meeting in her place.

Now Sophia was stuck beyond the shoulder of the road. Really, she was only three miles from the spa. An easy walk. Of course, she had on the creamy yellow suit and high heels she'd worn to town. But a pair of running shoes was in the trunk. And a T-shirt and shorts, as well.

Once she changed her clothes, getting home would be no big deal. Out here in the desert, the moon and stars were brilliant, more than enough to light her way. Yet the idea of climbing out of the car sent a shiver up her spine.

As she peered out the window, she saw headlights in the distance. Someone was coming, and hopefully she could get a ride.

She climbed out, waving a manicured hand as the lights approached. But whoever was in the other car roared past, leaving her standing in his backwash. Because he recognized her? Some people in town thought the Thalia sisters and cousins were witches because of the way they retained their youth and beauty.

She allowed herself another "damn" as she walked to the back of the vehicle and clicked the trunk release on the car key. The casual clothing was where she'd left it, in her carry bag. After changing into the running shoes, she reached to shrug off her suit jacket, then changed her mind. The idea of getting undressed on the side of the highway had her nerves jumping again.

To calm herself, she took a deep breath of the desert air. It smelled clean and fresh and reassuring, and she wondered why she was so spooked.

After slinging her purse over her shoulder, she started up the road, her eyes fixed on the white sign for the spa. It was a refuge for her and the other women of the Ionian Sisterhood who had come here long ago seeking a place where they could practice the ancient arts they had brought from their home in Greece.

As she walked, she heard the crunch of footsteps on the gravel shoulder behind her, and all her vague fears came crashing down on her.

She started to run, wondering if there was any chance of getting away from whoever was stalking her.

He answered the question by streaking past her at speeds no normal human being could attain, stopping about ten feet in front of her, blocking her path.

In the darkness, she couldn't make out many details, but she saw he was wearing a white T-shirt and tight-fitting jeans. His hair was dark, but the shadows hid his features as he walked slowly toward her, young and cocksure in the moonlight.

In that terrible moment, she knew who he was. Not his name. But everything about him told her that he must be a Minot, one of the men who had haunted the Ionians through the ages, ever since they had made a devil's pact with the ancient warriors.

None of them had attacked the Sisterhood in years, and perhaps that had made them too lax in their security measures. Of course there were wards around the property and a guard at the gate, but she should have had someone with her when she left the compound at night. Instead, she was alone and vulnerable on a dark desert highway. Like in that Eagles song.

Her throat was so tight that she could barely breathe, but she kept her eyes focused on the man who advanced toward her. Even while she kept him in sight, she sent her mind toward the resort that was only three miles away. Could she use her powers to get a message to anyone there? To Tessa, perhaps, her real sister, the one who was closest to her in all the world.

Help me, she silently called. *Help me. I'm on the highway. Just a few hundred feet . . .*

Before she could say any more, he raised his hand. He

was holding a small cylinder, and when he pressed on the top, a mist whooshed out and drifted toward her.

The second she breathed it, her head began to spin and her body stopped obeying her commands. Her mind told her to turn and run, but her legs wouldn't move. She was rooted to the spot, like a desert animal frozen in the headlights of an advancing vehicle.

The man waited a moment for the cloud of gas around her to dissipate. Then he tossed the cylinder away where it clanked against a rock as he walked purposefully forward, his gaze never leaving her.

When he stepped in front of her, she should have been able to see his face better, yet each feature was blurred. Still, she sensed that his eyes were large and dark, his brows heavy, his lips curved into a smile that was as arrogant as it was sensual. If she had met him at the spa, she would have seen him as a vital, desirable man.

And she might have made love with him. Totally on her terms. Because with the Ionians, that was the way sex went.

Yet she wasn't the one in control now, and she knew she was in danger. Centuries ago, the Ionians had reached out to the Minot for help. They were still paying for their mistake.

"I have you now," he murmured, reaching to touch her lips with one long finger.

She tried to speak, but no words came out of her mouth, and reaching out to her sisters had become impossible.

All she could do was stand facing him as his hand moved to her cheek in a sultry caress.

He smiled again, showing her his gleaming white teeth, while his hand slid down her neck, pressing against the pulse pounding there—and sending a shiver over her skin.

She hated responding to him, but sensuality was part of her being, and she was helpless to fight against the waves of sexual energy rolling off him—augmented by the paralyzing mist he'd sprayed on her. She knew it was affecting her senses—and her judgment.

Making a tremendous effort to speak, she managed to say, "Leave . . . me . . . alone."

"That's not what you really want, is it?" he answered in a confident voice as he slid his hand lower, pushing back one side of her jacket so that he could cup her right breast through her blouse. "You're a sexy, dynamic woman who needs a man to complete her. On his terms, not yours."

She closed her eyes, trying to shut him out as he rubbed his thumb back and forth across her nipple, making it stiffen.

Don't. Please don't, she shouted inside her mind, but she couldn't make the words slip past her lips.

This was so wrong. It wasn't the way of the Ionians. It wasn't the way any woman should be treated—being aroused against her will.

Somehow she mustered the will to speak. "Get off me . . . you . . . bastard."

He laughed, a rough, grating sound, and moved in closer. Keeping up the maddening caress on her breast, he slid his other hand lower, finding the juncture of her legs, then pressing through her skirt against her clit, sending an unwanted jolt of sensation through her body.

"You're as lovely as I knew you'd be. But all your sisters are so tempting. So young. So vital. So desirable."

What was he planning to do? Rape her out here on the highway?

She prayed that another motorist would come along and see what was happening.

Or was this like so many instances of modern life when strangers weren't going to get involved? Even if you were lying on the sidewalk bleeding.

Teeth clenched, she steeled herself against the man whose hateful touch sucked her into a vortex of his making.

Desperately, in her mind she said one of the ancient supplications that had sustained her Sisterhood throughout the centuries. Once they had prayed to the Greek goddesses, but their thinking had evolved so that they had come to see one divine force in the universe.

> *Spirit of the Earth,*
> *hear my plea.*
> *I am but a mortal woman*
> *standing before you.*
> *But I humbly ask for your aid*
> *in the hour of my need*
> *as the Ionians have done through the ages.*

Even as she clung to the ancient words, she could feel herself falling further under the attacker's spell, bending to his will no matter how she struggled against the unwanted arousal coursing through her body.

He tipped up her head, staring into her eyes, and she heard him gasp, "You're not . . ."

Before he finished the sentence, everything changed with the suddenness of a lightning bolt spearing out of the sky.

TWO

SOPHIA CAUGHT HER breath as another man came streaking out of the darkness and into the scene. Like the attacker, he was dark-haired and well muscled, although he wasn't close enough for her to see his face in the darkness.

His voice was loud and commanding. "Take your dirty hands off her."

"What the hell?" The guy who had thought he had his captive all to himself whirled to face the newcomer.

"Get away from her."

"You dare interfere." It wasn't a question; it was a statement of outrage.

"I do."

"I think you've made a mistake. She is mine."

"No." He bit off the one syllable as he charged forward, his fist flashing out, striking a blow to the first man's chin.

At least she thought she'd seen the punch because it happened in a blur of motion, the way both men had come out of the desert.

The man who had attacked Sophia struck back, but her

champion was prepared for the counter assault, dodging aside to avoid the fist before leaping onto his opponent, throwing him to the ground with bone-rattling force.

They rolled together in the red dirt, like two ancient combatants fighting without the need of weapons, each testing the weaknesses of the other and grappling for advantage. They moved with the speed of the wind, so fast that Sophia could barely follow the action. One slammed the other into the dirt with enough force to break the bones of an ordinary man.

Yet he picked himself up and sprang back into the fray, and she sensed it could be a fight to the death if they both kept up the intensity.

She heard the breath rushing in and out of their lungs, felt bits of grit spray in her direction as they kicked and scrabbled for dominance.

As she struggled to get a better look at either of them, one heaved himself away. She couldn't tell which one it was, but she saw him scramble to his feet. While his opponent was still on the ground, the one who had decided to cut his losses took off across the desert, running as fast as a speeding train and then climbing into the red rocks. The other one put on a burst of speed and almost caught up. They scrambled skyward, taking a path that would have sent any other man toppling to the ground, before disappearing from view.

She still didn't know whether the second man was really her champion or simply trying to steal what the other one wanted. But she must take this chance to get away. Before one or the other came back to claim his prize.

With every ounce of will she possessed, Sophia struggled against the effects of the gas that had immobilized her, dragging in great lungfuls of the clean desert air as she strove to clear her system of the poison.

To her relief, she found she could move her arms, then her legs. She shook her head and shoulders before taking a couple of wavering steps away from the spot where she had been rooted.

But she was still out in the open, and she knew she didn't have the strength to run. The best she could do was get back to the car. Lock herself in. Then use her powers to call for help, if she could make her brain function well enough. And pray that the vehicle would be enough protection until some of her sisters could come from the spa.

Doggedly, she staggered back the way she'd come.

As she wove her way toward the vehicle, she struggled to reach her sister's mind. This time she caught a stuttering of contact, as though she had almost closed the circuit but couldn't quite do it. Not in her present condition.

What she needed was to get back to the safety of the spa, where the collective power of her sisters would protect her.

With gritted teeth, she picked up her pace, hurrying to the vehicle as fast as she could. But not fast enough, apparently.

When she heard a sound to her right, like wind rushing down a canyon, she felt her heart thud in her chest.

One of them was coming back.

Which one? And did it matter?

She was reaching for the door handle when a voice spoke out of the darkness. "The bastard's gone, but you won't be safe until you get back home."

The words were both gentle and forceful. She knew that it was the one who had saved her from rape or worse. But she still didn't know *his* intentions.

Knowing there was no point in trying to evade him, she turned, backing up so that her hips were pressed against the car door as she and the man stared at each other across three yards of charged space.

He appeared to be standing in shadow, if that was possible when the world was all darkness except for the stars and moonlight shining down. All she knew was that she couldn't see him clearly.

Still, she could make out his dark hair, the outline of his

head, and the shape of his supple body. Like the other man, he radiated an aura of power and raw sexuality. Yet he stopped a few yards from her, keeping his distance, making no attempt to dominate her the way the other one had.

"Are you all right?" he asked.

She flicked her gaze into the distance, then back. "Yes. Where did he go?"

"Away. He ran. Like the coward he is." He spoke in a low, grating tone as though he were worried about her discovering his true identity from his voice, but she was sure she had never met him before in her life. He paused, then added, "You should not be out here alone."

Even though she'd had the same thought earlier, she raised her chin. "I take orders from no man."

"Sorry. I was just making a practical suggestion."

She swallowed, remembering what he had done for her. Risked his life, she was sure, to free her from the man who had stopped her on the road. And now he was keeping his distance.

"I should thank you."

"No need."

"Who are you?"

"A friend."

She wanted to tell him that no Ionian was friends with a man. She settled for saying, "Impossible."

"Why do you doubt me?"

"Because I know what you are."

"Maybe. Maybe not. But I will never convince you with words."

"Or any other way."

"We'll see."

Moving slowly, he took a step closer, then another until he was standing only a few feet away.

He was so close that she should have been able to see him clearly now, yet somehow clarity of vision was impossible. Her senses were still muddled, perhaps by the gas.

Cautiously, as though he were trying not to spook a frightened animal, he lifted his hand, touching her hair, running his fingers through the silky strands.

The other man had touched her, too. An unwelcome touch. But this was as different as the taste of wine and beer. She sensed that this man meant her no harm, although that could be as much of a trick as anything else that had happened in the last half hour.

A half hour?

Was that all the time that had passed since the car had gone off the road? She didn't know for sure, but she suspected that she hadn't been out here much longer.

He winnowed his fingers down to her scalp, and she felt something that she had never felt from a man. Something unique. It was almost as if she could sense his thoughts. Almost, but not quite. They were blurred—like her vision. Yet she hovered on the brink of a marvelous discovery. One that she knew would mean more to her than anything she had encountered in this life or any other.

Every instinct had commanded her to shrink from the other man's touch. Now she craved what this one offered.

A few moments ago, she'd been forced into intimacy with a stranger. Suddenly she longed for it.

A hum of sensuality flooded through her, and she clenched her hands at her sides to keep from reaching out and pulling him closer.

"Who are you?" she whispered again.

He didn't answer, only continued to caress her, his touch so different from the earlier one. The first man had been arrogantly possessive. This one was no less sure of his purpose, yet she felt need coursing through him as he touched her. Or was she only projecting her own feelings onto him?

His face was close to hers. He could have kissed her if he wanted. Instead he bent to press his cheek to hers, that touch as erotic as any kiss. When he slowly pulled her body against his, the breath caught in her throat.

She had thought the first man had aroused her. It was nothing compared to what she felt now.

Her senses whirled. Her mind spun. Her blood pumped hotly through her veins. She couldn't speak, but she felt a question form in her mind.

What do you want? she asked, the way she might speak to one of her sisters over a distance.

Again, she felt a flicker of something coming from his mind.

Everything.

Had he silently answered?

Whether he had or not, she felt a flood of longing coursing through her.

Or was she so off balance that she couldn't judge her own responses?

He pulled her more tightly against the length of his body, and she could feel his erection pressing against her middle, and the heat of his body overwhelming her.

"Sophia," he murmured.

"You know my name?"

"Yes."

"How?"

He laughed softly. "Modern technology. The spa has a website."

"Oh. Right."

And she was pictured there, with the others. Maybe that was a mistake they should correct.

She started to pull away.

"Not yet."

She turned her head—to look at him. And he turned at the same time, so that his mouth brushed hers. An accident.

But she was helpless to draw away as sensations assaulted her. She marveled at the softness of his lips, marveled at the currents of sensation surging through her as his mouth settled on hers, moving, pressing, urging her to open for him.

She accepted the invitation, drinking in the taste of him as his tongue pressed beyond her lips, teasing her and then withdrawing.

It was the most erotic kiss she had ever experienced, and it made her want more. So much more.

Somehow, she knew it was the same for him. They belonged together, in a way she could only dimly understand. But she would. She was sure of it. As sure as she was that he was going to make love with her here and now.

She wanted that. So much.

But before she could raise her hands to pull him closer, he let his arms drop to his sides and stepped back, putting a foot of space between them. As the heat of his body left hers, she felt such a sense of profound loss that she had to steady her hand against the side of the car.

Not yet. Not like this. It must be right.

Turning away, he walked to the rear of the SUV. "You need to get back to the spa."

"The . . . car's stuck," she managed to say.

"I know. Step back."

When she'd done as he asked, he grasped the bumper with both hands. As she watched, he bent and braced his legs in the shifting soil, then began to rock the car, moving it back and forth, freeing the vehicle from the unstable surface. With a mighty heave, he shoved the SUV back onto the road.

"You should leave now."

From *USA Today* **Bestselling Author**

REBECCA YORK

DRAGON
MOON

As a werewolf, Talon is no stranger to secrets, and he can sense that the psychic Kenna is keeping something from him. But he is powerfully drawn to the mysterious stranger, and the urge to claim her is just as strong as the instinct to keep himself guarded. With impossible secrets keeping them apart and the threat from the other world drawing near, their fate hangs in the balance—unless they can learn to trust each other.

penguin.com

Also from
USA Today Bestselling Author

REBECCA YORK

THE MOON SERIES

KILLING MOON

EDGE OF THE MOON

WITCHING MOON

CRIMSON MOON

SHADOW OF THE MOON

NEW MOON

GHOST MOON

ETERNAL MOON

DRAGON MOON

"Action-packed...
and filled with sexual tension."
—*The Best Reviews*

Penguin Group (USA) Online

What will you be reading tomorrow?

Patricia Cornwell, Nora Roberts, Catherine Coulter,
Ken Follett, John Sandford, Clive Cussler,
Tom Clancy, Laurell K. Hamilton, Charlaine Harris,
J. R. Ward, W.E.B. Griffin, William Gibson,
Robin Cook, Brian Jacques, Stephen King,
Dean Koontz, Eric Jerome Dickey, Terry McMillan,
Sue Monk Kidd, Amy Tan, Jayne Ann Krentz,
Daniel Silva, Kate Jacobs...

You'll find them all at
penguin.com

Read excerpts and newsletters,
find tour schedules and reading group guides,
and enter contests.

Subscribe to Penguin Group (USA) newsletters
and get an exclusive inside look
at exciting new titles and the authors you love
long before everyone else does.

PENGUIN GROUP (USA)
penguin.com